Carl Weber's Kingpins:

West Coast

Carl Weber's Kingpins:

West Coast

Raynesha Pittman

www.urbanbooks.net

Urban Books, LLC
300 Farmingdale Road, N.Y.-Route 109
Farmingdale, NY 11735

Carl Weber's Kingpins: West Coast

ISBN 13: 978-1-64556-205-4
ISBN 10: 1-64556-205-0

First Trade Paperback Printing July 2021
Printed in the United States of America

10 9 8 7 6 5 4 3 2 1

Distributed by Kensington Publishing Corp.
Submit Orders to:
Customer Service
400 Hahn Road
Westminster, MD 21157-4627
Phone: 1-800-733-3000
Fax: 1-800-659-2436

Carl Weber's Kingpins:

West Coast

by

Raynesha Pittman

To the little girl who needed healing, you no longer need the Band-Aid. It's time to embrace the beauty of the scar. You are my cousin, my mother, my sister, and one of my closest friends. Thank you for nursing my wounds when no one else would. Because of your love, teachings, and care, I am this woman, this healed woman. I'm at peace with God's decision to take you home sooner than most because you have always been more significant to me than this world and to everyone who was blessed to know you. I love you and miss you, Susan Mae Browne, sleep well.

June 9, 1967–January 27, 2019

Prologue

Troy sprang from the couch, snatched up the pile of clothes at his feet, and rushed to the window. He almost tumbled over as he lost his footing getting dressed. His nap was short, and the cause for it abruptly ending was unknown. However, the knots tightening in his stomach were enough for him to honor his gut feeling of getting the fuck up.

With space no bigger than the length of his cocaine-induced dilated pupils, he peeked through the broken blinds into the darkness of the night. The moonlight that usually graced the hood's urban decay had been replaced by what he feared most. Red, blue, repeat. Blue, red, repeat, and just for the hell of it, there was the steady glare of headlights positioned on high beam. The cycling lights were missing their usual serenade of sirens as each squad car pulled up and armed police jumped out. It was supposed to be a sneak attack.

"You three take the back, and the rest of you cover the exits," he heard one say as he slowly backed away from the window.

"Fuck," he hissed, unsure of his next move.

The time had come to raise the white flag and surrender. Though Troy had been nervously awaiting this day by staying higher than escort pussy, he wasn't quite ready to face the consequences of his actions. Hell, how could any man prepare himself to leave his three favorite girls?

The overheated, gooey crumbs of crack his pocket change could afford to buy didn't furnish the high needed to take his mind off the only threesome he'd triumphed over in years. His wife, still his favorite piece of artwork as her beauty continued to battle the effects of her addiction, lay in their bed stark naked, waiting for him to satisfy the hunger between her thighs. Knowing her hunger would eventually become starvation didn't sit right with him. There would be no makeup sex to fix their bedtime argument that sent him to slumber on the couch. He smirked. That argument of whose wrong was ultimately the better act of righteousness now seemed stupid. Truthfully, at this moment, everything they discussed outside of splitting the contents of a glass pipe seemed silly to Troy. *"Tomorrow isn't promised."* He felt that cliché weighing on him as the thought of not being able to touch his wife was seconds away from being a reality.

His mother, the woman who loved him through every unwise decision and more than any other woman could ever love him, would have to watch her only son be cuffed and hauled off again. Her house, the longest tangible memory she had left of the love she shared with her late husband, was minutes away from being barged into with the backing of an arrest warrant. To save her ass from Troy's latest mistake, she'd have to perjure herself when she willingly told the lie under oath that she didn't know her baby boy was a wanted man.

And the baby. What about the baby? She wasn't his baby. However, she was the only person he had the title of guardian over, and he loved his niece. He didn't want her exposed to his foolishness.

Dashing down the hallway in a sprint of hope, he decided to remain a free man as knocks rattled the metal screen door.

"Who the hell is it?" asked his mama, Jo, dragging her slippered feet across the dusty hardwood floor. There had always been a draft in the house. However, the room had never felt this cold. It was more than the Santa Ana winds sending the chill up her spine, she was sure of it. "I said, who in the hell—"

The police quickly answered her question as her door was knocked off its hinges and slammed against the wood, identical to the last domino played at a family reunion. She'd bitch about the door once the guns returned to their holsters.

"Get on the ground!" was all she could make out in the commotion.

"Where's Troy?" another voice shouted for what must have been adherence to protocol, seeing that the search of the premises was already underway.

Don't let go, Troy thought as his sweaty palms struggled to keep a firm grip on the rod. His knees were tucked into his chest, mirroring a half-completed set of crunches. Be that as it may, this was no exercise routine. It couldn't be. He was in the air while his feet rested flat against the wall. None of his body was near the floor. The hanging position he chose suggested he'd read one too many web-shooting and wall-crawling superhero comic books. The reality of being able to endure the discomfort of the situation was nonexistent.

"Y'all are asking me about the whereabouts of a damn crack ghost. Shit, I got questions too. Which one of you is paying to get my damn door fixed? Now answer that!" Jo yelled while lighting the cigarette that dangled from her lip.

Doors creaked open and slammed closed for more than half an hour. The police searched the house for Troy to no avail. At the discretion of the lieutenant, the search was seconds away from being called off. Then, Troy heard her voice. It was as if an angel had sung out to him.

"Why are y'all trying to take my uncle to jail? He didn't do nothing to nobody," Temper whined.

"Aw, sweetheart, don't cry. Your uncle did do something, something very bad, and we're only here because we have proof that he did it. Are you okay, sweetie? Why are you pinching your nose like that?"

Troy knew what was coming—an obnoxious hacking sound followed by her spitting—and he still couldn't hold in his laugh. Defeated, he let go of the rod, placed his feet on the junky closet floor, pushed the trench coats to the other end to make himself visible, and then put his hands in the air a second before the door flew open. Sighing, Troy walked out with guns pointed at him. The smirk on his face grew into a smile when he looked up and saw his angel.

"Did you hock a loogie in that pig's face, Temper Taz?" he asked as they slammed him into the wall and placed cuffs on his wrists.

"Yep, right in that coward's face, and it was full of *flam!*"

"It's phlegm, baby." He chuckled.

"Did you do something bad, or are they lying on the black man?"

Troy roared in laughter as tears filled his eyes. His mama stood on one side of his angel and his wife on the other. It was his makeshift trinity.

"Good and bad sit in the eyes of the muthafucka who's doing the looking. That shit ain't important right now, though." He stopped walking, and the police tried to drag him. "Damn, nigga, I know y'all mad I was hiding in the closet that you mark-ass bitches checked three times, but can I get a second to talk to my niece?"

"All you got is a second, nigga." The voice was familiar. He was sure it belonged to the man wearing his niece's mucus.

"Listen, Temper Taz, I'm going away for a while."

"No—" she shouted.

"Shut up. I need you to listen. I fucked up in their eyes, and they don't give out whippings with a belt. They punish you by snatching away your time. You might even be grown when these hoes let me out, but before I go, I need to drop this knowledge on you, and yo' Asian ass better not forget it. Are you listening to me, Chinaman?"

Temper nodded her head, her expression as cold as steel.

"Good. Now peep game. The only way out of the muthafucking hood is over a thirty-foot wall. Unlike the rest of us, you being born half black and Asian gave you a ten-foot ladder, and it's up to you to get the twenty or more feet to get over it. But that half-Asian and half-black shit don't mean shit. It'll only get you so far." He nodded his head toward a couple of white cops standing near her. "They don't give a fuck about your skin being pale or that your eyes slant. You're black. These muthafuckas will make sure you never forget it, and I don't want you to forget it. Promise me, no matter how life might twist, flip, or toss you around, that you're going to bust yo' ass to get those feet."

The room seemed to get lost in his words. They were ghetto yet militant and felt by all in attendance.

In a voice more mature than the eight years she owned, Temper locked eyes with his and said, "You can bet your ass I promise!"

Chapter One

It was nearly eight o'clock, and the signs of night approaching were slowly beginning to peak. Noctilucent clouds covered the sky in their beauty as the sun drifted away to its nightly hiding place. No one with vision would question why God was called the greatest architect of the universe. The sky was His canvas. The sunset was His painting, and He drew effortlessly for all the residents of Los Angeles to see. Well, everyone except Kei'Lani. She didn't get to enjoy the free art exhibit. Her best friend Temper's body perched on her bike's handlebars didn't grant her admission.

"Pedal faster, bitch!" Temper yelled.

Although little and malnourished from the junk food and beer she used as meal replacements, Temper's body acted as a solar eclipse blinding Kei'Lani's line of sight. She used memory to steer them to their destination. In cooler words, Temper was throwing shade, literally, and that shade prevented Kei'Lani from seeing her lap and the warm, sticky fluid that was covering it. That wasn't to say that she would have opted to glance at it if she could. The thought alone of blood dripping made her dizzy. It was paradoxical to the coldhearted gangster bitch Kei'Lani so desperately wanted to be.

"I'm trying to, but . . ." But seeing the blood was one thing. To feel it drip like a busted pipe in the ceiling over her thighs was another. An uneasy discomfort built in her upper abdomen and sent spasms to the back of her throat. If she gagged again, she'd throw up. Thanks to her queasy stomach, she didn't need smarts to assess the danger in the amount of blood Temper was losing. She knew only God would be able to make her friend's bleeding stop. Although, she was sure God was too busy handling more critical stuff than to make a trip to the hood for a sinner. That assumption reminded her of the deadly situation they were in. "Is it supposed to be leaking like that?" she questioned.

"How in the fuck am I supposed to know? Just keep pedaling. I think I'm about to die," Temper moaned, weaker than when she last spoke. The pain caused her lips to lock, suppressing her screams. She didn't want to scare her best friend with the answer. The truth was that the only thoughts Temper could formulate were those related to her death.

"I am pedaling, but your blood is dripping all over me, and you know my stomach is weak. What if Lena's not there? Doesn't she go to bingo with the church tonight? Man, I think we should stop at that mom-and-pop store on the corner and call 911 if you think you're dying. I can't ride around the hood with you dead on my handlebars. My mama gon' kill me."

"Damn, you got the bingo bus rider list memorized?" Temper teased, trying to make light of the situation. "Please do me a favor and shut the fuck up so if I do die, it can be in peace. We're a block away from her house. We might as well check, and why are you all in my ear complaining? I'm the bitch who might die on these fucking handlebars if you don't pedal faster. Does it look like I want your big undertaker-looking ass riding me through the hood dead on this raggedy-ass bike?"

"You're always taking shit as a joke. I'm here trying to help your crazy ass, and you still tryin' to burn on me like this shit is a standup comedy opportunity. I got your nasty-ass Asian blood dripping on me, bitch, and you don't give a shit about what I'm going through with yo' selfish ass. I am trying to pedal faster. I'm nervous and . . ." Her words stopped abruptly, and the not-so-easy-on-the-ears sound of vomiting replaced them. She didn't have time to warn Temper that the forty ounces of Olde English she'd gulped down less than twenty minutes ago were about to make their way back up and onto her back.

"I know you didn't just call Earl all over my muthafuckin' back. If I weren't dying, I'd jump off these handlebars and beat yo' ass."

"My bad. This shit got my stomach all fucked up, and I gotta shit, too. I need a blunt, a drink, or something. I can't believe you got me doing this. I swear if you live through this shit, I'm going to stop fuckin' with you like my mama said."

She continued voicing her ill feelings about making the house call instead of doing what was best, which, in her opinion, was taking Temper to the hospital. As she ripped Temper a new one, Temper lowered her head and focused on the squeaking sounds of the bike to take her mind off the pain of death moving near.

The gunshots a little while ago had seemed far away as the girls had dropped to the floor for safety behind the park's gymnasium. The tucked-away, graffitied, piss-smelling area, with shards of glass from every beer bottle known to Angelenos covering the concrete, had become the girls' sanctuary from the dangers that flooded their neighborhood. Whenever they needed a break from it all, they'd flee to the spot to smoke and turn up a beer or two without worrying about being seen by the wrong person or people. The girls knew everybody, and they hated that everyone knew everything about them, including their ages. Turning 18 was in their near future. However, 21 was years away. As far as the nosy adults and police assigned to their community were concerned, underaged drinking was still illegal. The girls didn't want to catch a charge nor have a grown-up snitch telling their guardians.

As they'd smoked the fattest blunt of weed Temper had ever rolled, the sound of the shots ripping through the noise barrier had acted as an alarm, and the best friends knew the drill. One and then the other hit the floor for cover. For the girls, it was overly rehearsed choreography. It was 1998 in L.A. Guns going off, police and ambulance sirens, and the loud, choppy sounds of the ghetto bird making its daily rounds were unwanted yet unremovable occurrences to that shitty side of the city where the girls grew up. Temper used to waste hours puzzled by why that part of Los Angeles had been called the Low Bottoms. It wasn't until she grew older that she realized it was a cool nickname given to those who lived in the bottom of the Hollywood-fueled city's barrel. In the 1980s and '90s, Hollywood still had the world trapped in its web of motion pictures identical to its heyday. The punchline was that Hollywood had yet to break away from L.A.

Nevertheless, being the rich and powerful Holly-Angelenos they were, they made sure to let the world know the city of Los Angeles was extremely large, so large that the city divided into multiple areas and sections. Holly-Angelenos got this message across by filming more movies and shows throughout the city so, no matter where you lived in this world, you'd know the bad sides of the city from the good. The poverty-stricken and underprivileged knew what Hollywood was doing and didn't give a fuck. Even with the movies filming on East Twenty-fifth Street and Naomi Avenue, the Low Bottoms were still the Low Bottoms. The drive-by shootings didn't stop on account of the cameras. Hollywood was fake, and the hood was as real as it got. Not everyone could call the Low Bottoms home. No one who made the mistake of visiting was allowed to make it home without the local gang's approval.

Out of mere habit formed from making it out alive after a shooting, Kei'Lani had burst out laughing until she looked over and saw her friend hunched over, gripping her side, with a growing puddle of blood beneath her. She'd wanted to call 911 and get help. However, Temper had her plan in mind. That plan had landed them on a bike ride to the neighborhood nurse's house.

"We're here. What's the plan now, smart ass?" asked Kei'Lani, out of breath as she backpedaled to bring the bike to a stop. There was too much weight on the bike. Her feet couldn't rest on the pedals like usual, so she used her Chucks as kickstands on the concrete.

Temper jumped off the handlebars the same way she did every other day, except every other day she hadn't been leaking blood outside of her monthly menstruation. The impact of her Chuck Taylors touching the sidewalk sent a shock to her already-pained side, and she nearly fell. Fortunately, Kei'Lani was there, ready to catch her as she always was.

"Like I said earlier, be ready to pull your daddy's heat out on this bitch as soon as she answers the door." Temper gave instructions in the slot where saying, "Thank you for having my back," should have gone.

Despite their frightening circumstances, Kei'Lani felt that a little gratitude would have been nice. If it weren't for the murderous look Temper gave her with the demand, "Bring yo' ass on!" she would have played taxi by dropping Temper off and cycling away.

The entire situation was more than Kei'Lani could manage, though it seemed to be as normal as starching khakis to Temper. Temper loved dangerous situations and found comfort in drama no matter whose drama it was. She wasn't enjoying the problem she was currently facing because this situation came with a level of uncertainty. Would she live to laugh about it another day, or would death headline an impromptu show? She didn't know, and the pain didn't ease to give her a chance to find out.

When they made it up the steps to the barred door, Temper let out her fears and frustrations on it through her knocks. "Don't act all weak and shit. Get yo' ass up out of yo' feelings, Kei-Kei. We made it and I'm still alive. All you have to do is keep the heat in this ho's face until she does everything I need her old ass to do. But if that ho acts crazy, pull the trigger!"

Kei'Lani nodded her head in understanding despite the fact that she didn't comprehend anything that was happening. The girls always toted guns and only planned on using them if they had to. To Kei'Lani, this didn't seem comparable to one of those forced times, though she knew it was always easy for Temper to make something out of nothing.

Temper pounded on the door harder and then lay on the bell.

"Who in the hell is banging on my screen door like they've lost their damn mind?" Lena yelled, pushing her window curtain back. She wasn't shocked to see Temper wearing an oversized khaki shirt and pants and looking every part the gangster bitch she yearned to be. What was surprising was that she dared to bring one of her little gangbanging friends with her, a fat one weighing 200 pounds or better and wearing too much black eyeliner.

Kei-Kei, which was the only name the hood knew Kei'Lani by, had the shit swirled around her eyes to accent absolutely nothing, and she'd heavily lined her plump, weed-stained lips. If her skin tone were half a shade darker, you wouldn't be able to tell she had any makeup on at all. Seeing that it wasn't, she looked a fool with thinning edges, wearing a Dickies jumpsuit and a one-inch ponytail to the side gelled with Pro Styl.

To make it worse, she stood next to a skinny, half-Asian, half-black girl almost twice her height who must have gotten lost in the hood and dressed consistently with the locals. She looked like she should be doing nails or ringing customers up for a pack of cigarettes and some lottery tickets. You could see the traces of black in Temper's DNA. Even so, the Asian was dominant. Everyone around Temper could see it, and she didn't care, because nothing inside of her felt Asian.

Lena grabbed her metal bat from its place next to her front door with the umbrellas, and she opened the door, prepared to swing. "I thought I told you that Khasema is in jail. Whatcha gon' do? Make him—"

Guns cocked in her face, forcing her to swallow her next words.

"Bitch, I'm not here for K-Mack. I came for you!" Temper said, moving the gun closer to her ex-boyfriend's mother's temple. "Now let us in so you can help me!"

"Help you with what?" Lena's heart hammered against her chest, causing her sagging C-cups to shake in her support bra. She'd warned her son not to mess with the neighborhood scraps, and now she was going to lose her life over the mistakes his dick had made. *He'd better be glad his ass is in jail. If he weren't, I'd kill him for this shit here,* she thought as she eyed Temper from head to toe, not seeing a cause for her to be asking for help.

Temper waved her bloody hands erratically in Lena's face.

"Oh, God, sugar, where are you shot? I heard the shooting but didn't think nobody was hit." She gasped and then gasped again as the smell of malt liquor and vomit invaded her nose.

"I'm not shot. I'm in labor with your weak-ass son's baby."

"Wha . . . what?" Lena stammered.

"There ain't no time for explanations. This is how this shit is about to go down. You're going to deliver this baby as if you're working labor and delivery, or my bitch Kei-Kei is going to put a bullet in the back of your head. So you can stop clutching your imaginary pearls as if you didn't know me and your son were fucking and get to work." Her demand came from gritted teeth as the contraction she tried to breathe through, as seen on TV, finally subsided.

"Since you put it that way, come on in," Lena said, making a mental note not to inhale through her nose. She looked from Temper to the gun Kei-Kei was nervously waving in her face with her right hand. Kei-Kei's left hand was up to her face as her thumb rested in her mouth while she sucked it. Lena cleared the entrance and then double-locked the door before she spoke again. "Kei-Kei, that's your name, right? Get your thumb out of your mouth and look in that hallway closet. Bring me every big towel you can carry."

Lena ran to the kitchen, began snatching every pot in view, and filled them with water. Even after years of working in Martin Luther King Jr. Hospital's trauma ward, she feared for her life. The hospital, better known by its street nickname of Killer King, had gotten a bad rap sheet over the years. It became known as the go-to hospital for victims of gang shootings. Lena had grown accustomed to working under hostile conditions. This wasn't the first time a patient's loved one had pulled a gun on her, demanding that she play God, and since she was far from retirement, she knew it wouldn't be the last. Despite her experience, Lena couldn't help the urge to run out the back door and risk being killed as she prepared for the delivery. She told herself years ago, when she realized that Khasema had sold his soul to the streets, that it was only a matter of time before his street life would find its way into her house.

Nonetheless, she never imagined it would be in this form. She assumed the police would be at her door to arrest Khasema for the dope he was pushing around the neighborhood, or one of those Crips he hung around with would be banging on her door to collect money he owed them. Having a young, worthless girl in labor, claiming it was her son's baby and forcing her to deliver it, was never a thought.

"Oh, shit!"

Lena heard Temper scream as the water began to boil and bubble out over the pots. She had another thought. This time it was about getting help. She could snatch the phone off the kitchen wall and dial 911 the next time the girl yelled in agony. She wouldn't need to say anything to them. All she had to do was speak loud enough to Temper or Kei-Kei about what they were forcing her to do at gunpoint so the operator could get the gist of what was going on. After a moment of giving it thought, she concluded it was too risky. *What if the girls catch on to what I'm doing, or the police show up at the door?* Lena didn't know a thing about the two thugs in training who'd invaded her home to judge if they'd shoot her before the police made it inside. *I should've taken my ass to bingo like I started to.*

"Kei-Kei, go see what she's in the kitchen doing. I want this baby out of me now," she heard Temper yell. Lena quickly turned the gas to high on another eye of the stove as she struck her match.

"What are you in here doing, Ms. Lena?" Kei-Kei questioned loudly enough for Temper to hear, while holding the gun in her shaky hand.

"I had to light the pilot to boil another pot of water. These pots aren't enough. There's more to delivering a damn baby than her pushing and me catching." She rolled her eyes and managed to catch the scared look on Kei-Kei's face. The girl's fear didn't go unnoticed, and Lena was ready to test her luck on it. *Fuck it,* she thought as she built the momentum to give it a try. "How old are the two of you?"

"Sixteen. Why?" Kei-Kei asked with her thumb back in her mouth.

"Because I don't think you understand how serious all of this is. Do you know how dangerous it is to deliver a child into this world even at a hospital? Women die during deliveries. Her chances of survival are slim to none having the child here. Are you ready to lose your friend because you didn't have the strength to put your foot down and take her ass to an emergency room? Yeah, if this goes wrong, I want you to know it falls on your shoulders, not mine. When the coroner comes for the body, he will want to know how she made it here while in labor. Are you ready to go down for her and the child's deaths?"

"This is what she wanted to do. I said, 'Let's go to the hospital,' and then she said you were the fucking hospital. Hell, I didn't even know my boo was pregnant for the past year or however long it takes to have a baby until she started leaking while we were smoking and shit. I hit the ground trying to dodge the bullets, and then my bitch screamed out her water broke." Kei-Kei couldn't hide her fear of possibly losing her best friend. Since kindergarten they had been besties, and they even went so far as making a blood pact when they were in the fourth grade.

The girls waited until recess and snuck into the bathroom with paper clips. It was Temper's idea, of course. "I'm tired of people saying we act like sisters. We will be sisters after this."

Temper retrieved a paper clip out of her faded denim skirt pocket and began to straighten it before speaking again. "We have to cut ourselves until we bleed. Then we have to mix our blood, and that will make us blood sisters for life."

Kei-Kei was scared of the effects of her blood mixing with that of a person who wasn't black. It was the nineties, and she'd heard the life-taking and career-ending impacts of HIV and AIDS. Uncertain of the outcome, she put her fears aside. There was no doubt that she loved Temper, and if hurting herself meant they'd have this special bond for life, she was ready to do it.

She didn't go through the trouble of straightening her clip. Instead, she pressed the point against her middle finger, closed her eyes, and twisted it until she was sure she had broken through the skin. Temper followed her actions, and then their middle fingers kissed as they recited the words Temper had told her earlier that morning had to be said.

"I will lie, cheat, steal, and kill to protect my sister. We are blood sisters for life."

Those words they recited meant more to her than they had in the past. She erased her fears of her fate and had her sister's back.

"Well, bitch, we're here now, and you're going to deliver my niece or nephew." She reenforced her words by pointing the gun against the middle of Lena's forehead. "If she dies, you die, and it's as simple as that. Now what else do you need me to do?"

Lena hesitated as she stared into the eyes of the little girl standing before her. All she saw was pain. She didn't know if the pain was from the current situation that faced them. Nevertheless, she was sure there had to be multiple sources mixing in with it, judging by her lifestyle.

"You don't have to do any of this, Kei-Kei. You can get help with whatever or whoever is hurting you. Is she hurting you and forcing you to do all this bad stuff? I can help you get away."

Lena stopped talking as Kei-Kei rammed the mouth of the gun against her forehead.

"Okay, I'll just help you with this then. Grab the box of gloves and those silver scissors out of the medicine cabinet in the hallway bathroom, and let's deliver this baby."

Kei-Kei returned to the kitchen with the items, and Lena lit another eye on the stove. Kei-Kei stood back and watched Lena grab the dish towel by the sink and wrap it around the scissors' handles before placing the scissors over the bluish part of the flame. Once she noticed the scissors' legs turning black, she removed them from the flame and walked into the living room to a fully naked Temper with the head of the baby crowning between her open thighs.

"I need to shit!" Temper yelled to no one in particular.

"Not just yet. Hold on a second. I'm almost ready. Kei-Kei, look in my bedroom closet for a duckbill hair clip. It's in a black duffle bag."

Kei-Kei heard her, yet she was too shell-shocked to move. The smell itself was enough to bring the remaining beer in her stomach up and out of her mouth. There was no way to describe the poisonous scent in the air besides labeling it as fishy sewage. She didn't know if it was supposed to smell that way, and she sure as hell wasn't sure if it was supposed to look that way. She was sure the dark mass was the baby's head making its way out of her best friend. Then again, that wasn't the way it looked. There was hair freckled with blood, a thick, creamy off-white substance, and slime leaking from a hole she had seen in its normal state and even had her tongue in a few times for the right amount of money. They weren't prostitutes. They just had prostitute tendencies. If their "get high" funds were low, they'd do what was necessary to get them back up. In those cases, for dollars from a dope boy or two, the girls would awaken their lesbian tendencies. To see Temper's pleasure tunnel stretched to fit a ripe cantaloupe, coupled with that smell, sent her into shock.

"Kei-Kei!" Temper yelled. She didn't get a response.

"Kei-Kei, don't forget our talk. Now go get the clip!" Lena said.

"No, you don't forget our talk. Black duffle bag in the closet," Kei-Kei repeated as she disappeared down the hallway. It took her a second or two to find one under all the sponge rollers in the bag, and when she did, the sound of a baby crying sent her rushing toward the living room. In a smoke ring that looked similar to a tribal ritual were the pots of boiling water around them. Temper had a big baby covered in blood and cream lying on her stomach.

"Congratulations, Auntie Kei-Kei. It's a boy. Now I need you to put that clip in the fire exactly how I did the scissors, and once you come back, you can have the honor of cutting the umbilical cord. Now hustle up. We're not done yet."

Kei-Kei was so excited that the metal burnt her hand. Lost in her thoughts, she placed the clip into the fire without shielding her hand from the heat. She sucked on her fingers except for one—her middle finger. It stole her attention as she stared at the spot where she'd punctured her finger so many years ago, earning her the right to be called auntie. She could still see the old wound.

"Auntie Kei-Kei," she mouthed with a smile.

Kei'Lani cut the umbilical cord, and Lena opened the clip. Using the fingers of a glove as if they were condoms, she covered the bills and clipped the baby's soon-to-be belly button. After that, Lena wrapped the baby in three towels and then handed him to Kei-Kei as she coached Temper through the removal of the afterbirth. Immediately after, she left the room with the baby to clean him up.

"Bitch, you did that shit like a pro," Kei-Kei cheered, and she even gave Temper dap for a job well done. "What's my nephew's name?" she asked, considering Temper's face for the first time since this began. She blinked twice. Her eyes had to be deceiving her. It wasn't her best friend looking back at her. It was a replica of the young woman she'd loved all her life. Temper never smiled to begin with, and knowing all the bullshit she had been through in her life, Kei-Kei understood her frown. On the other hand, the expression she was wearing now was one she had never seen. Temper looked like a pot as the water boiled away to nothing, leaving the whitish satin of the once-clear substance as a dusty coating.

"Whatever you want to name the little fuck boy. I don't care."

"Bitch, what's your problem? I know you're not going hard on your child because of his sorry-ass daddy. That's your fault for letting him nut in you, not my nephew's."

"Fuck him and his seed. Do you think I wanted to have his baby? When I found out I was pregnant, I put a gun in my mouth and—"

"Temper!"

"Don't 'Temper' me. I did, and the only reason you're not rocking an RIP shirt is because I thought about me. I didn't want to miss out on growing old, and it was too late to abort the mission, so I sat it out. He's here, that bullshit pregnancy is over with, and by force, I did my part. You and nobody else in this bitch or on this earth can force me to play mama to him. Help me sit up."

"I don't know if you should. I'll ask Ms.—"

"Bitch, help me sit up," Temper demanded, already trying to do it herself. After Kei-Kei propped her back against the plastic slip covering the couch, Temper grabbed her khaki pants and retrieved a joint. She sparked it and hit it three times before offering it to her makeshift sister, who declined. "I'm trying to get this money, and playing mama ain't for me. I'm not about to let a baby I didn't want by a nigga I don't want slow me down."

"So you're just going to do my nephew the same way your parents did you? What about when he grows up?"

"What part of 'little fuck boy' are you not hearing? He has that bitch in there and his ho-ass daddy whenever he gets out of jail. He'll get one of his hoes to play mama. This baby is his problem, not mine." Temper stopped talking. She heard Lena returning with the baby.

"Oh, hell no. I did my part. You will not smoke that shit in my house."

"I'm going to smoke this shit in your house until I leave this bitch, and you're not going to say a damn thing about it," Temper corrected her as she grabbed her gun off her clothes. "Kei-Kei, help me get dressed so we can leave this bitch's house. This ho got everything covered in plastic like she's painting the walls year-round." Temper chuckled at her own words as her high brought on humor.

"You think you can just throw your bloody, throw-up-and-beer-soaked clothes back on and walk right out the door with your ass all open? You need to rest, little girl. You got an infection in there"—she nodded toward Temper's baby exit— "that I'm going to get you antibiotics from work for. In a day or two, believe me, I won't try to stop you from getting the hell out."

"Yeah, I think you should rest for a while—"

"I don't recall asking for your dumbass opinion, Kei-Kei. You went into the kitchen and chopped it up with that bitch, and now your loyalty is to her. Is that how you're rocking?"

"Hell nah, it's not even like that." She could feel her temperature rising at Temper questioning her loyalty. She knew her best friend was living a nightmare. Nonetheless, Kei-Kei had to be her. She'd be committing fraud on herself if she let the slick remarks slide and said, "Bitch, you'll never find anyone as loyal to you as me, so put them weak-ass feelings back in yo' pocket. I'm telling you to stay here because you need to. Big Trice stayed in the hospital for two days after having OG Casper's baby, remember? We stole the diapers from the pharmacy and brought them to the hospital the day after she had the baby. If you say this is the hospital, you need to stay at least another twenty-four hours to get your shit together.

Where are you trying to go anyway? I hope not to your granny's house. That shit is filthy and full of junkies."

Temper knew where she would be going when she left Lena's. Still, her plan wasn't for Kei-Kei's hungry ears. She had enough of the life she was given and was ready to trade what she had for anything that looked better. Temper knew Kei-Kei loved her through her anger, and the only way she'd let her leave this house was by fighting her. Temper had energy, just not enough to use getting her ass whooped. However, she wasn't a match for Kei-Kei's heavy hands even when her strength was at its max. Temper was the brains in their sisterhood, and Kei-Kei was the muscle. She sat back down, not wanting to get fucked up.

"Well, damn, can one of you help me wash my ass? It smells like a fish market murder scene in this bitch."

Kei-Kei laughed, then hollered, "That's my bitch!"

Chapter Two

The longest day of the year had finally ended. One of the little homies drained the inflatable pool while another extinguished the grill. They'd do it all again the next day. The small gathering of the Low Bottom Rollin' Twenties Crips was moved from the backyard to the house except for those with less than OG to triple OG status. They were the little homies. They weren't invited inside, and they wouldn't be.

"Ay, cut that music off," Casper yelled after slamming down the last blank domino on the table. He locked the game, which was in his favor, but he knew the game playing was over when he saw the figure standing near the back door.

"Didn't I tell you niggas to page me about shit like this?" The voice was low and husky, yet it still managed to be calm and inviting. The shooting from earlier in the evening not only echoed off the gymnasium where the girls hid but off the houses and the lips of everyone who heard. The news traveled until it reached the ears belonging to the man in the shadows of the room, a man everyone in the house feared.

"I knew you were at work, cuz, so I told them niggas to wait," Casper responded, seeing that no one else in the room wanted to.

"So you're the nigga with authority to trump whatever I say? You calling the shots now, Casper?"

"That's not what he meant—" Big Trice started to explain, and the voice yielded her silence.

"Muzzle yo' bitch. As a matter of fact, all of you bitches, leave."

Before the order was in place, the room was frozen as if they were playing freeze tag. However, the heat in the man's words instantly thawed it out, and the women left with haste.

"Are you going to answer me, or do I need to call your bitch back? She seemed willing to talk to me."

The Crips who remained exited the room one at a time. They knew better than to act as flies on the wall while the supreme chief chopped it up with his chief enforcer.

"Man," Casper murmured once the room was clear. "Nah, I only got the authority you gave me, big homie."

"That's right. I knew you were smarter than that. So now that everybody knows that there was a shooting in the hood but no cars smashed off and no bodies were found . . ." He paused for a dramatic second and then said, "I hope! Tell me what happened and how you handled it." The figure lurking in the dark materialized with each step. It too was void of color. He was big, black, and beastly both outwardly and within. A goon. A monster. A living beast.

"What is there to tell? Those fools you fuck with from Pomona pulled up asking to buy a couple of bricks, but their money was funny."

"Funny how?"

"It was short a stack, and they tried to play us by stuffing dollars in between the C-notes to make the grip look proper. I guess they thought they could get one over on us since you don't be counting the bread they give you."

Casper wished he could take back his words as soon as he said them. Anger over the disrespect shown to him and his baby mama had taken over his words, and he was sure they had just cost him his life. When he woke up thirty minutes later to the taste of his blood on his lips, he was thankful that his OG decided to give him a pass by knocking him out instead.

Temper locked herself in Khasema's room with Kei-Kei by her side for eight hours. Lena wasn't allowed in, nor was the baby. She didn't want to see her son again, and if they wanted her to rest, they had to abide by her rules. It wasn't the first time Temper lay in Khasema's bed for hours. Experience had taught her to dodge the springs that poked through his full-size mattress whenever she shifted for comfort. Still and all, to Lena's knowledge it was her first time, and to keep the peace, she'd keep it that way.

"You don't have to stare at his bed like that. I change his bedding once a week out of habit," Lena told her, trying to wipe the concerned expression off her face.

"Good, then you shouldn't have a problem with changing them out again," Temper exacted and stood against the wall to give Lena space to refresh the bedding. The bedding hit the floor in a quick snatch, revealing the stained mattress.

Kei-Kei waited for Lena to retrieve the replacements before saying, "Ugh, it looks like he pees in the bed." She was joking, but Temper didn't join in.

She hadn't heard Kei-Kei's words. She was staring at the mattress. *Who else did he sneak in his mama's house to fuck?* Temper wondered, remembering the nights she had to stand on the water meter to climb through his bedroom window. That man deserved an Oscar for his role in their relationship. In the streets, he treated her the same as he treated everybody who moved work for him. She was the dealer, and he was the supplier. Aside from that, when they were together in the safety of his room, Khasema made Temper feel as though she was the only one for him. Not at the beginning of whatever it was that they shared. At the start of their sexual relationship, he'd get her to suck his dick. Then he'd strap up, bend her over, catch his nut, and then put her out. After two months of sneaking her in nightly, the condom usage stopped, and he'd lay face down in her pussy for hours.

Contrary to how he treated her outside of the house, he'd eat her ass to prove that she was his one and only. Though he never said it, there were strong feelings brewing. He stopped fearing the consequence that could follow from planting his seeds in her and began going to sleep with his shovel in her hole after sowing, with Temper cuffed in his arms. It became the only way he preferred to sleep. Temper wouldn't admit she had feelings for him, and if they ever showed without her giving the okay for them to, she'd go fuck a random homie to shake the shit off. No one knew their nightly routine, and that included Kei-Kei. The only information Kei-Kei knew was that they'd fucked twice, which was one time too many for Temper's liking.

She'd spent the last eight hours in his bed, reminiscing. "Hey, Tee, what time is it?" Kei-Kei yawned.

Unlike the hell Temper went through being raised by her alcoholic, always-gambling grandmother and crackhead uncle who was one step away from pushing a grocery store basket, Kei-Kei had both parents under her roof. Her father, Big Keith, was a retired gangbanger and former dope dealer who'd gotten his shit together. Rumor had it that he'd had kingpin status since birth due to sharing the same DNA as one of the founding members of the Crips. Now he was a paper-pushing supervisor at the oil refinery out in Long Beach. He did a lot of traveling up and down the West Coast and back and forth from California to Texas. His constant traveling for work worked in Kei-Kei's favor because her absence would go unnoticed by him. She wished that were true for her mother.

Her mother, Bridget, wasn't hood born and raised. She was a black girl raised in the affluent suburbs of the San Fernando Valley, who fell in love with a thug through letters, collect calls, and multiple visits to the Men's Central jail. Her best friend, whom she met in high school, lived in South Central L.A. and rode the school bus to Woodland Hills every day to attend school. It was she who encouraged Bridget to write to her boo's cellmate, and surprisingly to both Big Keith and Bridget, they had fallen in love through letters. Upon his release, Bridget made him promise to tuck his flag away and find employment that required him to clock in. Despite her effort to promote change, she forgot to enforce his move out of his hood. Keith was blessed to have been grandfathered into his mama's house at her death, allowing him to inherit her Section 8 voucher.

You don't throw away almost-free housing, and Bridget knew this, so she didn't push the issue of him contacting the powers-that-be to request to relocate. Although the shit she had to put up with wasn't worth holding on to the address. The neighbors aimed to disrespect her at every opportunity. They called her all kinds of four-legged bitches, three-hole whores, and two-dollar tramps, but only if they were sure that Bridget could hear them. It wasn't because she articulated her words well or that she was the only woman in the area who held multiple degrees. The dislike for her was because Bridget was the sore thumb. She never attended anything in the community, not the neighborhood barbeques, the food drives, and especially not the Hood Day festivities.

Due to her standoffish behavior, everyone assumed she had her nose turned up and thought she was better than everybody else. Her arrogance made everyone uncomfortable around her, and if the police happened to show up uninvited, the neighborhood assumed that she had covertly supplied them the invitation. Bridget knew she was the cold chill to those protected under the community's blanket of security, and she didn't give a fuck. A small part of her enjoyed the way they perceived her. It stopped the locals from bringing bullshit to her doorway.

For eighteen years, Bridget made the hour-and-a-half commute to teach African American history at California State University at Northridge. The commute to and from work was the only time she was outside unless she needed to make an unexpected trip to the local grocery store, which she dreaded. The produce catered to easily pleased farm animals instead of humans, and she hated bumping into women she knew couldn't stand her.

Bridget made it a priority to keep her daughter from being dragged into the hood life. However, with Kei'Lani being the daughter of the most beloved Crip in the area, it was more of a battle than she had foreseen. After watching her daughter transform into a hood chick after her transition from elementary to middle school, she had her daughter bussed to the Valley to attend high school, hoping to undo a portion of the madness she picked up. The education was better with the two-hour bus ride Kei'Lani had to take. The goal was to have her in a more diverse environment. Secretly, she wanted her daughter to see that she could make decent friends, unlike the gutter rat Temper she held so near and dear. Keeping Kei'Lani away from Temper was another battle she hadn't foreseen, and she knew if she interfered with the girls' bond, she'd be at war with her now-smart-mouthed teenage daughter.

Kei-Kei didn't want to be the first to mention that it was three o'clock Sunday morning and that if she didn't show her face soon, her mother would send the police. She didn't have to. Temper was already two thoughts ahead of her.

"Kei, you know your mama is going to be on that bullshit if you don't take your ass home soon. I already told you my granny said the next time your mama sends the police to her house looking for you, she was going to put her nine to her head." Temper chuckled as she rolled up another joint.

"Yeah, I know. But look at you. You're still in pain. I can't leave you like this. You're smoking more weed than Cousin Snoop at an all-you-can-smoke buffet in Jamaica. Why won't you just take the pain pills she gave you?"

"Don't play stupid. You already know why. Those shits have crack in them, and I'm not about to be nobody's junkie," she said, hitting her third joint in the past hour.

Silence captured the room as Temper remembered the last time she had seen the junkie she feared turning into her mother. She had been downtown school clothes shopping, better described as five-finger discount shopping, with Kei-Kei and a couple of other girls who followed them around the hood.

The day was going well. Temper had four new outfits and only came out of her pockets to pay for her shoes. The girls were munching on hard-shell tacos at Temper's favorite spot when a man attempted to use the men's restroom. The door was locked. He knocked and banged. Still, there was no answer. So he went to the cashier to get the key. The young manager repeated the man's actions and placed knocks on the door before using his key. He received the same fate.

"I bet you your other taco that the bathroom ain't empty," Kei-Kei taunted Temper.

"Here you go, you fat-ass bitch. If you were still hungry, that's all you had to say. I'm sure somebody is in there because that bathroom has a turn lock." Temper slid Kei-Kei her extra taco and continued eating until the girls roared in laughter.

"That bitch is in there washing her nasty ass in the sink," one of the girls screamed out, causing the rest of the customers to look.

It only took Temper a second to realize who the woman was. She tried to hide her face behind her taco wrapper, but it was already too late. Her mother was headed in her direction with only a pair of dirty, unzipped jeans on with no panties while she struggled to button up her shirt to conceal her braless raisin-shaped breasts.

"Temper, baby, is that you?"

Temper knew all the girls sitting with her had their jaws dropped and eyes on her.

"Hey, baby, how are you? How's mama doing? I see you have a lot of bags. You've been shopping?"

Temper slid out of the booth as her embarrassment turned into anger. *"Leave me alone, Dorothy,"* she screamed.

"I haven't done anything to you for you to be screaming like that. Can't a mama say hi to her fucking daughter? Shit, you act like I asked for a hug or kiss."

Temper had never disrespected her mother before, and unbeknownst to anyone, there was a part of her that hoped her parents would one day get clean and want her back. Sadly, the pressure of knowing her friends were watching was too much for her to bear.

"Bitch, I wouldn't hug you if the president paid me to. Get your junkie ass out of my face."

"Oh, I get it. These little bitches have you feeling yourself. Let me borrow five dollars, and I'll get out of your face. I'm hungry, baby."

Temper didn't know her mother that well, yet she could see the truth mixed with hurt in her eyes. Her grandmother told her all her life to never give her mother money because it would go to the dope man. Without saying another word, Temper walked up to the register, ordered, and paid for her mother's meal. She handed it to her as she made her way out the door.

"Thank you, baby, and I promise to pay you back. I'm going to a program that will help me kick the crack on Monday, and they will give me a place to stay and a job. Then I'll be back to get you. Wait until I tell your daddy how big you've gotten. He's going to be . . ."

Temper didn't hear her mother's last words as the door closed behind her. No one with her said a word until they were a block away, waiting for their bus to come.

"I can't believe that was your mama," the tallest of the girls said, hoping to get an explanation. Temper knew it, so she didn't respond. It wasn't until the youngest and supposedly hardest one in the group opened her mouth before anyone got a reaction out of her.

"I almost beat that junkie bitch down for calling us hoes. The only reason I didn't is because I didn't want her junkie blood to fall on me. I'm sure she has that hobo disease shit."

The tallest girl laughed, and it was on. Temper leaped in superhero fashion with her fists out and popped her in the nose, off target from her mouth. The impact crushed most of the bones like solid ice in a bag thrown to the concrete before being poured into a cooler to chill the drinks. Blood spattered and then shot out from the hole at the top of her nose where the bone that didn't crumble ripped through the skin. Seeing the gristle made Temple vow never to eat another piece of chicken down to the bone. When a drop of blood hit Temper's cheek, she got lost in her rage. She reached for the girl's shirt and slung her into the trashcan. The girl flipped over it and then fell to the floor.

"What the fuck were you saying about my mama, bitch?" she questioned as she kicked the girl from her forehead to her rib cage until her shoes were slippery from being covered in blood. "Talk that shit now, ho. I'm listening!"

Temper, consumed with stomping on the girl, almost missed the fight next to her. Being the ride-or-die friend Kei-Kei was, she put the tall bitch on her back with one punch that looked to have come from her soul and out of her fist for finding the shit funny.

"Why you ain't laughing now, bitch?" Kei-Kei said, hovering over the girl like a shade tree. Once the girl realized she was on her ass, she lay there and pretended to be dead. That opened the invite for Kei-Kei to join in on the stomp fest her best friend had started.

If you were standing far enough up the street and watching the chaos, you'd think the girls were in a double Dutch competition as ribs cracked underneath their feet. They beat the girls up so severely that when downtown security guards arrived to break it up, their focus was on the lives of the battered girls. The diversion gave Temper and Kei-Kei time to escape before the security could dispatch the police. They must have run ten city blocks nonstop from downtown L.A. to the fashion district before they slowed down to catch their breath. The girls broke out laughing in unison as they pointed out the blood that covered them. Temper wanted to say the right words to Kei-Kei to show her appreciation without getting caught up in her feelings. Kei-Kei beat her to the punch.

"Blood sisters for life. Them bitches didn't know that she's my 'junkie-ass mama' too. We left them leaking!"

Kei-Kei extended her arm so that they could dap it up, and to her surprise, Temper gave her the first hug of their lengthy friendship.

Taking the prescription of Vicodin was out of the question. She knew Kei-Kei didn't need the explanation.

"Knock, knock," Lena said, opening the bedroom door before being permitted to enter. "You say this handsome baby is my son's, and although I don't want to believe you, he looks just like him, and I feel it in my soul that he is. Look at him. He's as sexy as me," she said, slow dancing with the baby in her arms before continuing. "So being his g-mama, seeing that I'm too young to be called granny, he needs milk. This cow milk diluted with water will fuck his little system up. My grandbaby needs bottles and diapers. And how long do you think I'm going to let him stay wrapped in towels like Baby Jesus? You've been in this room for over eight hours without a gun pointed at me, and I haven't picked up the phone to call a soul. Let me drive out to the twenty-four-hour Kmart and get little man what he needs. And I'm beyond tired of calling him little man, too. What's his name?"

"I told you to leave me alone and that I didn't want to see him," Temper shouted.

"Oops, I must have forgotten. What's the baby's name?"

Temper wasn't in the mood to have Lena shooting things at her all at once. Nevertheless, she knew she wasn't going to let up until she gave in.

"His name is Emperor Charles and whatever the hell your son's last name is. I'll let you go grab your grandson's shit as long as you take my girl home and tell her mama she's been with you."

"Been with me where at this hour, the strip club?" Lena snapped.

"Hell, I don't know. Come up with a lie a mama would believe. Your son is a damn good liar. I'm sure he got it from you," Temper finished with a roll of her low, bloodshot eyes.

Lord, be a tongue depressor. I'm about ready to cuss this little bitch out and deal with whatever consequences come with it, Lena thought. Instead, she said, "Come on, Kei-Kei, and here, get the baby."

"I'm not watching that little boy. Take him with you!"

"I'm not taking this baby out in this night air, especially not wrapped in a fucking towel. He doesn't bite. All you have to do is sit here and hold him without smoking weed all in his face. Come on, Kei-Kei, so that I can lie to your damn mama. And, Temper," she said, now standing at the doorway, "you need to go back to the drawing board when it comes to my grandson's name. His daddy's last name is Charles, and I've seen you walk around this neighborhood with your head all high like you're hood royalty, but let me be the first to tell you you're not. There ain't no black men named Emperor coming out of this raggedy-ass neighborhood." She exited the room before Temper could speak.

"I'll be back to check on you later, Tee, but . . ." Kei-Kei hesitated as she walked to the door.

"But what?" Temper asked, clearly irritated by having to watch the baby.

"Um, I was just thinking. I know the baby looks like K-Mack and all, but are you sure it's his? You told me y'all had only got down like twice, and that you were fucking with a lame you met on the party line. How do you know the baby ain't that other nigga's?"

"Because I lied, bitch. The shit between K-Mack and me got real, and I didn't want you to know. Fuck that. I didn't even want me to know." Temper giggled. "We've been getting down for over a year. No condom, no pull out. His pussy, my dick. I know I should have told you, and you have every right to be fucked up with me about all this shit, but what can I say besides I'm sorry? It's my life that I fucked up, not yours."

"Shit, Tee, you still don't get it. If it's your life, it's my life too. I wish you had kept it real with me about all of this shit. That was a fucked-up way to find out you were pregnant, but I guess we all got our fucked-up secrets. I'll be back as long as my mama don't kill me." She chuckled and closed the door behind her.

Temper sat the baby down on the bed, and instantly he began to cry. She didn't know how to care for a child. Even when she babysat for her homeboys in the hood, she had a rule that the child had to be able to walk, talk, and use the bathroom on their own before she'd agree to watch him.

"Shh, hush, little nigga. Your granny will be back soon," she said, which seemed to make the child scream louder. She turned on the television to try to drown him out, but that didn't work. She went to Lena's room and grabbed the sports bottle she had been using to feed the baby and stuck it in his mouth. The milk began to spill all over his face as she attempted to feed him as he lay on his back. She scooped him up, and magically he stopped crying.

"Oh, you're like your sorry-ass daddy, I see. You like my touch. Don't get used to it because I promise you this is the last time I hold you. Once your granny gets back, I'm bouncing."

She didn't understand why the more she talked to the baby, the more relaxed he seemed to get. In a matter of minutes, the baby was out cold. Temper stared at him in disgust. He had his father's pointy nose, big, flat forehead, and bright yellow skin. Willful ignorance would prevent her from seeing the similarities the baby had to her. She refused to search for her looks in the child and credited his skin color to his father. She couldn't lie. The baby was beautiful. Not that she had been around enough babies to judge accurately. She'd only seen a handful of babies to compare and contrast. Using her memory, she concluded that he was born with more hair than average, and he didn't have the wrinkles most newborns had. Temper ran her index finger across one of his locks and almost panicked at the dent he had at the top of his head. She didn't know if all babies had that, yet she was sure that if it were a problem, Lena would have disclosed it by now.

"Damn, look at your purple lips. You've been smokin' that good too, I see." She giggled as she ran her finger across his bottom lip. Temper didn't realize that she was warming up to the baby. If it weren't for the phone ringing that broke her concentration, she would have kissed him on his forehead. She didn't answer the phone the first time it rang. It was four o'clock in the morning, and nobody should be calling at that hour. When it rang for a second time, she assumed it had to be Lena.

"Hello?" she answered.

"Hello? Who dis?"

The sound of Khasema's voice speaking his typical slang instantly pissed her off.

"Nigga, you called here. Who are you looking for?"

"I know where I called. I called my house, and nobody should be answering my mama's phone except her. Who the fuck is this?"

Not knowing what to say next, Temper hung up. She didn't expect him to call, and even if he did, she assumed it would be a collect call that she could deny. On the other hand, remembering the hustler he was, she was sure that he'd acquired a burner cell phone or had a three-way hookup, which meant he'd be calling back. When the phone rang for the third time, she had her thoughts together and was ready to spit fire at his ass.

"Man, who the fuck is this? Put my mama on the phone."

"She ain't here, and you know who the fuck this is, nigga. Don't play dumb."

"Temper. Bitch, I thought that was your voice. What are you doing at my mama's house? I told your young, stupid ass I wasn't fucking with you no more after you sent that bullshit letter trying to stick me for abortion money. Put my mama on the phone, ho, so I can tell her to put you out of our house."

"I already told you, she's not here, bitch, and don't worry about why I'm at your mama's house. You need to be worrying about keeping that ass soapy so you can have commissary while you serve your time, inmate. You have responsibilities when you touch down. Don't let them niggas raw dog your asshole until you're riding around this bitch in a wheelchair."

"Fuck you. The only thing I gotta do when I touch down is to have my bitch whoop your hood-rat ass. That shit right there is mandatory."

Temper fell silent at his confession of being in a new relationship. It was true that what they had, whatever it was, ended when he found out she wasn't 18 and began saying she was pregnant by him. He had been hounding her about hitting it for months, and she tried shooting him down several times. It was working until she began pushing nickels and dimes of dope for him. His hounding became worse. She didn't lie to him about her age for the relationship. She did it for the job. When Khasema asked her why she wanted to catch bites for him when her ass needed to be on a school bus headed to get educated, she told him she had graduated high school, and college wasn't for her. She never actually said she was 18, though she did make herself seem grown. When the pregnancy symptoms began hitting her hard, she confirmed her suspicions with half a dozen dollar pregnancy tests. When he'd called her from jail, she'd told him that she needed to talk with him and it was important.

"Tell me," he'd demanded.

"I don't think I can over this phone. That shit is suspect."

Not knowing if her words would incriminate him more, he'd urged her to come to visit. When the application was denied, saying, "Minors are only allowed to visit when an approved adult visitor accompanies them," he cut her ass off like a past-due electric bill.

"Fuck you and that bitch. Tell her to run up. I bet money that I'll put her on her ass. Ain't none of these hood-rat bitches in the Low Bottoms fucking with me."

"Bitch, please, you ain't fucking with Kei-Kei." He didn't mean to say her name. He promised Kei-Kei that he'd never tell Temper about what they had going on. It wasn't supposed to be anything more than homie love from time to time, yet more had sparked. Nevertheless, the cat was out of the bag. What could he do?

"Kei-Kei who?"

"Aw, I guess your best friend forgot to mention how she was riding this dick too, huh? I like fried chicken more than fried rice, you dumbass Asian bitch. You didn't have enough dark meat in you. Ain't no black man alive passing up barbeque sauce for a bottle of salty-ass soy sauce. So yeah, we're fucking, and if you don't get your ass up out of my mama's crib, I'm going to send her through there to fuck you up."

Temper felt heartbroken, and the battle she thought she was ready to fight had been won with just his simple words. She was going to hang up in his face at the same time the baby started crying in the background and caught his attention.

"Whose fucking baby is that?"

"Yours, muthafucka, and when you touch down, ask yo' bitch Kei-Kei to help you raise it. That spoiled-ass tartar sauce you're spitting out yo' fishy dick made a baby like I tried to tell yo' ass. I guess you better learn to love egg rolls, muthafucka, because your son is spitting soy sauce too!"

She hung up the phone and left it off the hook so that he couldn't call back. She wished she had said more than weak condiment jokes. She should have mentioned that he had broken up with one minor only to fuck with the next. Still, even with Kei-Kei stabbing her in her back, she couldn't help but feel the need to be loyal to her. A part of her hoped he was lying, contrary to her gut saying that he wasn't. *That's how that bitch knew his mama be on that bingo bus. She was leaving me hanging to dip over here Saturday evenings.*

Temper picked the baby up, but this time he wouldn't stop crying. She wanted to cry too and couldn't. There was something in Kei-Kei's betrayal that gave her the strength to hold back her tears and focus on the baby's. She tried feeding him the milk again, and he spit it out. She rocked him like she saw Lena doing, and that wasn't working either.

"Damn, all you do is cry. What's the matter? Are you hungry?"

Instantly, a lightbulb came on, and she remembered the milk that had been dripping from her breasts for months. She emptied the sports bottle and tried squeezing milk from her nipple into it. Only drops came out.

"Look, I'm going to put my tittie in your mouth, and you better not bite me," she commanded as if he had a mouthful of teeth or understood what biting was. She dedicated fifteen minutes without complaint to trying to get him to latch on to her now-C-cup breasts, and he wouldn't. Frustrated and ready to give up, she felt his jaws lock around her nipple, and he began to suck.

"Oh, shit, that hurts!" she screamed out in horror. Not only was her breast sensitive to his mouth, but the contractions she had during labor also came back to kick her in the ass. There wasn't a need to lie. She was cold-hearted. Giving up and letting the baby starve to save herself from the pain crossed her mind, except the thrill to do it wasn't there. Starving him felt like she was starving herself, and she couldn't go through with it. Whatever the feeling was that was taking over made her uncomfortable. It made her second-guess the decision she'd made months ago. *I can't keep this little nigga. He will slow me down. If I get straight, I'll come back for him,* she coached herself into believing. She leaned back and bucked up. Feeding him was the least she could do for him seeing that she was trashing him anyway.

When he finally fell asleep, releasing her nipple, Lena said, "Now you have to burp him."

She had been standing in the door from Temper's first attempt to latch the baby on to her nipple and planned to help if she hadn't had the thought, *this little heffa might have a motherly bone in her after all. Let me see if she can do it.* After watching her breastfeed successfully, she spoke up about burping him, knowing Temper wouldn't have a clue to relieve the gas from his stomach.

Lena put down all the bags she was toting, placed the baby over Temper's shoulder, and forced her fingers to massage his back. "See? At this age, he doesn't need all those pats on the back," she said once the baby let out an air-filled burp.

Temper laid him down and rushed over to the nightstand where she had laid her gun down.

"Peep this shit, here. You got everything you need for the little nigga, and I've been here long enough. I'm about to bounce, and you're not going to stop me this time. He's your grandson, and if you don't believe me, have a DNA test done on his bitch-ass daddy."

"I'm not going to try to stop you, trust me. I'm glad to see you go. I stood in that store, debating whether to call the police and put an end to all of this shit after the way Kei-Kei's mama talked shit to me, but I was more worried that you'd leave the baby here alone, impatient to hit the road. Instead of getting your little disrespectful ass locked up, I got a few things for you to take with you on your little trip. I was a young girl once, and I can tell by the look in your eyes that you're not trying to get home. Wherever you're going feels more like home already, doesn't it?"

Temper hesitated before answering, not knowing what tricks the lady had up her sleeve. She nodded, and then Lena handed her a bag with a sweatsuit in it, super-absorbent pads with wings, black house slippers, and a heart-shaped necklace that read MOTHER with a single stone on it.

"Go ahead and get yourself together. I have a grandson to raise."

Temper grabbed the bag, showered, and came out in the sweatsuit. She threw the clothes she previously had on in the trash and hightailed to the front door without taking another look at the baby. When she reached for the knob, Lena was standing behind her, holding her gun.

"You forget to grab this?"

"Nah. Where I'm going, I won't need that anymore."

"Umm, okay," Lena groaned, not wanting to be left with the gun. "Look at me, Temper. If you're sure this is what you want to do, why do you have tears in your eyes?"

Temper turned around to face her, and the necklace she was wearing turned on her neck.

"Never mind. I think I have my answer," she said as Temper stormed out the door before she drowned in her tears.

She glanced back once she crossed the property line and said, "Name the baby Symmetry Truth. You can give him his daddy's last name if you want to."

"You know you could have come up with something better than that shit. What kind of name is Symmetry Truth? Is it Asian?"

"No, it's not Asian. It's his name, and so are the meanings of the words when you put the two of them together if you raise him right. Tell him to let the world know they can suck his dick and drink his soy sauce if they don't like it." Temper laughed as she walked down the abandoned early morning street. For the first time in almost nine months, she walked the streets lighter.

Chapter Three

The only time the hood felt at peace was at sunrise. The chickens that the Mexicans housed in their backyards would crow, giving the deadly streets a warm, country feel to them. It was cold, yet Temper's body was on fire. She charged the rise in body temperature to the fleece sweatsuit she was wearing and kept it pushing. Normally she would walk in the security of the alleys and hop gate upon gate as a short cut through Kei-Kei's yard to get home, except climbing felt like a task she wasn't ready to complete. And knowing her anger, she would have been tempted to run into Kei-Kei's house to put a beating on her while she slept.

Temper spent the last nine months fighting her hunger pangs. Her craving for bathtub tamales, tacos, and dollar Chinese food won those fights most of the time. As she passed the Hispanic lady and her cart filled with beef and pork tamales, the smell of the combination made her feel sick. She called Earl twice, similar to an alcoholic having their first beer of the day.

"Ay, are you straight?" She couldn't determine whether it was the words or the person they belonged to that caused her to jump.

"Yeah, I'm good, big homie. That first sip of the day got me fucked up," she lied.

"You sure? I can drop you off to wherever you're trying to get to. You look a little sick."

Beast wasn't a person you comfortably said no to, nor did you freely decline his offer. Temper did her best to be anywhere that he wasn't so she wouldn't have to face that dilemma. Her day was off to a bad start.

"Yes, you know I live right there," she said, pointing two houses away. "But I appreciate the offer."

"No problem." He rolled his window back up, concealing himself behind the darkness of the tint, and drove off.

Temper didn't exhale until she made it to the gate that did anything except protect her grandmother's house from outsiders. Thanks to her uncle Troy's dope selling in the detached garage before he swapped it out for heavy usages, their yard welcomed the streets twenty-four seven like a hospital. The doctors were the dealers, and their patients were the dope fiends. Her uncle was an equal combination of them both.

"Where have you been? I've been waiting for you to get home so you can front me a dime until the third when I get my check. Is that cool?" Wiggles begged excitedly, twitching and scratching at the sight of the young, foolish girl coming through the gate.

"Yeah, I'll bring it out in a second."

"Hold the fuck up. What's wrong with you? You ain't never said yeah that fast without talking shit or threatening me first."

"You want the shit or not?" Temper snapped.

"Hell yeah, I want it."

"Then shut the fuck up and wait for me to bring it out to you, damn."

Wiggles sat down on the steps that led to the porch, reminiscent of a child on timeout. "I betcha I won't say shit else!"

No matter how often Temper had served this lady, she could never get over how beautiful she was and could be if she killed the habit that was consuming her. Everybody had a story, and Wiggles', as the neighbor nicknamed her, was one story that everyone knew. She had been a well-known blues singer from out of Chicago. The world knew her as Shirley Blu, and Shirley was everything every man wanted and what every woman wanted to be. Besides having a beautiful and powerful voice, she had a shape that most women dreamed of, and most men dreamed of being inside. Her skin tone was black as oil, making her brown eyes appear clear from the darkness surrounding them. She kept her short black hair relaxed and finger waved, and if she wasn't in the mood to groom, she'd wear it slicked down like a seal.

Like most singers, she'd started off singing in the church's choir. However, Shirley's spin on gospel music was banned from the church's doors and her parents' love. As the pastor's only daughter, she was an embarrassment and had to go. With nowhere to go except the streets, she began to sing at every bar, club, and pub that would give her enough money to get by. That exposure opened the doors to venues in New York and then all over the world.

Singing blues music to help deal with the pain of being disowned by the father she saw as a superhero wasn't a strong enough fix. Nor was the brandy she began guzzling a pint at a time. After making it to the world-famous jazz clubs that laced Central Avenue in Los Angeles, she was introduced to her painkiller. Her choice of Novocain, the medicine that could numb away thoughts of her father, was the highly addictive crack cocaine. She dived straight into smoking the drug out of a glass dick simply because she was scared to snort it, and since Shirley found that she could come across it with ease in Los Angeles, she made it her home, buying a lovely house on the west side in Baldwin Hills. She frequently used the drug, and it hadn't dug its deadly hooks in her all the way.

At the time of her relocation, it had only pierced her skin, and then she met Troy.

Temper's uncle Troy was what you would call an A-list dealer. He only supplied those who couldn't afford the loss they would take if their dirty secret were to get out. He was summoned to supply a party Shirley Blu was having at her house, and as they say in the movies, the rest was history. Troy fulfilled her demands both sexually and chemically, and she fell in love. She moved him in instantly, which caused a downward spiral for them both. She preferred her fix out of a glass pipe, and Troy had only used the drug in sprinkles in the joints he smoked. Before they met, he wouldn't smoke his weed heavy daily.

Nevertheless, he was now dating a musician, and he allowed the party lifestyle to wear its effects on him. The PP—party and perform—lifestyle had a seven-day schedule, and Shirley preferred to be high to get through it. It wasn't long before Troy never had enough dope on him to supply his buyers, seeing that the couple's personal stash had tripled in size.

Once he was out of the dope game completely, his income stopped. Shirley kept them high by performing for years until the drugs' effects ruined her voice and stage presence. Once that happened, vendors began turning her away for being too high to perform. Slowly, the tangible riches that covered her became the property of the pawn shop and whatever dealer was willing to give her the most dope for the items. She sold her house and downsized to an apartment for them, and eventually they were evicted for nonpayment of rent. Troy moved the now-married couple into his mother's house, and after robbing a mom-and-pop store at gunpoint unmasked to furnish their habit, he landed himself in prison.

As for Shirley Blu, having her poisoner locked behind bars, she tried to get herself clean. It would have worked if Temper's mother, Dorothy, hadn't been fighting the same monkey. Dorothy introduced her to the world of prostitution for a fix, which eventually forced Temper's grandmother to put her daughter out. Her grandmother blamed her son for Shirley losing everything and allowed her to stay, pledging that she had a roof over her head for life.

Temper knew the story and felt that same guilt her grandmother carried on her shoulders. Not because of what her uncle had done solely. Her mother's involvement collected its toll. She never layawayed drugs with anyone besides Wiggles, and fronting her always came with an explosion of her talking shit. Only today her response was different. Wiggles tried to help with Temper's upbringing since she was the only other female in the house, though oddly and inexplicably, Temper only accepted the not-so-bright advice of her uncle Troy.

"You look like shit, and I'm sure you smell like it. How many times do I have to tell you to at least come home to wash your ass daily?" Her grandma Jo knew the clothes she was wearing weren't the same ones she saw Temper leave in two days ago. She used the harsh words to let Temper realize she had been worried.

"My ass is clean, and I'm just tired," Temper returned.

Jo had been sitting in her favorite recliner, smoking a cigarette and attending church via television. She was wearing her Sunday best, which was a throw dress, which had to be fastened with safety pins to keep it closed because the zipper broke long ago, and worn house slippers that she wore out of the house more than inside. Jo replaced her cheap gin with a bottle of Seagram's, which meant she had taken her weekly turnaround bus ride to the Indian reservation to gamble and must have won.

"How much did you hit for? I see you're drinking top-shelf this morning." Temper laughed, and her grandmother gave her a crooked smile. However, it was a smile nonetheless.

"None of your goddamn business, Chinaman, that's how much I hit. I'll never trust a set of tight eyes on a two-legged bitch!" She dug in her bra and retrieved a hundred-dollar bill, except she didn't pull it out. She balled it up in her hand like a dirty piece of Kleenex and cased the room for her son. "Did you find out how behind in school you are like I asked you to?" she yelled, still casing the area, then urged Temper to come to her with her free hand's index finger.

"I already told you how far behind I am. I stopped going to school the second semester of the tenth grade, so that means I'm like three and a half years behind or close to that."

Jo shook her head, "You dropped out of school to sell drugs and don't even know simple fucking math. That makes your stupid ass a year and a half behind. I hope you count your dope money better than you figure out everyday numbers," she said, sliding the money from her hand to Temper's before whispering, "I know you'll be seventeen this Friday, so if I don't give it to you now, I'll be giving it to the bingo hall Thursday. Happy birthday."

Temper thanked her in the same tone as Grandma Jo started back, "Your ass will be grown in a year, and you don't have no type of education about yourself, and you're too fucking hardheaded for the military, so what do you plan on doing? I'm already taking care of two grown, smoked-out muthafuckas. There ain't no room in here for a third."

"Man, Granny, I already told you I'm not living in this nasty-ass house at eighteen. I have a plan. You just don't know it. I'll be out of this raggedy piece of shit by Friday."

"It's a raggedy piece of shit because you three raggedy muthafuckas are in it. I'm sixty-nine years old, and I'll be dead before I pick up a broom after y'all's asses. My room is clean. If y'all want to live in filth, that's your choice."

Temper reached in to kiss her grandmother on the cheek before disappearing to her room as she always did. The small action made her feel dizzy, and her grandmother caught it.

"What's wrong with you, girl? You're pale. Well, more pale than usual for your Cambodian ass, and you can't even stand up straight. What kite are you flying on? I knew it was a matter of time before you joined those cart pushers on that glass dick." She turned her bottle up and reached for another cigarette.

"I'm fine, just a little tired."

"Oh, I didn't know that not having color in your face meant you're fine. Whatever lie you want to feed me today is fine by me. Just don't forget you're supposed to have your non-rent-paying ass out of my house by Friday, little girl. Now get up out of my face. You're interrupting my service."

Temper held up a missionary finger and laughed as she went to her room. She prepared herself to stand on her tiptoes to retrieve the key she hid above her door. The key wasn't necessary. The door was already unlocked and slightly cracked. Even before she peeked in, she knew what— or better yet who—she would find if she walked in. She wanted to watch her uncle in action before she did.

Troy had fucked her room up in his search for money and was in the process of cleaning it up. He worked hard to cover his tracks besides the way he arranged her pillows on her bed. They would have given his intrusion away if she hadn't caught him red-handed.

"You're lucky I just tossed my heat, or I would have put a bullet right in your ass," she said, pointing her index finger with her thumb extended like a gun at his ass. He was bent over in her closet, lining up her shoes.

"You got a rat in here. I watched his dirty little ass go from the kitchen straight under your door. I told you about keeping food in here," he lied, trying to play it off.

"You're the rat, nigga. What did you steal out of my room this time? Empty them pockets, junkie."

"I didn't steal shit. I told you that was Shirley who broke in here the last time. I was in here trying to help your ungrateful ass out with that rat," he said, scrambling to his feet and pointing at a pair of K-Swiss that she hadn't rocked in years.

"I bet. Now empty those pockets before I do it myself."

"You stay with bullshit. What I look like stealing from you when I help Mama keep a roof over your head? I'm the nigga who taught you how to cook, cut, and package that shit up. I gave yo' ass the dope game, remember?"

He started with his back pockets first, and they were already empty. Next, he flipped the lining out of the front two. He had about sixty cents in pennies and a lighter in one, and his crack pipe wrapped in aluminum foil and a piece of steel wool in the other. "I told you I didn't have shit. There's a rat in here, and I was trying to be a good uncle and catch it for you. Since you're here now, you can catch his ass yourself and stop leaving food in here. I'm not going to tell your little bad ass again!" He made it through her bedroom door and down the hallway before she stopped him.

"Hold up. I need you to lift up that stinky-ass Boston Celtics T-shirt first."

"I'm not lifting shit because I don't have shit. Why are you always accusing me of being cutthroat? If I said I didn't take anything, that's what I mean."

Yeah, yo' junkie ass has something, she thought as she ran down the hallway and opened the junk closet's door that stored everything in the house they no longer used and were too much of hoarders to throw away. The steel baseball bat was in arm's reach. However, she decided to grab one of her grandfather's golf clubs to add nostalgia to the beating she was about to give him.

"You better not swing that muthafucking club at me, Temper."

As if his words gave her permission, she swung the 9 iron back and cracked him in the stomach with it. The impact of the club caused her hands more pain than it did her uncle's midsection. The collision even made a metallic sound.

"Lift the fucking shirt, or the next swing will be aimed at your lying-ass mouth. I promise niggas will be calling you No-teeth T around this bitch when I'm done."

"Mama, come and get your crazy-ass granddaughter. She's high off that shit again and tripping."

Grandma Jo didn't make a move. She had seen the two at each other's necks too many times to care.

"Y'all both high on that bullshit. I'm in church praying for y'all now. I'll pass God the message," she said, drinking another shot from her bottle. *I wish they would just kill each other and get it over with,* was what she thought.

Temper swung the club again, this time hitting him on his hip bone. The swing wasn't as powerful as the first. The first had exhausted the energy she had, yet it still caused him to scream out in agony.

"Lift yo' shirt, crack ho," she yelled, and he did slowly.

Tears filled her eyes, and Troy took a few steps back. He knew stealing the item would break her heart. He assumed that, since she had it stashed in the back of her closet, it would be a while before she discovered it was missing.

"Hold on before you swing that fucking club again. I was going to take your great-grandfather's medals to be polished. I promise I was going to put them back."

It wasn't the medals concealed in the box that caused the mist to form in her eyes. It was the gold hunter-case pocket watch that hung on its Albert chain that did. The dented watch belonged to her great-grandfather, and not only was it a family heirloom, but it was also a constant reminder that their bloodline meant to exist.

The solid-gold watch had saved her great-grandfather's life. It gave him his freedom to flee from France's control of Cambodia. He was considered a radical for his blatant disrespect for the French leaders. He wasn't a fan of Cambodia being a protectorate of the French because times had changed, and with the growth of the country, he felt it was time to let Cambodians run it themselves. The supposedly secret rallies he held landed him a meeting in front of Indochina's leaders. He was sentenced to death. After several months of imprisonment, he was privately walked into an abandoned rice field in Asia and received a single shot to his chest. He was left for death to take his soul and for his flesh to become one with nature.

After all their efforts to kill him, it didn't work out that way. The watch he stole from the French guard to use to barter with if he could ever escape had saved his life as it accepted the bullet for him. He didn't have a wife or children yet, and now he vowed to. He knowingly disobeyed his teachings of Gautama Buddha by failing to purify his conduct when he stole the watch. The stolen item showed him that he was meant to have the life he had been given, and he pledged to obtain both.

He married as soon as he made it into the northern half of Japan, and the irony was that he had four daughters, no sons. It wasn't until he was on his deathbed that he discovered his Japanese wife, twenty years younger than him, had given birth to their first and only son. He left instructions for the watch and legacy with his daughters to pass on to his wife post-labor, and then he died almost instantly, making those instructions his final words to his children.

The watch had made its way down the generations as Temper's grandfather tried to do away with his Japanese blood by marrying a Cambodian woman, who gave birth to only one male child—Temper's father, Davi, which meant Angel. Wanting more than what Cambodia had to offer post-Vietnam, Davi moved to America and made California his home. While working a random cleanup job on the east side of Los Angeles, he met the brown-skinned goddess Dorothy, fell in love, and married her. He provided the sperm that created Temper right before his love for the white substance swallowed him whole, and he found himself stuck in the belly of the crack beast.

His love for crack gave him more pleasure than exploding in Dorothy's warmth. He still made love to his wife from time to time. It wasn't until she went into prostituting full-time that his dick no longer reacted to her. The pleasure of his wife came from the drugs she provided. That was before he dived through the belly of the beast and was shit out through his death, a death caused by a drug dealer tired of waiting for his money. He passed the watch down to Temper. He knew the legacy, and the second chance for the men of his bloodline to make right with Buddha stopped with him.

The history behind the watch wasn't the reason her heart was heavy at Troy's thievery. It was what she held inside the hunter casing that did. She pushed her uncle into the wall as she ran to her room and emptied the case onto her bed. She placed the watch into the palm of her hand and sat on her bed as she opened it. The picture of her pregnant mother and stale-faced father outside of the late Marvin Gaye's residence following the singer's fatal shooting was still where she had put it. It wasn't a happy picture of her parents. They weren't high like she had always seen them, yet it was the only picture she owned of all three of them together. Drugs won ownership of her father's flesh and her mother's mind. Dorothy refused to admit that her husband was dead, and whenever she was around Temper, she'd make up a story for his absence. Crack killed her parents. All she had left of their lives together was a memory captured in a picture from before she was born. She was lost in the image and didn't know Troy had followed her until he sat next to her and spoke.

"I took that picture of y'all. Fucked-up part about it is I was out there working. Those rich-ass singers and songwriters who showed up needed a fix to deal with Marvin Gaye's death, and I supplied it." He laughed as he remembered the day and shook his head. "Hell, I even got that expensive-ass camera from a white cat who worked for the newspaper. He was short on cash, but that camera covered the difference. That was a sad-ass day in music history."

Temper looked up at her uncle, trying to see if there was a soul inside of the drug shell. She came up empty-handed. "What's sad is you. You'd do anything for the dope, and the dope ain't never done shit for you but smoked you more than you smoked it. You know you owe me big time for this shit, right?"

He stood up. "Yeah, I fucked up . . ." Troy forgot his next words at the sight before him. He checked out his skin and then Temper's. "Girl, you're bleeding all over your bed. Are you cut, stabbed—"

"Shut up before Granny hears you, nigga. I'm fine. I just feel weaker than a muthafucka right now. So look, you'll work for me until I get better. I shouldn't give your stealing ass shit, but I'm going to pay you when you're done."

"Whatever you need, Tee, I got you, but if you want me at my best, I'm going to need my medicine, too. You ain't the only one sick." He scratched his neck and then frantically scratched his head with both hands while she watched and shook her head in disbelief.

"I'll give you a dime piece to hold you until after you help me into the shower and clean this shit up for me. Get Wiggles, too. I need her help."

"I'm on it."

"Wait," Temper said before he exited her room. "This stays between us. Don't tell Granny or anyone in the streets shit about me, you hear? If folks come through looking for me, you ain't seen me. That goes for everybody, even Kei-Kei, and from now on, stop calling that fat bitch your niece. That ho ain't fit for our blood."

He saluted her and went to do her bidding. Temper sat on her bed, and her temperature kept rising. Her skin had gotten so hot that the charm on her necklace heated up and began to feel uncomfortable. She took it off her neck, removed the charm from the chain, and placed it in with her watch as her new keepsake.

"Hey, baby, that sorry, nothing-ass husband of mine said you wanted me." Wiggles came in with Troy behind her.

"Yeah, I do. Give me a second." She turned her attention back to her uncle. "Can you go get clean covers for my bed out of the linen closet? And while I'm in the shower, I need you to make it for me. I need to lie down for a while."

Once he was out of earshot, she locked eyes with Wiggles and let the tears fall that she had been holding back. "I made a move last night that I'm not proud of." She shrugged and then continued, "But fuck it. I had to and would do it again. I'm going to tighten you up, I promise, but I need your help first."

Wiggles didn't know the facts, and she didn't need them to figure out what was going on. She had been street poisoned young, and going to church every Sunday wasn't the poison control center as her parents had prayed. Wiggles had noticed the large gangster clothing Temper had recently switched to wearing. Then, Temper would send her into the Bloods' neighborhood for food at all hours of the night. She'd order chili cheese pastrami fries with a cup of Thousand Island dressing and a cheeseburger with avocado on the side every time. Wiggles knew she had been pregnant. What she didn't know was that Temper had given birth to the child. When she saw the blood on her comforter, Wiggles assumed she'd had an abortion or, even worse, she had miscarried. Aware of the pride the little girl wore on her sleeve like a badge from the Scouts, she decided to talk so Temper wouldn't have to.

"First thing you need me to do for you is run down this street to the dollar store. It's going to take a bottle of peroxide to get that out of the comforter, and do you have pads with wings? What are you doing for the pain? Never mind. I almost forgot that you have a thing about pain medicine. That shower should help a little. I'll bring the heating pad in here when I get back. What about a fever? You know you're wide open and can catch infection easily. Otherwise, I would have told you to soak in the tub." Wiggles was rambling as she placed her palm on Temper's forehead, which was on fire. "Lord, you're hotter than virgin pussy on sale on the stroll. I'll get you a bottle of fever reducer, and if that doesn't work, we'll have to get you to a hospital—"

"No hospitals and no doctors," Temper interrupted.

"You stupid little girl, do you know you could have killed yourself doing your own home-remedy abortion? I know you don't want to go to a doctor, but there ain't shit I can buy over the counter for an infection. But," she said, racking her brain harder than she had in years, "I do have a friend I might be able to get antibiotics from. We'll just have to wait and see."

"Wiggles, I need you to be my auntie Shirley right now, okay? Damn. Here's twenty dollars for the store. Get everything you think I need except for pads. I have a bag of them on the porch next to the door. I didn't want Grandma Jo to see them. I guess I'm bleeding heavier than I thought. Bring that bag in, look through my drawers, and find me an outfit comfortable to lie down in. Put it on my dresser while Troy changes my bed, and then go to the store."

Words never meant a thing to Shirley until Temper called her "auntie." Caught off guard by the affection, she wrapped her arms around Temper and rocked her as she sang. Temper didn't know the song. Still, she'd bet her last dollar that it was known around churches. The lyrics spoke of peace only found through God and giving her suffering to Him. That was about all she could take in as she felt the angelic voice take her to a place she never knew existed. The tears stopped, a smile grew on her face, and then she hugged her aunt back.

"Damn, you can still sing."

"Girl, that's nothing. I used to blow the wigs off the first three rows of the church." She giggled, releasing herself from the hug.

Troy had been eavesdropping at the door, and watching his wife love on the closest thing they had to a daughter made him remember why he had fallen in love with her. It wasn't the drugs. It was the long nights of talking and dreaming together. The drugs felt good at first, and then they didn't. It was too late for a do-over, but he vowed to get those conversations back.

He wiped the emotions off his face and walked in as Temper tried to stand up. "I got you, Tee, and the water is already on in the shower."

"Cool. Just help me get to the bathroom, and I got it from there."

He got her to the bathroom, and they both realized that she had lied. She didn't have the strength to take over from there. When the steam hit her in the face when she walked in, she got lightheaded and almost hit the floor. He grabbed the hair dangling from her ponytail and helped to remove her sweatshirt. The awkward silence in the room made them both uncomfortable. He had always been "Troy." There was no real uncle/niece relationship. He spit knowledge, and she picked over it, only taking what she felt she could use. He pulled on the waistband of her pants and then looked her in her eyes.

"Temper, do you remember what I told you the day the police kicked in the front door to get me for that robbery?" he asked, now pulling down her panties with his eyes locked on hers.

"Yeah, I'll never forget it. You said the only way out of the hood is over a thirty-foot wall. Being born half Asian gave me a ten-foot ladder, and it's up to me to get the twenty feet to get over it." She quoted him almost verbatim.

"Exactly, but there's more I need to tell you, and that's that I'm sorry we sabotaged you from getting the twenty feet you needed. None of us got ours, and we didn't do shit nor teach you how to get yours because we don't know how the fuck to get them in the first damn place. Look at us—smoked out or drunk off our asses. We gave up our ladders for a fix years ago. Lift your left leg, baby girl."

Fear of him seeing or having to touch her pad and panties flashed over her face, and he caught it. "We're family, Temper. I got you, and I should have stepped up and gotten you years ago. I'm sorry, baby girl. You have been through a lot of unnecessary shit, and if I had stepped up and forced the State to send you to foster care instead of volunteering to help Mama raise you,

you would have gotten your twenty feet." He had fully undressed her and even snapped her bra without ever breaking their eye contact. He kept that contact until she was behind the security of the shower curtain.

"Ay, I'm throwing all this shit in a bag and taking it to the garbage. I don't know too much about the health of pussy, especially Asian wonton-soup pussy. I've swum in the Red Sea a few times to know blood clots the size of plums ain't a good look, though. You got two of them muthafuckas looking at me like they might grow legs and attack. There ain't nobody you can talk to about this shit?"

Temper immediately thought about her grandmother. The thought dissipated as quickly as it formed. It was now close to eight o'clock in the morning. She was sure she'd be fully drunk by now. "Nah, Uncle. We will figure this shit out. I think I've also thought of a way for you to help me get my twenty feet. We'll talk about it later."

"Just let me know what I need to do to make shit right." He opened the bathroom door. "Let me clean this shit up before it attacks me," he chuckled.

Temper stuck her face out of the shower as she watched him clean it all up. Before he closed the door to give her privacy, she said, "Thanks, Unc. I love you." She hurriedly closed the shower curtain, realizing she hadn't said those words to him since that day when she was eight and he went to jail.

"I love you too, Temper Taz," he said, calling her by the nickname he had given her as a child. "Scream if you need me. I'll be back with a towel if Shirley's slow ass isn't back from the store by then."

Chapter Four

Big Trice wished she were alone in the desert without water or maybe in the back of a police squad car shackled to a shitty diaper. Hell, even sitting front row at her funeral would have been better than riding in the car for fifty minutes with Casper and Beast. Of all the bitches banging Low Bottom Rollin' Twenties Crips, Beast always called on her when it was time to put in work. Especially when her baby daddy was the reason they needed to put in the work.

"Say that shit again," Beast roared at her for the fourth time in the last twenty minutes.

"I'm gon' knock on the door and ask for that nigga Travis. If he answers, I'll hit him with the lines you told me to say—"

"What lines are those?" he interrupted, clearly irritated by Trice's summary.

"That I'm baby Capone's baby mama, and that he sent me over there to give him a burner phone so he can call him. I'll let him know it's an emergency, tell him the number is programmed already, and walk back to the SUV. If somebody else answers the door, I'll tell them who I am and walk back to the whip before he comes out. That way, he meets me away from listening ears."

"Good," he grunted.

"No disrespect, big homie, but why can't I just pop the nigga in his dome if he answers the door? His ass is grimy, and he tried to play us fuck ugly, cuz." She was talking to Beast with her eyes locked on Casper's.

The men were in the second row, loading clips and placing silencers onto their preferred pieces. Casper had been silent the entire ride besides responding to questions from Beast. He wasn't known to be talkative, which made the hood name given to him a perfect match. His ghostly moves gave urban legend a new meaning and fortuned him the right to save his words for giving out orders to his less-ranked subordinates. Trice hated his silence, and after investing enough energy into complaining about it, the couple adopted their language. Their language didn't require words, and if she was reading Casper's expression right, their plan after the robbery was still a go. Aside from being able to tell that he was scared shitless about making such a bold move, she knew he was ready to get it over with.

"No problem and no disrespect taken," was all Beast said in return.

The house they pulled up to had seen better days. Bullet holes had broken the two windows that faced the street. There were sun-bleached newspapers taped to the glass to make up for the lack of curtains. Broken shingles covered the ground more than they covered the roof, and the dirty canary paint wrapped around the house needed steam cleaning. Never-manicured hedges and wildly growing grass lined the broken gate that remained closed by the strength of a linked chain and lock holding it together.

Though the house seemed abandoned, there were a few telltale signs that lured you into believing that the house wasn't vacant. The driveway was clear, and there was a two-wheel freshly indented trail that led from the street to the back side of the house. Although the front exterior showed no signs that the house had running electricity, a lone light at the house's rear was proof that it did. Vertical black security bars lined every window, and the wrought-iron security door placed in front of the wooden door couldn't have been more than a year old.

Trice pulled into the driveway and parked with the butt of the SUV in the street. The other entrances and exits to the property were blocked. She unzipped and removed the sweater that shielded her cleavage and granted stardom to her double-D breasts. If her titties didn't get her the pass she needed to make the plan flow smoothly, she hoped the extra-glossy lip gloss she applied would.

She made it halfway to the back before being met by one of the dope spot's henchmen. "Damn, sexy, what do you got going on?" asked the man with green eyes now hindering her path.

He was bright yellow with peanut butter–pigmented freckles. The word "goon" could describe his size and dress. However, it didn't define his face's angelic features. He was handsome, and if she hadn't met him with a plan in place, she would have pushed flirting with him to the max. She wondered if his dick was as wide and long as his arms and neck, then seductively asked, "Is Travis here?"

"Travis who?" Hearing his OG's government name used by the stranger snapped him out of the trance her flesh had put him in. The girl didn't look as if she could be a Fed, nor did she reek of probation officer. Nonetheless, she wasn't identifiable, and only those banging Pomona Hustling Crips were allowed at the spot. He wasn't sure who she was, nor did it matter, because he was sure she was banging his hood.

"Um, I don't know his hood name. My baby daddy, Baby Capo, gave me this address and sent me over here to give him a burner phone to call him on. He said it's an emergency. He said there's a lot of bullshit floating around the pen about his big homie Capone," she said with a shrug.

"Baby Capone said that? Damn, has he been smashing on them niggas who got the big homie's name in their mouth?"

She shrugged again, and then he continued with a stone expression etched on his face. It was the first time that "goon" could describe his full description.

"I don't know if I know anybody named Travis, though."

"Okay, cool," she said, turning on her heels and walking toward her vehicle. "I don't like running his gangbanging errands anyways. If his ass hadn't left me to do twelve years in Chino state prison, he wouldn't have let me come to his hood. I'll tell him what you said."

She was ten feet away from the car when a different voice told her to wait. It was Travis. He was wearing a white muscle shirt, navy blue khakis, and a pair of white and blue paisley house slippers. He hit the blunt he was holding in his hand before he spoke again. "You Candice?"

"Hell nah, I ain't Candice. Do I look like a snitch-ass bitch to you?" She said it the way Beast had instructed her to. "I'm his first baby mama, Audrey."

Travis hit the blunt again and then passed it to his henchman. He started walking toward her, and she rushed to meet him as far away from the SUV as she could.

"What did my nigga say was up?" he asked when they came to a meeting point.

"He didn't. He told me to give you this burner phone and tell you to call him. The number is already locked in the recent calls."

"Good looking out," he said, accepting the phone from her outstretched hand. He dialed the number as she made her way to the car. Before she could pull off, he flagged her back down.

"Ay, my nigga needs you to drop a package off for him," he yelled, and she pulled back into her same parking space. Quickly he beckoned her to pull around to the back. Beast had told her he would. "Pop your hatch, little mama, and come on in. It's going to take me a minute or two to get this shit together."

"I'm not going in nobody's house full of thirsty-ass niggas. I'll wait right here," she snapped.

"There ain't nobody else here. It's just me and that nigga Dice you just met, and we don't bite."

She hesitated and then got out. She followed both men in the house. Once she was seated in the living room, or what should have been the living room, her phone rang.

"Is it just those two niggas in the crib?" Beast asked.

"Yeah, Mama, I'll be back soon. You stay trippin' on my kids like they ain't your grandkids, too. Damn, I'm on my way back now."

The call ended, and the show was about to begin. Both men entered what looked to be the master bedroom. She reached in the waistband of her pants and gripped the handle of her piece. Dice came out of the room first and headed out the back door with a duffle bag in tow. Once she saw Casper walk through the door, she made her way to the bedroom.

"Ay, go back and wait in there. I'm sure my nigga don't want you caught up in this shit no more than you already are. If the supreme chief, OG Casper, sent word to Baby Casper in prison to get this done, there's some shit about to pop off with them Low Bottom Twenties niggas in L.A.," he urged.

Sadly, the sound of her pistol cocking told him otherwise.

He had a decision to make. Should he tackle her for the piece before she could get off a shot, or should he run to the adjoining bathroom and grab his piece? With adrenaline fueling his decision, he leaped toward Trice, and Casper sprayed him with bullets before he could get close. As planned, she cleaned the room of all the guns, money, and drugs she could find while Casper did the same. They weren't sure where Beast had gone. They were under the impression that he was in the other bedroom, mirroring their actions, until they heard their echoes against the house. Once the couple was sure the house had been emptied of everything worth value, they loaded the SUV.

"Where's Beast?" Trice asked after confirming he wasn't in the house or their ride.

"I don't know. He had his pistol on that light-skinned nigga last time I saw him. Check the side of the house, and I'm going to check the garage."

Trice ran around the house twice and didn't see anything or anyone.

"He's in here, baby," Casper yelled, and she exhaled her anxiety. Now it was time for her to put on the real show. Three made the trip to Pomona, but only two of them would make it back.

Casper felt it was time to retire Beast. He had become self-fulfilling and disrespectful to the couple and the code of the Crips. He'd talked to Trice about killing him and running away with the profits from the lick they had hit, and she'd agreed with her man. When she walked into the garage, she pulled her heat out, and before either man could draw their guns, she shot Casper in his stomach. He hit the floor, clutching his gut in agony. Within seconds blood filled his mouth.

"Did you really think this bitch was more faithful to you than me?" Beast questioned, his words as calm as the weed smoke he exhaled. "You plotted to rob me and take me out, and you thought my bitch would help you do it? Trust no bitch or her nigga, my nigga."

"Trice baby," Casper moaned as blood spewed out of his mouth, "he's playing you. The Pomona Crips are his—"

"Shut the fuck up," Beast muttered after swiftly kicking Casper in his mouth.

Casper wanted to finish his sentence. Instead, he used the last bit of energy he had to try to scoot away from the dark blob of evil hovering over him. Every inch he gained deleted seconds off the time he had left. His sight began to darken, and seconds before death fully welcomed him, Casper got one last clear picture. It was the picture of the woman he loved and had birthed a child with executing the shot that would take him out.

"Now do you trust me?" she asked with the barrel of the gun still pointing at Casper's corpse.

"More than I trusted you yesterday," he said, pulling the vapors of weed deeper into his lungs before passing her the blunt. Once he exhaled, he turned to her and asked, "What do you know about that little Asian bitch Temper who works for K-Mack?"

Temper didn't realize how tired she was until she woke up hungry Monday night. Troy stayed by her side until she closed her eyes, and after giving him and Wiggles the gram of dope she'd hidden in the fish sticks box in the refrigerator, she knew he wouldn't be there when she opened them.

"Damn, stank bitch, I didn't think you'd ever wake up," Kei-Kei said, smiling, "How are you feeling with your extra-loud snoring ass?"

Temper didn't answer her. She had more important things to tend to first, like her pad. Kei-Kei coming to check on her was a sure sign that she hadn't spoken to Khasema. Nonetheless, with the rotten smell of a Red Lobster chain whose refrigeration system went out coming from in between her legs, she decided to use the time to wash her ass before snapping off on her.

"How did you get in here?" Troy asked. He'd stuck his head in the room to check on Temper. Instead of seeing her, he saw small blood stains on her sheets and Kei-Kei rolling a joint at the foot of her bed.

"Through the front door. How else do you think I got in, nigga?"

"I know that, dumbass. I'm trying to let you know, big stupid, that Temper ain't here. You got to come back another time," Troy said, grabbing Kei-Kei by the fatty meat on her arm.

"Don't touch me, smoker. She is here with your lying ass. She went to the bathroom and then grabbed her things to get in the shower."

"Oh, so y'all are good again?"

"Why wouldn't we be? You need to stay off that shit. It's eating at what little brain you have left. Wait, don't you owe me two dollars?"

Before Troy could say another word, the swing of a golf club had cut across his peripheral vision, and Temper had connected it to Kei-Kei's shoulder. The weed hit the floor as Kei-Kei screamed out in horror.

"You thought I wouldn't find out that you were fucking Khasema?" Temper yelled with the same vacant look she'd had in her eyes after giving birth. Where pain should have been, there was nothing except anger.

"Hold up, Temper. You got me too fucked up," Kei-Kei said, using Troy to shield her from another swing of the club. "How are you going to take the word of the streets over me?"

"Bitch, stop lying. He told me, ho. Smiling in my face and fucking my trick behind my back. You're a dead bitch."

Temper advanced on her, and her uncle extended his arm to hold her back.

"Stop, Tee. I can't let you beat this girl down with that club. You're better than this shit here."

"He's lying. I swear he is, and when he gets out, I'm going to have his ass fucked up. I put that shit on my mama. I ain't never fucked his grimy ass."

Kei-Kei couldn't get the lies out of her mouth fast enough, and Temper's face said she didn't believe them. Her neighbor, Tiny, used to push weight for Khasema and let Kei-Kei put money on her phone to accept his collect calls. As of late, Tiny was going through her own jail shit with her baby daddy, and she was never home. It had been weeks since she had heard Khasema's voice. They wrote to each other every day, though. Kei'Lani was catching feelings for him in a big way, and seeing that she was the only person with freedom who was writing him consistently, he shared those feelings.

It wasn't her goal to stab Temper in her back. Kei'Lani asked her all the time about their relationship, and Temper assured her that there wasn't "shit between them." If she had known it was a lie and there was a baby on the way, she would have cut off the pussy before it got this serious. She was invested now and didn't know what to do with the love she had for her blood sister's baby daddy. Her only sister of any sort had just given birth to a baby by the first man she'd ever loved. She was sure their situation would make them prime guests on *The Jerry Springer Show*. After going back and forth with Temper, she broke down and told the truth, albeit only half.

"Y'all were beefing when I strolled up to buy a sack from that nigga, and he wanted to smoke, sip, and talk about you. You know how I get off that gin and juice. He took advantage of it. He ate my pussy or whatever. I promise you that was all. I haven't even talked to that nigga since."

"So you gon' sit here and tell me you're not writing him?" Temper said, lowering the club.

"Hell nah. You know my mama wouldn't let me get any letters from a nigga in jail without opening and reading them first. I'm sorry I didn't tell you, damn. When you told me that you were in labor with his baby, I knew I had to put you up on that small shit. I wanted to make sure you were good first. Ain't nothing or no one more important to me than you."

"Fuck you, bitch. You should've told me. It's not like the nigga was mine anyways. I thought we were better than that shit." Temper's voice was back to its normal tone, and the anger had left her face.

"We are better than that. Ain't no nigga coming between us, ever. You know I don't rock like that."

Troy put his arms down and slowly moved from between the girls. *Did fat ass just say Temper was in labor? Then all that blood is from her having a baby, but where's the baby?* He decided now wasn't the time to ask.

"Y'all good?" he spoke up, ready to terminate his position as the middleman in the club fight.

"Yeah, Unc, we're good. We just need to talk this shit out. My bad, Kei-Kei. I should have known that nigga was lying. He's a bitch, and that's what bitch-ass niggas do."

"It's all good. He's just locked up, stressing. That second strike they gave him was a wakeup call. Mr. Untouchable did all that hustling in the streets and can't deal with the charge. Girl, fuck him. He's missing the outside world and trying to stir up shit out here to keep himself relevant in the hood."

As Temper placed the club down on her dresser, Troy made his way out of the room. He got in his favorite position at the door and eavesdropped for a minute or two to gather more information. Once he confirmed that Temper did have a baby, he watched television with his mama, feeling heartbroken.

"So how are you feeling? I saw the blood on your covers."

"I'm straight, just bleeding heavy as fuck. It's like having a year's worth of periods all at once, and that shit funky," Temper said, locking her door.

"I still don't believe I didn't know you were pregnant. We're together all day every day, and I couldn't tell. So what did you decide to do with my nephew?" Kei-Kei asked on her knees, trying to salvage as much weed as she could out of the brown carpet.

"I already told you what was up. Stop calling the bastard your nephew. What you need to be talking about is what the fuck we're doing for my seventeenth birthday. I'm trying to get so fucked up that I don't even remember it."

"I heard that shit. Are we staying in the hood, or should I call up them white bitches I go to school with? You know those hoes stay with that good green, and their parents don't ever be home."

"Hell yeah, call those bitches up and tell them to re-up." Temper laughed as she pulled a packed suitcase out of her closet. She'd packed it months earlier when she planned on leaving before giving birth, except her money said otherwise. What she had in her pocket would only allow her to get as far as San Bernardino, California, at the time. Now that she had saved up a little over $3,000 and she didn't have pregnancy holding her down, she could bounce.

"You know I got you. I'm going to make sure your birthday is the shit. My bad about that weak shit with Khasema's three-ounce-dick-having ass, but on the real, he could eat the hell out of this pussy." Kei-Kei laughed, and Temper joined in as she removed her birth certificate and social security card from her dresser drawer.

"Man, that nigga ate pussy like he was sucking up the last Oodles of Noodles in the bowl," Temper said, laughing harder than before.

"Bitch, you ain't lying. A washrag to the pussy ain't got shit on the vinegar-and-water moves he busts with his tongue."

"What was his tongue made from anyways?" Temper laughed, then quoted a line from her favorite movie, *Coming to America.* "'What is that, velvet?'"

"Naw, I think that muthafucka was patent leather or made from that same shit they use for the Slip 'N Slide mat. It had a slightly rubbery yet glossed feel."

"Bitch, you're dead wrong for that one." Temper squealed, "Oh, 'extra baby oil on a condom' tongue-having ass."

"He was gargling with Turtle Wax. I bet my next nut on it," Kei-Kei hollered with tears of laughter forming in her eyes. "His tongue felt like a bowling alley lane after you cross that line, ol' strike mouth."

"Damn, I can't believe they gave the clit whisperer his second strike. Guess it's a good thing his grown ass used to suck his thumb. Makes it easy to adjust to dick." She shrugged.

"Them niggas already tried him in there. He was on lockdown for like two weeks for fighting and couldn't even write me back," Kei'Lani added as she laughed until her head hurt.

Temper walked into the living room with her bags in one hand and the golf club in the other. After cracking Kei-Kei over her back with it, she went upside her head with it for good measure, leaving the girl knocked out, face down on her bedroom carpet. She was going to hit Kei-Kei before she left the house regardless of what her uncle said. She knew Kei-Kei was dumb and would get caught up in her lie about not writing him just as fast as she told it.

"Let's go, Unc. I'm ready for my twenty feet."

Troy saw the club and then shot down the hallway to Temper's room as she made her way to her grandmother.

"I told you I'd be out of your house before I turned eighteen."

Grandmama Jo believed in raising Temper with tough love, and it would be no different upon her departure.

"You ain't walked out yet. I'll believe it when you come back in a year or two to visit me if these cigarettes haven't sent me to glory first," she said, lighting another one.

"I'm not coming back, Granny. This is it."

"That's good to hear. Well, I guess you can give me a hug goodbye," she said as Troy walked back into the room with his jaw open from finding Kei-Kei out as though she hadn't been to sleep in months.

They hugged tightly, and Grandmama Jo let go after planting a kiss on her granddaughter's forehead.

"It's not going to hurt you to write every now and then to let us know you're okay. You're turning seventeen, not eighteen, but I think you can handle yourself. I'll tell you one thing, though, if you fuck up before eighteen, I'm telling the law your ass ran away. Oh, and if you run across a stack of money, don't forget about my trips to the casino. Go on and go. You're making me miss the news."

Temper smiled when she saw the tear fall from her grandmother's "good eye," as she jokingly called it, and walked out the door with Troy on her tail.

"You got your ID, don't you?" she asked.

"Yeah, I do, but didn't I tell you not to hit that girl with that club? She's in there snoring and shaking on the floor. You know her mama is going to have a fit over this shit, and if I have to give her the dick to calm her down, it's gon' cost you."

"Fuck her and her mama. That bitch will live."

The cab pulled up with perfect timing, and Troy got in without asking any questions.

"Take us to the Greyhound station and keep the meter running. He'll need a ride back here."

Troy didn't question her. He had a more important question he needed to ask. "Where's the baby, Tee? Is it a boy or a girl, and why isn't it with you?"

"What baby? If there were a baby, he would be leaving with me and not at home being raised by his daddy's mother." She left the twisted lie at that.

"No good can come of this, Temper Taz."

"You might be right, Unc, but you never said getting those twenty feet would be easy, nor that I would like what it takes to get them. Whatever happens from here, I already chalked it up as collateral damage. My life can't get any worse than what it is," she stated with a shrug.

"As long as you know to expect shit, I don't have shit else to say."

"Where are you getting this ticket to?" he asked when they stepped inside the bus station.

"One one-way ticket to Las Vegas, please."

Temper smiled at him while she handed her information to the desk agent who listed Troy as one of her legal guardians, and Troy gave the lady his ID.

"The next one leaves in forty-five minutes. It's the last one going there tonight. If that's too soon, there's one that leaves at—"

"That's perfect," Temper interrupted, handing her the money and giving Troy the hundred-dollar bill she had gotten from her grandmother. "That's for the cab ride home, and you can keep the change."

"Why Vegas?" he asked, pocketing the money.

"It's the fastest place to get out of California so I can get ghost."

The agent handed her the ticket before Troy said another word.

"Well, you might want to stay in the restroom until your
bus arrives, because I'm keeping this money. Hell, I can
walk home from here, but that cab driver will be coming
inside looking for us."

Temper laughed as she nodded her head in agreement.
"You're never going to change."

"Nope. I'm fine as is, but I hope you do." He kissed her
on the cheek, grabbed a bag sitting unmanned by the
counter, and made his way out of the building through
the emergency exit.

Chapter Five

Temper didn't know where her final destination would be, yet she was sure she wouldn't get there by Greyhound. She wasn't 18, which meant buying another bus ticket wasn't an option. She didn't know anyone in Vegas, and truth be told, her immaturity and lack of education made her choose it. She couldn't think of anywhere else to go and hadn't researched other cities. Vegas was where all her big homies went to move their work, pimp the bitches who were foolish enough to believe that they were selling their ass for love, and to have fun. Temper didn't have to research Vegas. From what she'd heard, it was precisely where she needed to be.

The usual four-hour ride was six thanks to the unnecessary stops the bus made on the way. She wasn't in a rush to get there. The rocky bus ride made her body ache, and the bathroom wasn't fit for her to freshen up with the heavy bleeding she was doing.

When she arrived in Las Vegas, the first thing she noticed was that the bus station mirrored the one in Los Angeles. It was covered in bums and beggars too. The loiterers weren't begging for bus tickets. They were there to beg for money from those traveling to Sin City to gamble. She was approached by one before she could grab her bag.

"I'll tote those bags for you if you want," a voice said over her shoulder.

"I'm good."

"Can I have a dollar then? I'm hungry."

"You can't have shit, and you can get the fuck away from me before I beat yo' ass," Temper said louder than she usually spoke, and brought everyone's eyes to her situation.

"Leave the young girl alone, vato, before I help her kick your begging ass," a Mexican accent said from behind her as the shadow of a woman began to cover the light Temper was using to get her bags.

"Get your bags, chola. I got you."

Temper grabbed her bags, feeling protected by the stranger. When she turned around, she couldn't believe that the voice belonged to a five-foot-two gangster-looking chick and not to a much taller woman by the way the shadow had covered her.

"You gotta be careful down here. These fuckers see young girls and see an easy target. I'm Blanca, by the way. Where's your ride?"

Blanca must have attended a gang meeting before arriving at the bus station. She was wearing a white T-shirt under a creased black Dickies shirt that buttoned at the neck. Her khaki-colored Dickies pants had been cut at the ankles, and the strings hung past her calf-high socks to her brand-new white-and-black Nike Cortez shoes. Her face was partially covered by a black-and-white paisley bandana that covered her forehead from her drawn-on eyebrows to where her bangs began on her head. Her eyes were dark brown like the heavy makeup she had around them, and the crease of her eyes had a black tail made from an eyeliner pencil that stopped at her temples. Above her thin lips, painted black, was a drawn-on mole that was too big to be confused with being real. Although her neck gave proof that she was naturally shades darker brown than Temper, the foundation on her face was white, almost ghostly.

Everything about Blanca read that she was a real-deal chola, even her heel-to-heel stance. It wasn't until Temper read the fake-looking gang tattoo going across her neck that she was sure Blanca's gangster image was tied to a Mexican gang.

"So what's up? You gon' tell me where your ride is so I can get you there safely, or are you going to keep checking me with your eyes, chola?"

"I don't have a ride."

"Big, bad chola bitch is on her own, huh? Well, what side of Vegas are you headed to? I got a few lame-ass vatos picking me up. I can give you a ride or whatever."

Temper had slept during the entire ride to Vegas to avoid dealing with the pain she was in, so she'd failed to plan her next move. Getting out of California had been her only goal. "Nah, I'm good, but can you do me a favor and buy me a cigar from that tobacco shop? My ID isn't legit for a few more days," she lied.

"I got you. Wait, do you know where I can get a sack of mota around here? Those fools I'm with do that heavy shit. I like to float when I'm high." She laughed.

"Call me Mary fucking Jane. Get the cigar and meet me in the family restroom when you get back. I'll have it already weighed out. How much are you trying to get?"

"Shit, I'll take whatever you can spare to sell."

"Okay, have a hundred dollars with you when you come back, and I'm going to get you straight."

Temper didn't plan to sell half of the pound she had stashed in her suitcase. It was her smoke supply. She sold it because the Mexican gangster stepped to the junkie for her. She felt obligated to show her that same kind of love back. She didn't have scales with her, so she eyeballed the ounce and weighed it out in front of the mirror. When the knocks fell on the restroom's door, Temper made herself ready for the quick transaction, and she decided to take her up on the ride.

"Damn, what's up with the change of clothes?" Blanca asked. "You're not on the run, are you?"

"Hell no. I, um, I started my rag and fucked up my clothes. I had to change. Here you go." Temper stretched out her arm to hand her the sack of weed.

"Hell yeah, all this for a Franklin? Can I get your number? I need to be a returning customer. Fuck that," she giggled.

"Shit, being real with you, this isn't my weed," she lied just as her Uncle Troy had taught her. He told her never to claim ownership and watch who you're talking to because they might be the police. "This nigga in Cali stashed it in my bag before the Feds locked him up. I forgot he had put it in here until I got off the fucking bus. I smoke that shit. I don't sell it. You can have the weed for free. I want the money to get me a room tonight. I'm not feeling too good. I think I need to rest."

"I can tell. Your face is pale, like you've lost a lot of blood. Your period has you looking all messed up. You know what? Fuck a room. You can stay with me. I know the shit sounds weird, but I got a little house not too far from here, and you're more than welcome to crash a night or two. What did you say your name was again?"

"My name is Temper, and I appreciate the offer, but I'm straight. Can I get that ride you offered me instead?"

"Sure, let's head out. I'm sure they are tired of waiting for me. So what are you? I mean, like, your nationality?"

"I'm black and Asian."

"Damn, for real? What are you, Korean?"

"Naw," she giggled, "I'm Cambodian. Everyone always says Korean."

"My bad, no disrespect. You just look like one of those chicks at the nail shop with a dark tan, but your voice sounds like a black girl's. That shit is trippy as fuck. Let me guess, you're like nineteen, huh?"

"Yes," Temper lied.

"I hated being nineteen. Too young to buy alcohol, and too old to keep living in the house with my parents. Nineteen was a fucked-up age for me, but how's it treating you? Oh, there those fools go. They're parked over there." She pointed.

Temper followed her finger and thought she was pointing at a new-model car. Instead, they walked up to a dark blue Astro van with tint parked beside it. She couldn't make out who was in the driver seat or front passenger seat as she climbed in because the sun hadn't fully risen yet.

"Thanks for the ride. Can you drop me off at whatever motel is the cheapest on the strip?" Temper said as Blanca slid the door closed once she was all the way in.

"Sure, no problem. I'll take you wherever you need to go after you straighten a few things out for me, Temper Chey. I talked to your bus driver, and I want to know, what's a minor doing traveling by herself from Los Angeles with no place to stay and weed?"

The heavy Mexican accent she had been speaking with was gone, and she was holding a badge in Temper's face. Instantly, Temper began crying.

"I think I'm dying. I'm not trying to ignore your badge, but I need to go to the hospital."

"I agree with you and will make sure you see a doctor, but first I want to talk about this weed and why your guardian got a one-way ticket to Las Vegas for his sixteen-year-old niece?"

"I already told you I didn't know the weed was in my bags until I got here, and he didn't have enough for a round-trip ticket. He told me to call if my mom didn't meet me tonight like she said she would, and he'd get me a ticket back. I didn't want to sell you the weed. I needed the money for a hotel. I feel real bad. That's the truth."

"That's a lie, and a horrible one at that," the guy sitting in the front passenger seat announced. He was another pretend Mexican who you could quickly tell was white with a tan. "Exactly how much weed are you transporting from California?" he asked as he made his way to the back of the van to check Temper's bag while Blanca slapped cuffs on her wrists. In less than thirty seconds, he said, "Oh, shit. It's not the jackpot, but I'm looking at a brick. I say we get her down to the station now."

"No. We don't know if her connect is watching," Blanca stated.

"I don't see a tail," said the driver, speaking for the first time.

"We've been working the Greyhound for four months straight, and this is the biggest bust we got. Weed ain't dope, and that's the white bitch we're looking for. Take her to the hotel with the others, Matthew. Let me question her there and see what else we can get out of her." She turned her attention back to Temper. "If you tell the truth and answer our questions honestly, we will let you go. No arrest and not one night in jail, understood?"

She shook her head as snot dripped from her nose to her shirt. Her eyes felt as though the moisture in them was drying out, and if she exhaled too hard, she was sure she'd spit out fire. Temper's stomach began to contract as it had when she was in labor, and everything in between her legs began to irritate her. "I think I'm—"

"You think what?" Blanca asked with concern in her voice that wasn't there before. She could look at the little girl in front of her and could see that something wasn't right. If she spoke up, though, her partners would chalk it up to her being a woman. Knowing they wanted her off their undercover case, she bit her tongue as she placed her palm to the girl's forehead. "You're on fire. Are you okay?"

"No, something is wrong with me," Temper announced as her body began to shake uncontrollably.

"Damn right something is wrong with you. You're going to jail, drug dealer," Matthew stated, making an announcement that wasn't intended only for Temper. He wanted his estrogen-filled partner to know that her woman's intuition wasn't going to interfere with this drug bust. He made a series of unnecessary turns, aiming to hit every bump that he approached before they pulled into the parking lot of a motel in sight of the Greyhound station.

"I'm going to take these cuffs off and let you walk into the room freely, but if you try anything—"

"I won't. I just want to get this shit over with, and afterward, can you please take me to the hospital?"

The undercover officer nodded her head in agreement, and five steps later, Temper blacked out.

The phone vibrated in Keith's pocket every fifteen seconds. If he were still pushing weight, it would be a dream come true. Unfortunately, he was out of the game. No one called his phone, family included. For it to be going off meant there was an emergency at home that needed his attention. His common-law wife of the past twenty or so years never bothered him while he was working. She understood how dangerous his job at the oil refinery was and waited for him to reach out when he deemed it safe.

He excused himself from the meeting as if he weren't the host. There were too many of his bosses in the room who he aimed to impress. He needed the promotion to safety inspector like he needed air in his lungs. The title was excellent, and the work would be less strenuous. However, it was the pay increase he was gunning for.

For years he'd listened to his wife complain about living in the hood. Though it didn't bother him and his baby girl Kei'Lani, it drove his wife mad. Everything he loved about her was slipping away with each year she spent in his hood. She didn't smile as much, and he couldn't recall the last time they'd lain in bed and laughed together. Keith was thankful his current position kept him on the road 40 percent of the time because her nagging about everything hood and Crips drove him crazy. If he could land this promotion, he could buy her a house in a city along his commute to work and retire her from teaching. The benefit of the promotion for him would be the increase in travel to 70 percent, and that would save him from pretending that he was still in love with her.

"What's wrong, baby?" he asked with urgency at the sound of her voice.

"It's . . . it's Kei'Lani. She's in critical condition and—" Bridget began to say through sobs, and he cut her off.

"What hospital?"

"They don't know if she'll—"

"What fucking hospital is my baby at, dammit?"

"You watch your tone—"

He hung up on her. Even in a time of peril, he couldn't fake interest in his wife. She irritated him like a thorn in his side or a corn on his pinky toe in tight shoes. She talked shit, too much shit, and he could no longer stand the smell of her. When they were young, he thought it was cute. Having a sassy mouth, an Oreo from the Valley fit perfectly with the kingpin lifestyle he was living. She was sexy, educated, and overly opinionated. She knew a lot about everything, and if she didn't know it, she'd research the subject until she did. He never foresaw the result of her metamorphosis being her transformation into a selfish, self-absorbed, uppity, and bigmouthed bitch he'd eventually despise. He assumed she'd grow to love his neighborhood as much as he did. She just needed time to adjust to the change. He thought she'd be so busy getting her degree and finding work that she'd stop tripping on their surroundings. He was wrong.

"How am I supposed to study with police sirens going off in every direction every second? I wonder which one of your Crips friends is getting chased this time?" She paused, knowing he would be too pissed to answer, and then said, *"You want me to get used to this trash receptacle you call home?"* She snickered until her beautiful, big brown eyes transformed into slits. *"As a matter of fact, King Crip, when are you going to stop Cripping and grow the fuck up? You can't sell nickel bags of weed all of your life."*

"Who said I was going to stop doing that?" he growled.

Keith was a Crip. Bridget knew it before she ever sent her first letter to him, and he never mentioned retiring from gangbanging in any of the letters he wrote back.

Yeah, she voiced ill feelings about his choice of organization, mostly about how stupid gangbanging was, which left him bewildered, seeing that he had never asked her to join. If she didn't see the similarities between the sorority she belonged to and street gangs, then it wasn't for him to be the person who pointed them out.

"The baby in my stomach says it."

It broke his heart when she threatened to abort their child if he didn't give up his street life and secure a job to provide for them. Nevertheless, he loved her and would have done anything to keep them together, so he tucked in his flag and became a family man.

Bridget didn't understand that there was no getting out, especially when someone was in as deep as Keith was. His was a second-generation Crip. His flag was passed down to him and his brother not only from their father, but from two of their uncles who'd lost their lives for banging and believing in everything blue. His mother bled blue. He would be lying if he said that he heard his mother bang Crip out of her mouth, but he was sure she was down for his father and everything that came along with him, the gang included.

He announced he was out of the gang, although none of his homeboys seemed to get the memo, nor did his enemies. Bridget must have dwelled in a land of make-believe if she thought you could shoot up Bloods and then tell them you weren't a Crip anymore and the beef disintegrated. You couldn't hold all the hood's secrets and walk away to hold hands and skip around scot-free. There was always a price, and Keith wasn't ready to pay it.

California Hospital. Come quick.

Bridget sent the message to his two-way in the midst of her calls, and he was glad he thought to check it. After responding, which was his way of apologizing, he jumped in his Excursion and hit the freeway speeding.

"I know Beast has a hand in this shit," he said, tightening his grip on the steering wheel. It was a wild assumption, seeing that this incident involved his daughter and not him. However, he had his reasons for pointing the finger at him.

For the last three days, every piece of bad news that had made its way to his ears involved that reckless nigga Beast. First, his protégé Casper was found shot up in Pomona with niggas who Beast had welcomed in their hood against his better judgment. It wasn't that Keith knew the Pomona Crips were shady, and that was his gripe. He didn't know shit about them except for one, OG Capone. They used to be tight years ago, almost inseparable. Nonetheless, that changed, and the pair hadn't spoken a word to each other in years. Crips weren't created equal. That was a fact he'd tried to drill in Beast's head, but since Keith was no longer the supreme chief, his words didn't mean shit.

He didn't need to know all the details surrounding the Pomona tragedy to know that Beast played a part in it. Instead of pulling up to Big Trice's house and consoling her over her baby daddy's loss, he met yellow police tape. The rumor was that she'd committed suicide over losing the love of her life, and Keith didn't believe it. Suicide didn't fit her character, and there was a baby involved who needed raising. Not even a broken heart could force her to leave her son's side. Keith was pissed that everyone could believe the Romeo-and-Juliet tragedy so easily, so he did his own little investigating. He found out that Trice's moves before her death gave the impression that she was uncovering a truth that wasn't supposed to get out. Lady Chocolate, Trice's right-hand woman, told him that Trice was fucked up over Casper, but it seemed she had more important shit to handle.

"What do you mean, more important shit?" Keith asked as he passed her the bottle of gin back after taking a long swallow.

"My bitch was asking questions about nobodies. I answered what I could, but when I asked her why she wanted to know about a dumbass little girl, she got all secretive and bounced." She swallowed until she needed a break to get oxygen, then passed it back. "I don't know what's going down, big homie, but what I do know is that she didn't kill herself. She loved little man too much to let these streets raise him."

"Yeah, I was thinking the same." He stood up and handed her the bottle back to let her know it was hers to keep. He asked, "Who was she asking questions about?"

"That little young tramp Temper. You know, junkie-ass Troy's niece. She ain't from the set, but that little Asian ho act like it."

Hearing Temper's name was beginning to make his ears ring. She was Bridget's biggest complaint when it came to their daughter. She thought the girl's friendship was toxic, and he agreed. He just made sure that he never agreed with her when she said it.

One thing was for certain, if Kei'Lani was in trouble, then there wasn't a doubt in his mind that Temper was in trouble too. Bridget had asked him multiple times to have a talk with the girl and to run her off. He hadn't. His daughter loved the little mixed breed, and Temper was her only friend. He couldn't see himself tearing them apart. Keith wouldn't deny that the girls seemed to stay in mischief together. Even so, he felt like the girls needed each other. He knew Temper's mama and her uncle. He'd gone to school with them. Back then, every nigga prayed Dorothy would let them fuck, and every dope boy wanted to be Troy. It was sad to watch crack fuck them both over. Temper didn't have anybody left except for her drunk-ass grandmother, and her bond with Kei'Lani gave her value in her world of nothing.

As for Kei'Lani, she was exactly like him. If he couldn't stand Bridget, he knew his daughter couldn't either. If it were up to Bridget, she'd lock his baby in the house until she was able to ship her off to college. He couldn't have that. Nor did he want his little girl to miss out on the valuable lessons that could only be taught by the streets. Letting her hang around, Temper gave her those lessons. However, Keith didn't believe in coincidences. If there was heat on Temper, then there was heat on Kei'Lani. If Trice died trying to hunt down a truth involving the little girl instead of grieving, then the shit that was taking place was monstrous. It was Beast.

"What happened? Why aren't you in the room with her?" Keith questioned as he stormed down the emergency room corridor. He didn't expect to see Bridget heading toward the exit doors. In fact, he thought he'd have to pry her away from their daughter's side.

"No one can go into the room with her. If you hadn't hung up in my face, you would have known that. I'm going outside to smoke."

"Smoke what?"

"What do you think?" she sassed back.

"I don't know because your ass don't smoke."

"You don't pay attention to shit, do you?"

Keith was at a crossroads. He couldn't decide if he should find a doctor with an update on his daughter or follow Bridget out the door to see her smoke with his own eyes. After weighing his options, he headed to the parking lot, sure that Bridget wouldn't have left Kei'Lani if she'd had the opportunity to stay.

"So you smoke Newports now?" he asked, firing up the Black & Mild cigar he kept in his shirt pocket.

"How about asking me about our daughter before you start judging me and shit?" she snapped, and she was right. He didn't have a clue of what was going on.

"What happened? How's my baby?"

Bridget rolled her eyes. She hated it when he used the word "my" when it came to their daughter. It confirmed that he enjoyed that his daughter was becoming the lowlife he used to be.

"Our daughter is being put in a medically induced coma," she said as she fought back the tears. "Nobody seems to know what happened, but the Mexicans across the street from us found her in their backyard having a seizure."

"A seizure?" he yelled.

"Lower your damn voice," she snapped. "Yes, a seizure. Somebody used a weapon to beat our baby's head in. Her body is covered in bruises, and she keeps having seizures. The doctors said they have to put her in the coma as an attempt to save her life."

The strength Bridget was pretending to have washed away with the tears streaming from her eyes. Keith grabbed her and pulled her into him. He didn't acknowledge the heat from the cigarette she was holding against his arms. Instead, he snatched it out of her hand without complaint. Tears began to fill his own eyes, though he couldn't decide if his ducts were overflowing from hurt or anger. He wanted to see the bruises. He wasn't an expert in forensic science, nor had he been a medical examiner or coroner, yet seeing the wounds would lead to who had done it. He didn't see the need for a man to use a weapon to subdue his daughter. Nevertheless, he wanted to confirm it.

His mind was running a fact check over a plethora of his thoughts. Could Trice have taken her beef with Temper out on Kei'Lani before she died two days ago, or did her little investigation lead her to Kei'Lani being the problem? To answer that question, he would need to know the last time Bridget had seen their daughter and the time difference between that and when the neighbors found her. Questions filled his mind, and he knew who had the answers—Temper. He needed to talk to Temper.

"Did you hear what I said?" Bridget said, interrupting his train of thought.

"No, baby, I didn't. What did you say?"

She pulled away from him until her eyes met his. There wasn't an indication she had been crying besides a slight puffiness under her eyes.

"I said you need to come out of retirement and kill the muthafuckas who did this to our baby. Understood?"

"Perfectly. That's on Low Bottom Crips. I'm gon' handle this shit."

Chapter Six

"Ladies, down the hallway. When you hear your name called, step out for transportation. I'll repeat it for those of you who have a problem with listening and following directions. Step out for transportation only if you hear me say your name. B. Adams, K. Boyd, T. Chey, and T. Washington, step out for transportation, ladies. Bring your dirty linen and all of your personal belongings with you. You might not be coming back here after court."

The correctional officer's voice echoed down the hallway. For a second, you'd think she was using a megaphone to give orders by the volume her voice carried. Barry J. Nidorf Juvenile Hall was in Sylmar, California, twenty-eight minutes from Central Juvenile Hall. Temper had court next door to it at Eastlake Juvenile Courts. In Los Angeles traffic, that trip could easily be an hour and a half. Still, the wake-up at four thirty in the morning seemed unnecessary, and one of the girls didn't have a problem with showing it.

"I see one of you is deaf. There should be four girls in my hall dressed and ready for court with their dirty linen rolled up and their brown bags in hand. When I say your name, take a step into the center of the hallway, follow the white line down to me, place your dirty linen in the bin, and have a seat in the dayroom for breakfast," she said, unfolding the list clipped to her board. "Brittney Adams, Katrina Boyd, Temper Chey, and Tyger Rae Washington. Washington, step out!"

"Permission to speak?" Brittney Adams asked as she turned into the dayroom.

"Permission granted, Ms. Adams."

"Um, Washington is probably in the room asleep. She normally stays up all night talking to herself. She's probably too tired to get up," she relayed, holding back laughter.

"And how do you know she stays up all night talking to herself, Ms. Adams?"

"Because she was my roommate at Los Padrinos Juvenile Hall a few months ago, and that chick is weird. Like, crazy weird. She was up like three days straight doing math, and when I asked her what she was doing it for, she said to graduate early. She said she would take over the world and make criminals like me her modernized slaves since we enjoy the defeated mentality."

"What? You're telling me Washington, the girl down my hall, said all of that?" the correctional officer asked with a slightly uncomfortable giggle in her tone.

"Yes, ma'am. I remembered it word for word. I didn't understand what it meant, so I asked my mama. She told me to tell the CO to switch my room because that, um, B word was crazy."

The other girls and the CO erupted in laughter. Temper's jaws didn't flinch.

"Ay, Debbie, can you come sit with these girls in the dayroom while they eat breakfast and wait for transportation? I might have a little issue to handle down this hallway with the fourth girl."

"Shit, you should sit with the girls, Kim. You know I'm all about handling issues, especially after my damn vacation was denied again." She unsnapped the pepper spray off her belt loop and said, "What's the problem?"

Kim brought her up to speed as the girls ate the food in front of them. Then their ears got full of the story Debbie shared of what she knew about Washington.

"Something is wrong with that girl, Kim. Adams ain't lying. That's the girl I told you about, the one who hit her public defender during court. She couldn't get sentenced after that shit. They sent her crazy ass straight to loony lockup to await a therapist. That's probably what she's headed to court for now. Yeah, I got this one. Watch how I do her."

"Hey, Chey, do you have a problem?" Kim asked Temper, who didn't seem to find anything amusing.

"No, ma'am."

"Then why are you looking at my partner like that? Are you cool with Washington? Because you look like you have something you want to say in her defense."

"I don't know Washington," she said, taken aback, "and I wasn't looking at your partner in no type of way. I'm just here to do my time. I don't want any extra problems. If you thought I was messed up about it, my bad."

"Listen to you. Who taught you how to talk black?" Kim questioned and then laughed at her own words. The other girls joined in.

"Man . . ." Temper moaned.

"Man what, Chey? Answer the question. Who taught you to talk black? I didn't think Asians were allowed to have black friends, but then again, you're kind of on the darker side of Korean. Aw shit, Chey might be one of us or at least half of one of us. Who got jungle fever, your mama or your daddy? It looks like you got you a black card, girlfriend."

The laughter picked back up as Debbie entered the room with Washington hogtied in shackles. She had one connecting her legs and another wrapped around her waist. The only part of her body she could move freely was her mouth.

"How about Miss Washington here told me to come and get her when transportation arrives because she's reading and didn't want to stop for breakfast? She said that it's poison, and she's sure the additives in it cause cancer."

The irritation growing throughout Washington showed on her face, yet she opted to use her words. "You're fabricating, and you know that's not the truth. I told you I was up, dressed, and ready for court. I wasn't hungry, and my linen was clean since I hadn't used any of it. Yes, I did mention the cancer part, which was the only part of my words you didn't add to. You woke us up at four thirty in the morning. Transportation doesn't arrive until six. We aren't allowed to fully groom, so the extra time we waste staring at the dayroom walls isn't beneficial to any of our futures. I was reading, and you interrupted me because you could, not because it was necessary. That's what I said."

Temper giggled.

"What are you laughing at with your Chinese ass?" Debbie snapped.

Washington had an answer for that too. "That was more of a giggle than a laugh. If she were a boy, you'd call it a chuckle, and her last name is Chey, a common surname for Cambodians. But then again, how would you know that? To become a correctional officer, a college degree or special knowledge isn't necessary. Not even a criminal justice course is required as long as you're a citizen, at least twenty-one, have a high school diploma, and are in good physical condition. I'm not sure how you passed that portion. You must have taken your physical years ago and must not possess a felony conviction. Then they'll hire you to babysit us. You take a few self-defense classes, learn to use pepper spray, and get CPR certified. It sounds like those qualifications aren't much more than what's needed to operate a neighborhood liquor store or strip club or become a middle school PE teacher. Nothing impressive to brag about there. Chey is Cambodian and black, which means she's black, or so says the one-drop rule," she finished with a shrug.

Neither correctional officer said a word. They just stared at her. Temper had to grit her teeth to prevent the smile that longed to grace her face. She was more than impressed with Washington's smarts, and through their pissed-off expressions, she could tell the correctional officers were too.

Surprisingly, it wasn't until transportation arrived that the officers sought their revenge. "Hey, Debbie, can you shackle the CCs together?"

"CCs? Who the fuck is that?"

"The crazy one with the Cambodian. I think they're made for each other. Let's make them best friends for the day."

"No problem!"

The ride to court was quiet and quite painful as the shackles dug into Temper's ankles with each pothole they hit. The sheriffs demanded it be silent, and since they had the power to bring their threats to life, no one debated their authority.

It had been five months since Temper's arrest and hospitalization. At that point in her life, she didn't want a life and would have happily traded it for a room six feet deep. There was a baby she'd never mother, and an unknown infection and STD that would have taken away her life if they had gone any longer without being cured. She had a drug trafficking charge over her head. To save her ass when the police came questioning how Temper could hide a pregnancy and why Temper wasn't enrolled in school while in her grandmother's care, her grandmother told them that Temper was a runaway and that her granddaughter must have used her son's drug addiction to manipulate him into buying her the one-way bus ticket. She told the courts that Temper was too wild for her to handle and that she didn't want her back. The shit storm she caused had fallen on her head, and death seemed to be the best option for her to use as an umbrella. Then she received a visit that changed all of that.

"What do you want?" Temper asked, suddenly feeling disgusted by the visitor sitting across from her.

"I want to help."

"The same way you helped me in Las Vegas? If that's the case, I'm already locked up. You can leave, Blanca."

"I'd rather stay, and Blanca is my undercover name. My name is Isabel."

"What do you want, Is-a-bell, ringer, and whistleblower? I'm somewhat busy serving time for trying to help a fellow weed smoker get high because she stood up for me to a junkie. I just wanted to return the favor, and look at what I got out of it." Temper pointed at the orange jumpsuit she was wearing.

"I know what you got out of it, but you don't see it yet."

"Yeah, I need to get my eyes checked. That's why I smoke weed. What is it that your perfect police vision sees that my eyes don't?"

"I can tell you, yeah, that's the easy way, but you still won't see it. Why were you running from California, Temper?"

"I'm not answering shit without a lawyer," she snapped. "You've already set me up once."

"I'm not here as a cop. I'm here as a friend."

"Damn, a friend? Well, I'm going to decline your friendship invitation. I don't want any friends, especially the kind who will put me in jail. I know I blacked out because of the infection growing inside my pussy, but weren't you the same cop bitch who put the handcuffs on me? Fuck your friend request."

"I knew you would have your guard up, but I'm trying to win your trust."

"That's the problem. You keep treating my life like it's a game. Don't play with me to win my trust. Earn it. Now tell me the truth. Did you cuff me? Are you that same cop bitch who set me up for a hundred dollars' worth of weed? Am I sitting in this hellhole because of you?"

Isabel stood and paced the small space for a second before returning to her seat. She didn't have a problem with answering the questions truthfully. Her delay was because she wasn't sure if Temper would accept the truth for what it was.

"Yes, I got you to sell me the drugs so I could arrest you. I placed the cuffs around your wrists, that's the truth, but I will not lie and take the blame for you being in this hellhole, as you call it. You're here because of all the bad choices you've made. You're so busy being mad at the world that you forgot to be mad at yourself. Don't you realize you could be dead right now if I hadn't cuffed you?"

"Yes, I do," she interjected, "and if I were dead, I wouldn't have to deal with any of this shit."

"That's the coward's way out. That little girl who birthed a child and traveled two days after having it, with a temperature of 103 or better, with nothing but the clothes on her back and a few dollars, she thought she was defeating her problems, not running from them. You didn't neglect your child. You gave him a better life. The only person you keep cheating is you."

"So you did a little research, and now you think you know me?"

"No, I did a lot of research, and I won't pretend to know you, because you don't know yourself. You're too busy turning all the hurt in your life into anger and releasing it through sex, drugs, and violence. Your parents *were on drugs, and they left you, so you went to school and whooped everyone's ass that you could. Half black isn't full black, is it? And in the hood where you grew up, they constantly pointed that out to you, so you suppressed the Asian in you to prove you were blacker than everyone around you. You thought that by keeping yourself caught up in the bullshit, you'd earn the respect the lack of melanin shorted you, huh?*

"Your granny is an alcoholic, and your uncle is on crack. That pisses you off because you don't understand how they could love you in their addictions to raise you, but your parents jumped ship. So you sell drugs to feel above the addiction, but I bet that I couldn't give you cough syrup or a children's Tylenol without you panicking from being scared you'll get addicted to them.

"Your dad is dead, and your mom lies about it. Truthfully, she's too high to believe the truth. That's why you'll never love. You have a fear of loss. You've had sex with everyone you could and didn't feel anything from it. Open those beautiful, tight, slanted eyes and see the truth, Temper. You didn't do your son as your parents did you. You gave him more than you ever had. You said that I'm playing with your life? No, sweetheart, you are, and the saddest part of all is that you don't see that you won. Your uncle was high as the tip of Mount Everest when I sat down with him, and after telling him everything that happened with you, he smiled, clapped, and do you know what he said?"

Temper didn't respond, and it didn't matter because Isabel wasn't done.

"He said, 'She finally got her twenty feet.' I thought he was high and rambling, but when he told me his theory behind it, I couldn't help but agree." She slammed the picture Troy had taken of her parents outside of the legendary singer's house on the table in front of Temper.

"Now that you have your twenty feet, what are you going to do with them? Can you let go of the anger to finally get mad at Temper and fix the shit in your life? You're still a kid and can erase a lot of this shit, and what you can't erase, there's Wite-Out for.

"I'm here to help. I don't know why, but I am, and I want to be. The way you looked at me before you passed out said you did not only need help, but you wanted it, too. I'll be back to see if you still want that help next week. If you decline my visit, I won't make another trip from Vegas to check on you again. If you do, be ready to work, because that court-appointed public defender is an hourly employee. No one has to pay you to defend yourself."

Isabel left Temper sitting there with a lot to think over. The anger made her want to scream, "Fuck you, bitch. Don't come back." Though, for the oddest reason, the words wouldn't come out of her mouth. By Wednesday, Temper had grown impatient waiting for Isabel's return visit.

"Thank you," Temper shot out before Isabel was seated in her visitor's chair.

"Don't thank me yet. I need to know everything. Are you ready to trust me?"

With six months of Saturday afternoon visits, Temper was ready to defend herself in court.

"You're smiling. That's normally a sign that court went well, or you could have thought of something funny and I caught you in that moment. If you don't mind, I'd like to know which it is."

Still in shackles, Washington was placed next to Temper outside the courtroom with a large manila envelope stuck to her chest under the chains. She hadn't said much to anyone while serving her time, yet here she was, ready to talk to Temper.

"Um, court went good. I got what I wanted."

"Court went well, and that's not true. You wanted your freedom, but you received the next best option."

"No, I actually didn't want my freedom. At first I did, but the truth is I'm not ready for it."

"Wow." Washington turned in the chains the best she could to get a look at Temper's face. "That was beautiful. You've accepted your wrongs and considered what it would take to not only make them right but to ensure you make better decisions in your future. Freedom isn't free. At times, it costs us a piece of our time to grow. I knew you were different from the other girls here, but I didn't think you knew it. I mean, there aren't a lot of Asian girls in the juvenile disciplinary system to begin with."

"Why does me being half Asian matter to you mutha-fuckas so much?"

"I've never fucked anyone's mother, so please don't label me, and you're so much more than your nationality."

Temper laughed. "My bad, didn't mean to label you, but everybody always brings the shit up like it means that I'm special. I'm not special. I'm black."

"We've been brainwashed to think higher of Asians than we do ourselves. Excuse my warped way of thinking. I'm foul for that, and I thank you for waking me up. But again, you're greater than what's flowing in your blood."

"Yeah, and how do you figure that?"

"The same way I figure everything. I deduced it using reason and logic like my uncle taught me. He's a bio-chemist, which means absolutely nothing, but it opens the door for me to say he's well-read. He has relation-ships with all sorts of people. Race and money don't matter. He taught me never to judge a book by its cover completely, but make sure to include the cover to add accuracy to my findings. Please pay no attention to the additional facts I always seem to shoot off after giving answers. In other words, I tend to rattle off unnecessary information at times. I'm correcting that flaw now."

"So what are you, a genius?"

"I wish. I know a lot but use only half of it by choice. My strengths are that I'm a good listener and loyal, but those are my weaknesses, too. My other weaknesses are spelling and that I tend to use science and logic in place of feelings, making me a bad friend or easily used and abused by bad people pretending to be nice. I tend to be loyal to those types of people too."

"Girl, you are—"

"Crazy," Washington said, interrupting. "I know. I hear it half a dozen times a day. I prefer to think I'm just misunderstood."

"I wasn't about to call you crazy. I was going to say you are special, and those half a dozen people who are calling you crazy are dumbass losers who are jealous of your mind. I hate haters."

"That is very nice of you to say, Temper Chey, but I'm sure you heard the rumors of me hitting my public defender. That alone made me crazy to everybody, including the courts. They even sent me to therapy afterward, but I wasn't allowed to explain my reasoning. I was misunderstood." She nodded at the envelope strapped to her as she said, "I got what I wanted in court today too."

"What's that?"

"Suitable placement while I go through an emancipation program."

"No, I meant your reasoning. What was your reason for hitting your public defender?"

"Ultimately, I hit him for my freedom."

"No, hitting him should have gotten you more time."

"Exactly."

Temper, lost by the victory smile Washington wore on her face, had to know more.

"Can you please explain? I'm not smart at all. You might want to tell me everything like how you even got arrested to be able to hit a public defender in the first place. You don't seem like you should be in here with us."

The smile was wiped off her face at Temper's request for her to tell her story, and a new look crossed her face. Temper knew that look. It was anger.

"You shouldn't be in here either, but it took you to get here to know that and make a change. My story, well, it's a very long story to tell. I don't want to bore you."

"Then it's a good thing that I have time to listen."

Tyger wasn't planning on ever telling her story to anyone. It wasn't in her plan. She didn't know who Temper was, but it didn't matter. She decided, at that moment, that she liked her and would answer.

"My uncle is my favorite person on this earth, and I've always wanted to be just like him. Not the biochemist part. In my opinion, he aimed too low, but everything else. I played basketball like him and—"

"You play basketball?" Temper inquired with her eyes locked on Washington's stomach.

"Yes, chubby people play basketball, and so do short people. Any more stereotypical questions before I continue?"

"Nah, go ahead. You play basketball and . . ."

"And I joined as many educational groups as my school and neighborhood offered. It's what my uncle did at my age. I was always busy with extracurricular activities, and my mama worked a full-time job. She reserved her weekends for me, but my mama found other things to do with her time as my schedule grew. She never made it a priority to be at my basketball games or school events, so I was shocked to look out into the audience and see her cheering me on as I was inducted into the Black Honors Union. I ran to her when it was over, and she hugged me tighter than she ever had before. As she released me, I noticed she was wearing a wedding ring set, and that's when she stepped to the side and introduced me to Marvin, her husband. I was beyond surprised, but that was my mama, and despite everything we had been through, which is another long story, I was glad she found love and was happy. Anyway, a month had gone by, and all my events, clubs, and group meetings had slowed down except for basketball, so I was home more. The first red flag I saw waving was that my mama started dodging me. I could finally be at home with her alone while her husband hunted for a job, and we could spend time together. I wanted us to sip tea and watch a movie like we used to do, yet she refused to come out of her room."

"Why?" Temper asked, finding it to be weird with the little information she'd given.

"At the time, I didn't know, but the next morning, the Marshals kicked in our door to arrest him for violating his parole. It took my mama all day to tell me why he was originally arrested because it would force her to confess how they met. Come to find out she was his prison prayer pen pal while he was serving the last three years of a ten-year manslaughter sentence. Marvin had killed his wife, and I don't know the story behind that. She told me he got off with manslaughter for doing it."

"What the fuck? Your mama married a convicted murderer?"

"Yes, but please don't interrupt. It's kinda a long story. To speed it up, Marvin goes back to jail for less than a year and has his parole switched from Florida to California since his new wife lived here, and when he got out, I became his number one priority. He wanted my mama to himself, so he had to find a way to get me gone. Everything I did was wrong. He said I spent too much time with my uncle so I could hang around boys and that I used the clubs and groups so I wouldn't have to do chores. My mama knew better, although, for reasons I'll never understand, she started agreeing with him. I wanted to run away and live with my daddy, but that meant I'd have to tell my daddy about Marvin, which wasn't an option, so I cut out everything except for basketball. My mama's new favorite game of ducking and dodging me got worse. I finally caught her one morning in the kitchen and reminded her I had my championship game that night and would be home late, which she okayed, of course. We won, and I called home to tell her I was getting a ride home. She told me to invite the team over, and she'd cook for us like she used to do. We were partying, and my mama had everyone's stomachs full, and then Marvin came home."

"Oh, shit. Marvin didn't like coming home to a houseful of kids, did he?" Temper asked.

"No, he didn't, to answer your question after I already asked you not to interrupt."

"Damn, my bad!" Temper snapped.

"Yes, it was," Washington snapped back. "Anyway, Marvin didn't like coming home to a houseful of boys and seeing his wife serve them food. He kicked everybody out and cursed them out as he did. My mama ran to her room, and I heard them arguing but didn't think anything of it. The house was a mess, and I didn't want that to be the next issue to piss him off. I started cleaning up. After about twenty minutes, I thought I heard my mama in the kitchen. I shot in there to ask if she was okay. Her right eye swollen shut and her busted nose said that she wasn't. She was trying to hide behind the open freezer door as she grabbed more ice, but I saw it. I won't lie to you, Temper, and I didn't lie to the judge, either. When I saw my mama's face, I saw red.

"All my life, I was told I was just like my daddy, and for the first time, I hoped I was. I ran up in his face, and we yelled and screamed at each other until we reached the staircase that led to our front door. Marvin called himself kicking me out. His bad, because I didn't have plans to go anywhere. My mama jumped in between us and told me to leave until I calmed down, and then I could come back. Marvin must've taken it as if she were overshadowing his words. He cocked back and punched my mama in the mouth. I ran behind the door that separated the house from the steps and grabbed my baseball bat. He thought I would crack him with it, and I wanted to, but that wasn't the plan. I needed to scare him into thinking I would, and I did. Marvin fell down all twenty-two steps, and his big ass landed on his neck. He didn't move. He just lay there with his eyes open, and we couldn't tell if he was breathing. I was scared, and so was my mama. I didn't know what to do next, and leaving felt mandatory. I grabbed my backpack, filled it with books, and grabbed my camera so I could run away."

"What in the hell did you think you could do with a backpack full of books and a camera in the damn streets?" Temper was livid with her hand raised.

"I don't know what I planned to do with the camera, but I wasn't going to let being a fugitive stop me from educating myself, just like you're not going to let my words stop you from interrupting me."

"Exactly. So you might have committed murder, and the first thing you think about is educating yourself? But you can finish telling me what happened next."

"Next, I had to climb over him to run away. I felt like I was crossing a graveyard on Halloween as my mama watched me go. When I made it to the door handle, his hand shot up, and he grabbed my backpack to keep me from running. We played tug of war until I began unzipping it. I started lying about having a weapon inside of it that would make him let go. I thought my protractor had a sharp point on the end of it and I could stab his hand with it, but when the police drew their guns on me when I went to the police station for help a week later, I learned that Marvin turned my protractor into a large black gun."

"Don't get me wrong, this story is better than anything I've seen on TV, but where does hitting the public defender fall in?"

"If you'll listen and stop talking long enough, I can finish," she said, rolling her eyes, and Temper placed her hand over her mouth. "I was arrested with a protractor, books, a camera, and two pairs of panties in my personals, and my story seemed to be fitting together like a puzzle as Marvin's crumbled. When they asked him what happened that night, he said I was high on drugs and had attacked my mother. He told the courts he tried to stop me to no avail, and I attacked him with a baseball bat, pushed him down the stairs, and put a gun to his head to rob him for his money. When it was my turn, I told the same story that I just finished telling you. Since our stories were day and night, it went to trial, and my mama was the key witness. She took the stand and said she didn't remember which one of us hit her. If she had to guess, she'd have to say it was me because I was high. Her words didn't sit right with the judge, especially since they didn't find any drugs in my system. He was about to send me home with them on probation with court-ordered family counseling because he wasn't sure if I had truly committed a crime. I guess I had a moment when I used feelings over logic and asked my mama who hit her again, and she looked me dead in my eyes and repeated what she said. 'I don't know which one of you gave me the black eye and busted my nose and lip. I was knocked out.' My heart broke, and I asked the judge if I could stay in jail instead of going home with a woman I'd never trust again, and he said no. He said they didn't have enough evidence to prove that I had committed the crime. They couldn't keep me."

"And that's when you punched your public defender."

Washington nodded. "I punched my public defender with everything in me. They charged me with assault with a deadly weapon inflicting serious bodily injury for breaking his nose once the judge found out that I spent every summer in the boxing club at the recreation center my uncle worked at while in college. That's a felony. My plan somewhat backfired on me. After the therapist spoke to my judge on my behalf—I had no priors, straight A's since daycare, and was set to graduate high school two years ahead of my class—the judge sentenced me to an emancipation program inside a suitable placement."

"Why couldn't you just go live with your uncle or your father?"

"My uncle is a single man, and I didn't want him to be the middleman between his sister and her daughter, and my daddy is . . ."

"Your daddy is what?" Temper quizzed, and Washington didn't answer.

Washington had her eyes locked on the three older girls walking their way. The way the girls had Washington's attention made Temper pay closer attention. Temper knew the girls, but not well enough for them to stop to speak with her. They lived not too far from her grandmother's house in the adjacent Bloods' hood. They weren't friends. Everyone Temper hung around was affiliated with the Crips.

"Say, Blood, are you that bitch Temper I keep hearing foul shit about?" the tallest and darkest-skinned girl questioned as she stood securely in her spot between the other two girls, who were both bigger than her when it came to waist size.

"Depends on who's asking and why?"

"A simple yes or no will do."

"That's not necessarily true. She has the right to screen who she shares her identity with," Washington said as she gave a smile to the sheriffs down the hallway with their eyes locked on the gathering.

"She wasn't talking to you, was she?" the girl on the right said and then jumped at Washington, who didn't jump nor blink at the action.

"I'm asking because," she said, making sure to emphasize the letter B, "if you're the bitch who got my nigga K-Mack that statutory rape charge by pinning that baby on him, I'm stomping a mudhole in your ass."

Temper had wondered how the neighborhood was taking the news of her hiding her pregnancy, forcing his mama to deliver the baby and then getting slammed with a statutory rape charge that landed him his third strike. Not to mention she also named him as the person who stashed the drugs in her bag as an added "fuck you" for that shit he pulled with Kei-Kei. With time, the thoughts had faded away, more so after she realized she'd never have to see nor deal with any of those people again. Isabel told her Lena planned to sell her house and move away, too, so her grandson would never have to hear about the tragedy surrounding his birth. She had pushed her past out of her mind, and now it was standing in her face, threatening her.

"Please shut up!" Washington got out the words through her exaggerated yawn. "If you're going to whoop Temper's ass, just do it and get the shit over with," she urged as she looked at the girl's left wrist to read her jail name badge. "Theresa Stockton, all that fly-ass talking isn't necessary."

"Ay, Resa, do you want me to go ahead and shut this bitch up for you?" the girl on her right asked.

"Nah, that's just Washington. You see they got her tied up. That ho crazy."

"No, I'm not crazy, ho. After meeting Temper, I think I'm special. My daddy does too." Washington cleared her throat by letting off a broken, dry cough, and when she spoke again, her voice tone and vocabulary changed. "Y'all bitches must've forgotten that warning your big homies sent you about there being a chick in here you're not supposed to fuck with, huh? Heard me shoot a little vocabulary your way, throw on a crazy act, and thought I was the bitch you could fuck with, huh, ho? You little bitches never learn, do you?"

Temper froze in her stance at Washington's split personality. However, she didn't miss the fancy finger work she flashed at the girls from under the shackles, nor did she miss the fearful looks on the girl's faces when they saw it.

"We don't want no problems with you, big homie. We got orders from up top to handle Temper."

"Fuck those orders, and tell whoever sent them that Temper has my blessings. She's off-limits!"

"What about us? Are we good?" Theresa asked as she stepped back to get out of Washington's face.

"As long as I remain a ghost with no face, we are." Theresa had placed enough distance between them to turn her back and walk away. Washington needed to make sure her words were exact. "Theresa Stockton of the East Central Block Bloods, if anyone knows who I am, even if these bitches you brought with you are the ones who spread the word, I'm going to make sure to close casket everybody you love and that everyone you bang East Central Block with buries you, too, out of respect for me. So who am I? That ain't a trick question. You already said it."

"Crazy-ass Wash . . . Washington," she stuttered.

"You damn right. Now get the fuck out of my sight before I make one of those sheriffs looking down here beat the fuck out of you!"

The girls started running as if they were playing a game of tag and Washington was it. When they were out of sight, she looked at Temper and, in her intellectual voice, said, "My daddy is an evil man, and I couldn't live with him if I wanted to. I have a restraining order against him."

"Umm, who's your daddy?"

"A very well-known, bad man who has pull with every gang, pimp, hit man, and dirty cop, FBI, CIA, and Interpol agent from coast to coast, but I think for the safety of the rapport we're building, you don't want the answer to that question, do you?"

"Hell nah, I don't, but can we be best friends then?"

Washington laughed until she realized she was laughing alone. "Oh, you were serious? Guess I'll have to research what exactly a best friend is, and I'm tempted to decline based on the timing surrounding your inquiry. It seems like you're interested in being my best friend for the perks that come along with my birthright."

"You don't even consider your birthright a perk. You're not hiding it for safety reasons. You're hiding it because you hate it. You already said your uncle was your favorite person, and that nerd shit comes too natural, unlike the act you had to put on to hit those bitches up, so why would I find what you hate a perk you'd give to your best friend? Yeah, I deducted, deduced, or whatever the hell you said you do too. I'm in it for your brains and your loyalty. Real shit, I actually like the version of Washington everyone calls crazy. You can keep the gangster kingpin daughter's version to yourself."

"Temper, you are special too," she giggled, "and to be honest, I prefer an equal combination of both sides of me. Incarceration and fair sentencing forced me to suppress anything I might have inherited from my father's status. I'll give you a definitive answer to your question in time. Still, we can be best friends on a trial basis now, as long as you knowingly never have me in police presence for obvious reasons, and stop calling me Washington. Call me Tyger."

"Why, Tyger?" Temper laughed, anticipating another wild explanation.

"It's my name. Tyger Rae Le'shay Washington. I guess my parents thought they were poetic."

The girls both broke out laughing as a friendship built under the juvenile court's dim hallway lights.

Chapter Seven

The judge warned Temper it could take up to 180 days to be picked up by the group home. Three days after court, Temper was breaking down her bunk and retrieving her property. She hated putting on the clothes Isabel had arrested her wearing. They were reminders of the past that her sentence was supposed to erase. There was a deadly omen living in the clothes. Every second she wore them felt like her last—her last seconds free from the clutches of juvenile jail and the last with life in her body. Although she was technically still in jail, she felt they'd arrest her again if she didn't take them off. As proof of life for the omen, the MOTHER necklace Lena had gotten her was the first item the sheriff handed her after she dressed.

"Fuck that," she mumbled as she threw the necklace in the trash along with the duffle bag she'd packed eight months ago that held her family heirlooms. Now Temper's past was in the trash except for the picture Isabel gave her of her and her parents. Isabel told her she'd taken the picture out of her property in Vegas, not wanting anything to happen to it. For a few minutes, Temper battled the urge to retrieve her family heirloom from the discarded bag. After debating it, she decided that she had to get rid of everything from the past if she genuinely wanted a new life.

"I'm sure you want to burn those clothes. Everyone who regains their freedom does. Don't worry, we're going to stop at a department store and a pharmacy so you can grab a few personal items before I take you to the Perky Lane group home. I'll do all the talking on the ride there, and your job is to listen. If you have any questions, by the time I drop you off, I'll be able to predict your future. How? Because I'm Elenore Bentley, your probation officer, and until you turn eighteen, I'm in control of the blueprint of your life. Get in the back, and don't try anything stupid."

"Are you saying you're God? Because He's the only person in control of my life."

"I said no questions."

"That was a statement," Temper corrected her.

"Do you want to taste freedom today? I can come and get you another day. The judge gave me a hundred and eighty to get you suitably placed."

Temper didn't answer immediately. At that moment, the actions of her new best friend Tyger played in her mind. She'd hit a public defender in front of a judge to get freedom the way she required it. Yes, Temper wanted freedom too. However, a fresh start was a requirement. It felt like a continuation of her past. She had to stand up for the sake of her future.

"No, I'm good. You can walk me back inside," she declared, closing the rear door on the SUV she was supposed to get into. "And when you come back to get me, can you please bring me new clothes to put on? I'm not picky. Grab whatever you like in an adult small. The way I see it, if I'm erasing my past, I'm not going into my future with any part of it."

Elenore hadn't expected Temper to call her bluff, and her pride made her feel the need to show her power.

"Wrong answer. I gave you direct orders, and you disobeyed them. You violated your probation conditions, which you didn't allow me to explain to you. That's a new charge."

She removed the handcuffs from the holder on her hip and began reading Temper her Miranda rights. Temper didn't know she was violating her probation if she offered her a choice. She thought about apologizing and asking for another chance. But if she made wavering an option this time, she always would.

She was roughly taken back inside Central Juvenile Hall handcuffed, and Tyger was on her way out with her camera hanging around her neck and her backpack on her back. She gave Temper a smile after deducing what had gone down and approving of it.

As expected, Temper's probation officer lied about the incident. Her violation sentencing was the same as the previous—suitable placement. When Mrs. Bentley came back 179 days later, she had new clothes for Temper to wear out of the juvenile hall's door, and out of respect for Mrs. Bentley's request, Temper didn't say a word on her ride to Perky Lane.

With two weeks to go before she'd turn 18, and a month left in the probation system, she was thankful for Isabel's weekly visits and therapy sessions. Though many of the sessions were painful, like a scab being slowly torn away from an unhealed wound.

"I dreamed of it again," Temper said softly, almost inaudibly.

"Of 'it'? We talked about this, Temper. Your son is not an 'it.' He is a person, and until you realize that, I don't think the dreams will ever stop."

"I know he's a person. Damn, can I just tell you about it? You said talking about it . . . I mean, talking about him more should help me deal with my feelings about him, right?"

Isabel nodded.

"Then let me talk."

"I'm listening."

Temper took a deep breath, lowered her head, and closed her eyes. "I was alone. I couldn't tell if I was in an empty jail ward or a hospital by the beige walls because everything was dark. The EXIT sign at the end of the hall gave off a little light, but the only thing I could make out was the closed doors lining my path. I felt cold, so I looked down at my body to see what I was wearing, and all I had on was a T-shirt, his T-shirt. I knew it was his by the way it made me feel—safe. Whenever he would sneak me into his house to sleep over, he'd give me one of his oversized shirts, and I'd feel safe."

"Why do you fear saying his name?" Isabel whispered in hopes of sounding soothing, but of course, Temper took it as an attack.

"Ain't nobody scared of that nigga. I don't want to say his bitch-ass name because he ain't important and you already know who I'm talking about."

"You're right, I do. Please, keep going." Isabel thought it would be best to hold off on pointing out the psychology behind Temper's name avoidance.

"Like I was saying, he'd give me his shirt to sleep in, and that was all I had on. No shoes, no pants, and no underwear. Another thing that was weird was my hair was down. Like, straightened and hanging over my shoulders. I never wear it like that. It makes me feel . . ."

"Feel what?" Isabel asked, encouraging her to say it.

"Feel less black. Not that I'm embarrassed about being Asian or anything, but the chicks I hang around are chicken heads, so I keep my hair braided or pushed back in a ponytail. You know, so they won't feel bad."

"And so you don't feel different," Isabel added. However, Temper pretended not to hear her.

"But that part isn't important. It was just weird. Anyways, I tried to grab one of the doorknobs to see what was behind it, and it was locked. I checked a few more doors, and they were locked too, and then I heard him crying. He was crying like somebody was hurting him. I tried to get into the room where he was, but I couldn't. I beat on the door, and nothing was happening. He kept getting louder, and it seemed like I was getting farther away from him. I wanted to save him, and I couldn't. He screamed for a few seconds more, and then he said some fucked-up shit to me."

"What did he say?" The suspense had Isabel sitting on the edge of her cold metal seat. If she were any closer to the glass that separated them, her heavy breathing would fog it up. Temper had told her of a couple of dreams that involved her being pregnant but none where the baby had spoken directly to her.

"He said, 'Mama, why you not saving me?' But I was trying to save him. I really wanted to, and then I heard a big boom behind the door where he was at, and I woke up. I couldn't catch my breath, and then I threw up. I know it was a dream, but I felt like shit for hours because I didn't save him. Why though? It's not like I want to raise him. I just wanted to help him."

Isabel shook her head in disbelief as she came up with the right words to say. "The why is a truth that lives inside of you. I can speculate or form a theory, but ultimately only you know what that dream means to you."

"I thought you said you were here to help," Temper giggled.

"Hell, I thought I was here to help too," Isabel said as she joined in on the laugh. "But seriously, you sharing your dream with me did help. You just don't see it yet."

It was visits like those that ultimately helped Temper "Wite-Out" her past and start anew.

When Temper's time was served and Mrs. Bentley released her from probation, the only thing she kept as she walked out of Perky Lane's doors was her friendship with Tyger. The picture was the last piece of her past she had to trash. She didn't feel a thing as she tossed it.

Hey Best Friend,

I'm sorry it took me so long to write you, but Isabel has kept me busy since I moved in with her. It's like having a roommate, friend, therapist, and mama all in one, and she's driving me crazy. In my first month here, she enrolled me in a GED program and got me a job at the skating rink. After that, she started adding more to my plate by the week. Now she has me volunteering at a runaway shelter, going to church with her, and I'm learning to speak Khmer, which is Cambodia's official language, and Spanish, which is hers. The funny thing is, I'm catching on to both quickly. Las Vegas is better than I thought it would be, but I still haven't made any friends besides Isabel. I found out that I can visit you once my juvenile record is officially closed, which should happen in the next month. How is the emancipation stuff coming along? Before I left Perky Lane, I heard the staff say you had made unbelievable progress in the six months you were there before I moved in, which doesn't surprise me because you're an incredible person. Just in case this letter doesn't get to you before the last day of this month, congratulations on completing high school. I can't wait to brag about my best friend who graduated from high school a month before her sixteenth birthday. You are something special, Tyger!

Can't wait to read your response,

Temper

It took Temper four months to send her first letter to Tyger, but she didn't have to wait that long to hear back from her.

Temper,

Your life is so tossed, but that's what makes you you. Yes, best friend, I am officially a high school grad, and next week I'll be spending my sixteenth birthday moving into my dorm room at USC. In other words, there's no need for you to come from Las Vegas to visit me here when your record gets sealed. Unfortunately, I'm still on probation or, as they call it, a ward of the court until I complete my emancipation course, but that is less than six months away. Besides all the scholarships I received, I also qualify for financial aid thanks to the arrest. Life is funny like that. It will throw you under the bus, run you over, and all the pain you're going through is delivering you to your next destination.

I think it's cool that you're learning two new languages, and I hate to be the bearer of bad news, but the fact that they are coming easy means you are smarter than you think. Congrats on the job and the GED prep. Once you take the test, you should look into taking a few history courses so we can work together in the future, but I'll go into details about my full plan for us later. Oh, and I guess I'm a lesbian now. There's this girl in the Cutie Cakes therapy group who goes to school here on campus, who kissed me in the timeout room when I was homesick from public school. She told her friends that the nerd wasn't that square, and word of me being gay spread. Next thing I know, I'm being moved to the opposite end of the hall, near the nurse's station on the way to the kitchen to a room by myself, and different girls started sneaking in after lights out to test out these lips. To keep it short, I had an intimate encounter with a girl here while the overnight staff slept on the couch inches away from my door, and I enjoyed it.

Placement life is taking its toll on me. That means it's time for me to go. I'm also starting to get too attached to the staff at Perky Lane. Mostly all the ones who graduated from USC. Maybe it's because the majority of them hooped and they're the coolest nerds I've ever met. FYI, I hate my therapist here, and we will never get along. She got word of my nighttime activities and moved me out of the main building to one of their satellite houses. She waited to announce it the same day I made it to level C and could control the van's music and ride in the front on group outings. It's only been a week, but I miss being around fifty girls every day. Their personalities were beginning to entertain me, among other

*things they had to offer. And before I forget, I'm
your only friend, and Isabel is only a fill-in until
I'm free. Smile. Don't bother writing me back here.
I'll write once I'm in my dorm. Counting down these
days until I'm out of here.*
  I miss you, best friend,
  Tyger Rae Washington

Months passed before Temper received another letter
from Tyger, and she didn't bother reading it after opening it. Once she saw the number written on the bottom of
the letter, she called her.

"Nine months? It took you nine months to write to me?
What kind of fucking friend are you?" Temper jokingly
yelled into the phone at the sound of Tyger's voice.

"A very busy best friend. I know we have a lot to catch
up on, but did you take your GED test yet?"

"Yes, and I failed horribly, but why was that the most
important question?"

"Because I was going to tell you that if you haven't
taken it and passed, I found a way to get us working together without you having it. Are you ready to move back
home? I moved out of the dorm when they sealed my record, and got an apartment."

"I can't move back to L.A. Are you crazy?"

"Why not? You are off probation, your record is sealed,
and—"

"And my past life is there. But even if my past moved
away, California isn't the place for me. My family is here
in Vegas."

"Isabel isn't your family. She's the reason you were in
jail if I recall correctly, and be honest, the only reason
California isn't for you is because of your past."

Tyger was right, but Temper wouldn't confirm it. During the almost year and a half when she lived in Vegas, Temper had become colorless, and her nationality couldn't be judge by any other title but human. She even chose "other" when selecting a race on multiple-choice forms. She spoke four languages now, and her style had grown to a business-casual look, which was a trick Isabel taught her from working undercover on maintaining a neutral front. Meeting Isabel was destined, and though she was growing fond of Tyger, she had a bond with Isabel that not even she could touch.

"She is my family, and you're right, it is my past. Did you forget there was a hit put on me when we went to court? Or what about the bitch who tried to fight me at Perky Lane? She said she was sent by her hood's chief enforcer to get me. Why would I willingly move back to be killed?"

There was a moment of silence that sent a chill down Temper's back. It felt like she was paying homage to the dead. She didn't want to think about the past nor discuss it, but that time had come.

"You never told me why, though. What did you do to get both the Crips and the Bloods after you? Better yet, who did you cross?" Tyger's questions were valid, and Temper knew she deserved an answer.

Thanks to Isabel, Temper wouldn't have to supply it now. "Hey, I thought we should go out for dinner tonight. I'm not really in the mood to cook," Isabel whispered after sticking her head in Temper's room and seeing her on the phone.

"Is that that bitch talking?" Tyger snarled.

"Whoa, what's up with all of that name-calling? Hold on."

Temper put the receiver down and pushed it into her pillow so Tyger couldn't hear her conversation with Isabel. Not that she had anything to hide, but she could see the jealousy brewing. That was how she used to feel whenever Kei-Kei hung out with her cousins instead of her. As an extra precaution, she responded to Isabel in Spanish.

"*¡Hablas español mejor que yo ahora!*" Isabel laughed after telling Temper that she spoke Spanish better than her now, and Temper laughed with her. When she put the phone back to her ear, Tyger's vibe was worse.

"What were y'all laughing at? I hope not me."

"Why would we be laughing at you? Isabel knows you're my best friend, and she doesn't have anything negative to say about it or you. Like you shouldn't have anything bad to say about her. She's helped me a whole lot. If anything, you should like her just off the strength of that."

"I do like her for helping you, but she's a cop. I asked you never to have me in police presence knowingly, and then you go and shack up with one."

"I'm not forcing you to be in her presence. I'm asking you to stop calling her out her name. As a matter of fact, how about I stop bringing her up since she's a cop, so we won't have to talk about her at all?"

"That's fine with me. We are supposed to be catching up anyway. So tell me what's been going on with you."

"I can't right now," Temper stammered, not wanting to say the next words. "We are going out to eat dinner, but I'll call you when I make it back, okay?"

"Okay, that's fine. Wait, I have a study group tonight. How about we plan to talk all night Friday? That way we have more than enough time to play catch up."

"That's the plan! Can't wait to talk back to your crazy butt."

"Me either, and I'm sorry I crossed boundaries or whatever."

"Me too. Let's act like it never happened."

"Cool."

It was close to noon on Saturday when the girls got off the phone. They talked each other's ears off. Temper told her about life at the skating rink, the few dudes she flirted back and forth with, and the personal changes she'd made in her life. Running her mouth gave her the courage to answer Tyger's question from their previous call.

"I fucked over a Crips dude in a real way. He wasn't ranked up or anything like that, but he was close to a few homies who were," she said, hoping her summary was enough.

"Okay, that was vague. How about answering this, was the fuck move you made gang related?" Tyger questioned.

"Strictly personal. We had a relationship, or so I thought, and when I found out he fucked me over with a bitch, I fucked him over worse. It didn't put his life in danger. Well . . ." Temper said before falling silent.

"Umm, I'm going to need you to finish that sentence," Tyger snapped.

"It got him his third strike."

"You snitched on him?"

"No," Temper sighed, not knowing how to explain it without giving Tyger all the details. "He was already in jail before I did what I did. He's just not getting out now that I did it. That's why everybody wants to beat my ass."

"You know what? I don't want to know if you don't want to tell me, because it's not making sense. I could understand if his homeboys from his hood were after you, but why would his enemies come for you? The only way that could happen is with the blessing of a . . ." Tyger's thoughts moved from her thesis statement to her supportive argument, then stopped at the conclusion. "A kingpin." She didn't wait for Temper to try to explain or for her to change the subject. Tyger changed it and took over the call.

She gave Temper the day-to-day life of a double-major college student and a small piece of the plan she put together for her life. They'd laughed and joked all night. Sleep wasn't why they ended the call. Tyger had a Saturday class to attend, and Temper had to get ready to volunteer at the runaway shelter.

Before that night, the girls didn't know much about each other. Eventually, they decided that neither wanted to talk about their past ever again. They agreed that whatever they did or whatever happened before they met didn't matter, and they would never bring it up. With juvenile records sealed, and neither having ties to parents or family, what would be the point of talking about their individual histories? They were reborn at the courthouse, and if that was true, then they had been best friends since birth.

It became a daily routine to be the last person they would talk to before sleep, which made the distance between them disappear. In the two years of talking daily, the girls got along 98 percent of the time, but they both had their moments. Temper would fuss about Tyger not driving to see her now that she owned a car, and Tyger fussed about Temper not moving home now that she upgraded her apartment to a two-bedroom. Neither had to say it, but they were no longer friends. They had become sisters. With everything flowing correctly, they weren't surprised when tragedy finally found them.

"What time will you make it into town? I want you to help me pick out my birthday outfit. It needs to be nice and slutty," Temper affirmed.

"Damn right it does. You're turning twenty-one, and you're newly single. I didn't want to say anything back then, but I knew Kevin wasn't going to turn out to be shit. Twenty-five, still living with his mama, and he only had part-time hours emptying trash at that casino. That shit adds up to absolutely nothing. Ay, I hope your pussy doesn't have a thing for scrubs!"

Tyger had purposely dodged answering the question about the time of her arrival because she wanted to surprise Temper. Temper meant the world to her, and hearing that her first attempt at having an adult relationship had left her hurt made Tyger want to be there for her even more.

"Then you should have said that shit when I first told you about him, ho. What good is the information now? Girl, my pussy misses him so much, and I'm trying to help her ignorant ass get over him, but her stupid ass went and gassed my heart up to think we got feelings for him. My pussy is going through it. Please pray."

"You are so stupid you make my ass hurt." Tyger laughed. "You need a skimpy black dress, pumps to show off all them bony-ass legs you got, and a pair of crotchless panties so you can let your scent attract your next piece of dick. If you want your pussy to beat her battle with depression, you will have to keep her distracted with other dick. That's the only pussy medicine on the market that can help you beat that shit. Yo' pussy needs a hug from a new man."

"Okay, madam sexy doctor, go ahead and tell me how you know that prescription is going to work. Aren't you a lesbian now?"

"Fuck you," Tyger retorted.

"Nah, that's too much of a distraction for her. I'm not trying to have my pussy confused, but I appreciate the offer."

"Remind me to kick you square in the ass when I see you. I told you I had a lesbian experience that I enjoyed. That doesn't make me a lesbian."

"Bitch, you licked a whole pussy. You rocked another bitch's scent over your lip like a fragrance mustache, but if that doesn't make you a lesbian, then I know I'm a virgin because I've sucked more dick than I've let fuck me, hands down."

"I hate you!" Tyger screamed jokingly.

"The feeling is mutual, carpet muncher."

"But seriously, science has proven the best way to get over one person is to get under the next. It's the lonely and unwanted feeling that got your pussy caught up. Let's be honest. What was it about him that makes him the one you wanted to be locked down to anyways? And don't say anything involving sex."

"Then I can't say nothing, bitch. I hated everything else. Whatever I couldn't stand about his Polo Assassin–wearing ass the dick made up for," she said as she squeezed her legs together, hoping to stop the tingling feelings from thinking about those chubby nine inches he'd used to beat her down.

"Exactly. Just because you don't have book smarts doesn't mean you're unequipped for pussy smarts. You have to get you a ho mentality or a ho cheat sheet. I keep a ho translation of the male language in my pussy for times like these. You better get you one."

"Bitch, I hate every word you let out of your mouth," she said through her laugh. "But I have to get off this phone. Everybody can't get paid for going to school like you. Unlike you, I have to work for a living."

"Yeah, you're the one who took six years to finish four years of high school by a GED test, and I do work. I told you I'm in an internship with the museum."

"'Internship' and 'job to survive' aren't the same things. Now that I'm a counselor, I can't do my 'come in late' volunteer stroll anymore. I'll call you tonight when I get off."

"Bye, bitch. And, Temper, happy birthday, ho."

"Damn, it took you all day to say it. I was waiting to see how long it took you to remember your only best friend's birthday. Thank you, and be ready to hit the road headed my way tomorrow night. Bye, bitch."

Temper rode in the cab to work with a mixture of Tyger's words and confused feelings for Kevin. Tyger didn't know her past in detail, and she was thankful for it because that meant Tyger didn't hear the truth in her words about being in love with the dick. From the day Temper gave away her virgin status, she replaced it with daily dick trips. She didn't care if it was from the dick she had the day before or a new dick owner. As long as she covered one in cum, she met her daily goal. That was part of her problem, and from the second she realized she was pregnant, she swore to wean herself from daily dick until she was in a relationship with the right person who could give it to her as often as she liked. Her decision to date wasn't rash. Her choice in a mate was because her pussy couldn't hold off any longer, and her fingers had never worked. They only bought her time.

"Hey, are you getting out or what?" the driver asked, and by the tone in his Arabic accent, it wasn't the first time he had asked her the question.

"Don't rush me. You should be glad I'm running your meter up. That's more money for you," Temper countered, and his eyes shot up to the rearview mirror.

"I'm sorry, beautiful. Please take your time."

Seeing the lust filling his eyes, Temper stepped out of the back of the cab and took one step toward the shelter. She retrieved the money to cover the ride, but the shelter didn't look right. The entry hall lights were off, and the smoking area was empty, which never happened. From the busy street, she couldn't see the parking lot in the rear of the building.

"Here," she said, handing the driver the money and a small tip. "Can you wait a second before you pull off? If that door is locked, I'll need you to take me back home. I don't have a key."

"No problem," he said with a flirtatious wink of his eye.

Temper couldn't think of any reason for the shelter to be closed, but if by rare chance it was, she wouldn't complain about having her birthday off. Initially, she was scheduled off by request to spend the day with Kevin. Once she learned Kevin didn't mind using the little paycheck he made cleaning rooms at the casino to buy prostitutes off the strip, she dropped his freaky ass and canceled her day-off request. She should have known the best sex she ever had in her life had to come with a fucked-up tie to it. She was sure her luck had gotten better with all the changes she had made in her life, and then Isabel had delivered the bad news.

"I almost arrested Kevin's nasty ass tonight. That makes you officially done with him, understood?"

Isabel wasn't completely inside the house before making the announcement. If Temper didn't know any better, she would have thought that Isabel ran straight home with the news as her chest heaved up and down, a sign she was out of breath.

"What do you mean you almost arrested him? What did he do?"

"I don't want to tell you the details. To make it short, I was working undercover to catch johns to question

for our murder investigation of that young girl. You know, the one you asked me about from the news the other day? I got a tip on where I could find him, which was bullshit because I ended up catching Kevin at the spot instead. Don't get me wrong, he was in legal limits of prostitution, but for me to have to bring him in as a known client of the night makes you done with him, understood?"

"Yes, but are you positive that's what he was doing?"

"You know what? Call him. Companionship has you blinded. Ask him about our encounter tonight. He'll tell you the truth. I'm sure of it!"

"Nah, I believe you. I'm done with him," was what Temper let out of her mouth, but once Isabel snatched her workout bag and headed out the door, Temper made a call.

"Why are you fucking calling me? Didn't your big sister tell you that I'm through with you?" Kevin's words held no emotion. He seemed bored by the contact alone.

"How are you through with me when you're the one out buying pussy?"

"Are you serious? Your sister is a cop. You had me around a pig like you didn't know I smoke weed."

Temper couldn't help but laugh. Kevin was the biggest square she had ever spread her legs for, and even his weed smoking was small and far from addiction. She didn't bother continuing the confrontation. It wasn't like she'd ever feel comfortable having sex with him again. The dick was good, but an STD had almost taken her out. Hanging up was the easiest way to end it.

She turned the knob on the door, and it was open. "Hello, is anyone in here?"

"Yes, we are in the back, Temper. The power went out, and we're in the kitchen waiting for it to come back on now."

"Is that you, Shelia?"

"Who else would it be? Bring your scary ass on. Once you come down the hall, you'll see the candlelight." Great spirit, warm personality, a little on the big side, and always talking shit—those facts about the 45-year-old black woman from Brooklyn Temper loved, and they were why she looked at Shelia like an aunt. Though her voice wasn't what Temper questioned. She thought she had seen a dark shadow move across the doorway in the opposite direction of Shelia's voice.

She waved to the cab and closed the door behind her.

"I'm not scary, but wouldn't it have been smart to put a candle at the entrance?" She had to squint her eyes to make her way to the hallway. "I'm just saying that's how everybody comes in the build . . ."

She couldn't talk, let alone take another step. Candles did light the hall once she turned the corner, the candles from her birthday cake.

"Surprise," the room screamed in unison as the lights came on. It took a second for her sight to adjust and confirm her second surprise. Standing next to Shelia and Isabel was Tyger. The three were wearing full-teeth smiles.

Shelia sang the birthday song to Temper.

Isabel said, "Take a second and make a wish before you blow out your candles. You only turn twenty-one once."

"But I don't know what to wish for. This is already more than I would have ever wanted."

As the room said, "Aw," at her heartfelt words, Tyger stepped up. "Cut the drama and make a wish. You love us, and we love you too. Just promise me that the wish is for you and will benefit only you. Can you do that?"

Temper nodded in agreement, closed her eyes tightly, inhaled, and blew out all twenty-one candles as she released her wish through her breath. She ran straight to Tyger and hugged her for what seemed like hours. In truth, no more than a minute passed.

"Why didn't you tell me you were already here when we were on the phone, and when did you make it?" Temper asked.

"How about you cut the cake before you start asking a million questions? We're all hungry from sitting in the dark waiting for you. I hope that wish didn't have anything to do with Kevin's dick, too. I already told you we are going to fix that depression shit y'all going through," Tyger said as she turned her back to Temper to face Shelia. "Can you please grab the paper plates for me? I'm going to my car to grab the cake cutter and her birthday gift."

"Of course, precious."

The ladies went in separate directions, and it was Temper's turn to thank Isabel. "Why do I have a feeling you put all of this together, including Tyger being here?"

"Because I did. I wanted this to be special for you, and this is only the beginning. Friday and Saturday, I have a few things planned for us to do, and Sunday, we'll have brunch before Tyger leaves. You know it's killing her to miss class all these days. You didn't tell me your best friend was a nerd pretending to be a gangster." Isabel giggled as she looked over her shoulder to see if Tyger was on her way back. "I did a little snooping into her background, and I . . . You know what? None of that matters because I know her now, and she's a grade A geek. Beautiful in and out, but she's a total Poindexter. That girl was studying the entire time we waited for you." She pointed to a table in the rear of the kitchen covered in books.

"That's Tyger for you. I didn't tell her much about you either. I just felt like it was best not to let the two worlds collide. Plus, you're a cop. I'm normally allergic to pigs, and so are the people around me."

"Understood. I vomited every day for a week when you moved in and had diarrhea the next. Being around a criminal full-time affects me like I've eaten a pot of old refried beans. You would have died if you smelled the dump I took after spending time with Tyger yesterday." Isabel winked at Temper when she finished talking and joined Shelia to help organize the cake distribution. Tyger came back with nothing but a key ring in her hand.

"Here you go," she said, handing her the keys. "It's your birthday. You go get that shit."

Tyger blew the surprise with the excited look on her face. Temper didn't hesitate to snatch the keys out of her hand nor to run to the door. The bow wrapped around the luxury four-door beauty in silver made Temper fall to her knees in a happy cry.

"Happy birthday," Isabel, Tyger, and Shelia screamed as they jumped for joy at Temper's response.

She cried until there weren't any tears left in her ducts and hit the unlock on the doors. She sat in the sedan's driver seat, adjusted the mirror, and then said, "Thanks, Isabel, it's the exact one I wanted."

"Then you should thank Tyger for hunting it down for me and then thank her again and Shelia for helping me pay for it. We didn't want you to be stuck with a note. Oh, and there's a few bags in the trunk for you, too. Don't stay out here long. There's a party going on in here for you."

"I won't."

"Yes, you will," Tyger whispered when the women were out of earshot. "You have to drive it around the block at least. I don't know anyone whose first car was a big-body Benz." She nodded at her own car. "I had to settle for a two-door Benz with the top missing." She giggled as she got in on the passenger side.

"You don't look anything like I remember. It's like I knew another person," Temper noted, finally getting a good look at her best friend.

"We both are other people. Don't you let anyone tell you differently, and you don't look the way I remember you either. You have meat on your bones, and you look a hundred percent Asian besides that butt you're growing and that desert suntan you got. I thought Asians couldn't hold on to weight."

"Whatever. This Asian got ass, but I won't lie, it's a benefit not looking black. No offense to your extra chocolaty ass, but people treat you differently when they don't see the black. It's not until I open my mouth that they know what time it is. I can't change my voice tone, and I wouldn't want to if I could." She smacked her lips and then pinched Tyger's hips, which looked like they'd tear through her jeans. "Look at all of this. Ass, ass, ass. Yo' ass looks like the end of a damn horse. You've been doing a lot of fucking it seems, Miss Lesbian."

"Study, fuck, eat, class, and then repeat, and this is donkey fat," she said, slapping her ass, making sure it sounded painful in a freaky way. "And I thought I told you I had a lesbian experience. Keep fucking with me about it, and I'm going to give you one. Them little bitty titties are sitting up nice," she joked as she reached for a nipple.

"Fuck you!"

"When? We can hop in the back seat now and break this bitch in," Tyger teased.

"You know I love you, right?"

"Um, I was just playing with you. We both know you can't handle this tongue. Take me back to the center, you freaky Asian bitch. I haven't even breathed on the cat yet, and you're confessing feelings."

"Stop playing, Tyger. I'm trying to be serious. Your being here means everything to me, and so does our friendship," Temper confessed. "Thank you for making my day special, boo."

"You're welcome, my love-face. There's no place in the world I'd rather be, besides at home alone studying."

"Ugh. I hate you because I know you mean that shit."

"Yes, I do, as I sip on a flavored coffee in my panties."

"Sorry, boo, I'm not going to let that fucked-up statement kill my joy. It's my twenty-first birthday, and I'm spending it with the two people I love most in this world."

"Man, fuck that bitch!"

"What? Why did you say that?" Temper asked, confused. She thought for sure whatever problem Tyger had with Isabel had to be squashed after the communication it took to come together for her.

"Because he is a bitch! Did you think I'd let you spend your day with Kevin's weak ass?"

"I was talking about you and Isabel."

"Oh, I thought you were talking about Kevin's raggedy ass," she lied.

Spending time with Isabel was for Temper. She still didn't like nor trust her. By the questions Isabel asked over lunch, Tyger knew she'd done her homework on her and her family. She expected that from a cop, but to have someone follow her was crossing the line. Whoever the big, dark blob she'd hired was, hiding behind the tinted windows of his Grand Marquis, he was doing a terrible job. Tyger had clocked him when she pulled into her hotel room the night before, and he'd passed her and Temper twice since they'd been in the car. She wanted to tell Temper what her so-called sister had done, which would have wasted time she'd never get back. Either Temper would piss her off by taking Isabel's side, or she'd assume her past was still haunting her. Tyger chose to be the bigger person, but only for Temper's sake.

"Look, no more trying to make memories with jack-asses. How about that? We'll throw the entire birthday away before we spend one with a nigga who ain't our husband or we don't know for sure we'd marry. That way, if we run across dick while we're celebrating, we get to have celebration dick with our cake."

"Sounds good to me." Temper giggled. "Let me get us back before Isabel panics."

The girls made it back, but Isabel wasn't there.

"You know she can never stay still long. She got a call and changed clothes like Superman in a telephone booth," Shelia grunted to voice her disappointment. "She didn't want to go, but you know how that goes."

"Yeah, I do."

"Well, Temper, you still got us, and Tyger is welcome to stay your whole shift. Just brief her on what to do if we get a 911 incident. I don't want her scared to come back." She laughed, cut herself another slice of cake, and went to the front of the building to check on their guests. The runaway shelter also functioned as a "soda pad home," which was an in-between spot for kids waiting for foster care or a group home setting. The doors never closed, and there was never a day when they didn't get someone new.

"Help me clean up, and then I'll take you to my office," Temper said with a smile that didn't go unnoticed.

"Aw, shit, Temper has her own office. How you pull that off with your six-year-high-school-diploma-holding ass?" Tyger jokingly asked as she wrapped everything up on the table in the cloth and threw it away.

"Please give me all my props. I have a six-year high school degree and my GED. There ain't too many people who can say that shit."

"Right, people who graduated within the four years allotted say 'isn't,' not 'ain't.' I see grammar wasn't a major part of the required credits."

"Everybody can't be a hood genius like you." She rolled her eyes at Tyger.

"Well, technically," Tyger articulated in that irritating genius voice that Temper was first introduced to her using, "unless there's a disability present, anyone can be taught what I know. Most don't have the discipline to retain the information nor to use it. That's the real issue."

"Please discipline your mouth to shut the fuck up." She giggled and then looked around to see if anything else needed cleaning. With Tyger knocking out the cleanup in one quick move, Temper said, "Come on, my office is up front."

The girls chatted about everything they talked about over the years by phone but with the facial expressions as Temper did the live-ins' daily logs. Tyger took that as an opportunity to study, and just when it felt like they were making progress in their projects, everything stopped. Chaos skipped through the building with glee, looking for its old friend, and when it found her at the highest point of her new life, it did what it did best. It tossed Temper's life.

"This must be one of those 911 situations Shelia was talking about," Tyger said. She saw all the cops fall in before Temper did.

"Yeah, it looks like it. You stay here, and please don't come out. Since they're minors, we have to protect their privacy."

"Bitch, I'm only nosy when I know the folks involved. Go do you and close the door behind you. I'm studying."

Temper took a couple of steps toward the forming crowd and froze once she realized everyone's eyes were looking in her direction with grief etched on their faces.

That dread Temper felt the first time her probation officer picked her up in the clothes she was arrested in was back. As it embraced her, she couldn't take another step, nor could she breathe. It was the same tragic death scene from the hood movies she grew up watching where the dead were announced, there was a high-pitched, heartbroken scream, and then that heartbroken person yelled, "No!" in disbelief. Yet this time it had a fucked-up twist.

"Hey, Temper, can you please come here for a minute? There's something we need tell you," announced the taller of the two officers who Temper quickly identified as Isabel's partners.

"If it ain't 'happy birthday' or Isabel sent the two of you to tell me something for her, then no, I can't come here." Her words were shaky as the chill in the room entered her lungs.

"Oh, Lord," Shelia whimpered as she dreaded the inevitable.

"Oh, Lord, what, Shelia? If you know what these pigs want with me, then you tell me."

"Temper, now you know better than that," Shelia snapped while the tears she was holding back surfaced and covered her cheeks.

"No, Shelia, I don't."

Tears mounted in the wells of Temper's eyes. The progress she'd made under Isabel's love and care felt like it was a sentence away from washing away with her tears.

"Isabel was killed in the line of duty. I'm so sorry, Temper."

Temper didn't know which officer gave her the news, but whoever it was should have been arrested for murder. His words had killed her too.

"No!" she yelled repeatedly before falling to her knees drained of life. Hope for all that could be good and just ran over her eyelids and met her lips with a salty aftertaste.

Motion pictures didn't capture devastation accurately. Temper needed someone to get with the writers and coerce them into rewriting this movie. Instead of the officers announcing the murder of a well-loved civilian, they were there to comfort Temper. The same two officers she met that night at the Greyhound station with Isabel were the ones with their arms open, ready to place them around her and comfort her through the horrible news. The sick irony was too much for her to take or deem as real. Temper's beloved Isabel was dead on her twenty-first birthday. The murderer had rewritten more than a hood movie's script. The killer rewrote Temper's life.

Chapter Eight

The Southern California Natural History Museum's tour schedule had no vacant spots available for the next six months, and that's how Paula, the director, had to have it. She wasn't sure about hiring such a young girl for the curator position, but Tyger's resume was impeccable. She'd graduated high school at the age of 16, earned bachelor's degrees in anthropology and history before her twentieth birthday, and began volunteering at the museum. At the same time, Tyger pursued a Master of Liberal Arts in museum studies with ancient African artifacts as her specialized area of study ten minutes away at USC.

Not long after, Tyger wrote her dissertation for her PhD in anthropology. She was even cocky enough to base her thesis on a theory she created as the discussion topic for two of her four published books. There was no way Paula could pass her up. When the board of trustees, known as the "money people," politely told her they weren't comfortable giving a black girl that much power, Paula didn't have a problem reminding them how much money they could bring in from making Tyger the face with those accolades. Once she painted the picture for the board, calls were made. Within days, the museum received a large donation from a black-operated, but not black-owned, television network. They also began running commercials to get donors and the African American community to support the museum. To top it off, Tyger hired a drop-dead gorgeous Asian and black woman to fill the docent position, which made the $18 an hour they paid her a steal with all the traffic Temper's beauty brought in.

"The exhibit designers outdid themselves with the *Escape to the Safari* display. It's created a huge buzz, and the board upped the in-house budget. So you know what that means?" Paula said with her eyes shooting from Temper to Tyger.

"Yeah, it means you can finally hire me a boss and give yourself and Tyger a break from doing it," Temper responded.

"Or I can promote you to the museum educator position, on the grounds you remain the docent, and pay you more to be your own boss. I believe you can handle it. What do you think, Tyger? Can Temper handle it?"

"I know she can handle it. For a girl who graduated high school six years after starting, Temper knows her stuff." She giggled. "It's like she was born to work here. I've been on a lot of museum tours, but I've never enjoyed one as much as I enjoy Temper's. You got it going on, girlfriend."

"Whatever. Don't forget, I also hold a GED, thank you very much. I had to perfect my exit from high school. That's what took me so long to complete it. If you're going to tell history, make sure you check the facts. But then again, I guess that's why I'm the best docent in the western hemisphere and you're not," Temper teased.

"So do you want the position or not, Ms. High School Degree Holder?" asked Paula.

"How much is the pay increase? Managing me is going to be hard work. That's a lot of talent to handle. I'd need to see at least two dollars more an hour."

Tyger was already shaking her head in disappointment. No matter how many years Temper had been around her, she still didn't see it. It was hard to watch Temper finding value in everything around her except herself, but she knew why. Temper had never fully forgiven herself for her past mistakes, whether she talked about the past or not. She added blaming herself for Isabel's death to her self-hate list, and though she never admitted it, she thought of herself as a burden who Tyger pitied.

"How about going from twenty-eight thousand a year hoping that you get thirty-hour workweeks to a mandatory forty hours a week at fifty-five thousand a year?"

"Um," Temper hummed, taken aback.

"Okay, you're right. Two jobs deserve more pay. Sixty thousand a year and a possible performance increase after two years. That's the best I can do. What do you say?" Paula begged, clearly taking Temper's shock for disappointment.

"Two questions—where do I sign, and when can I start?"

"It's effective immediately, and there's nothing for you to sign. I've had the approval to promote you for a month but wanted to monitor your performance myself. Not that I don't trust Tyger's words. It's the bias of them that makes me curious. The two of you are best friends and have an unbreakable sisterhood, but your work ethic put my doubts to rest. Congratulations!"

"Thank you kindly," Temper said, then gave a curtsy in her slacks.

"Hold on. Before you get ready to celebrate, I have good news to share too," Tyger announced. "I spoke with my academic counselor about a few concerns I was having, and he took those concerns to the board of directors of anthropology. Not only am I up for an honorary doctorate for the anthropology work I did last year in Africa, but they also found a way to accredit it as well."

"So what does all of that mean?" Temper asked, cutting her off. "Don't look at me like that. You know I hate suspense."

"You can kill a punchline in a wet dream starring Idris and Denzel with your short attention span," Tyger snarled, rolling her eyes. "All of that means I finished my dissertation last month." Her attitude began melting away, and her words were choppy as tears materialized. Tyger didn't have to say another word as the ladies added their tears to her joyous, silent cry.

"A fucking doctor. Crazy-ass Washington is about to cross the stage at USC to get her doctorate. Bitch, I was happy for you when you got your master's, but, ho, I'm proud this go-round," Temper rejoiced as they walked into their shared apartment in Venice.

Seeing that partying was no longer warranted in the days after Isabel's murder, Temper had used the three days she had left with Tyger to pack up her belongings and hit the road back to California with her. There was no way she would continue living in that house. Isabel's mother and father assured her she could stay, and that's what their daughter would have wanted, but she wasn't for pleasing the wants of the dead. She was in California with her driver's license updated to her new address before the funeral and was too hurt to drive back to attend. She was running again. However, this time she had a plan. She'd bust her ass and be the best at whatever she decided to do and prove to the curse that had been following her her entire life that she'd make it.

Temper loved her decision to move in with Tyger. It helped her get over Isabel's death. Tyger kept their schedules too busy to grieve, and then six months later, time froze.

"This letter came for you today. I held it to the lamp but still couldn't read shit. Hurry up and open it. It's from a lawyer in Laughlin, Nevada." Tyger handed her the letter and stood over her shoulder. They must have read it at the same pace, because when Temper made it to the closing, Tyger shouted, "Ain't that a bitch?"

Isabel named her the beneficiary of her estate with one catch: Temper wouldn't receive a dime of it until she was six months into her thirty-fifth year of life, or earlier if she were married with a child. Isabel wanted to make sure she was mature enough to handle the blessing her death would bestow on her.

"I don't want her estate." She was about to rip the letter into pieces, but Tyger snatched it in time.

"What the fuck? Are you crazy or utterly stupid? If you don't accept it, everything your mom, big sister, and friend worked for goes to the State. The same State that didn't find her damn killer."

"I don't care. The shit doesn't feel right. I want Isabel, not her damn money. As of today, I don't need money from nobody."

Finally, the hurt broke through the blocks of ice that Temper had placed around her heart, and she cried. There was no room left inside of her to store the pain. Beyond that, there wasn't any room left to hide her fear of going back in time to become that same clueless little girl Isabel help her erase. It eased her past fears knowing Isabel would be there to stop the old her from coming back. Tyger's friendship helped. However, at that time, they were in separate states. It was Isabel who had functioned as her personal security. Taking the money didn't bring her back, and that was what she wanted—her Isabel back. She cried until her sorrow attacked Tyger, and then they cried together.

"Why are you crying?" Temper asked.

Tyger cried with a smirk on her face. "Bitch, I'm happy." She laughed. "Look at us. We've come a long way since juvenile hall."

"I asked you never to mention that. The last part of that bullshit died when I turned twenty-one. Can we be happy about our accomplishments without digging in that raggedy time capsule? Damn," Temper barked.

"Yes, you did ask me never to bring it up, but it's only us. Calm down!" Tyger wasn't feeling Temper's tone, and it irritated her that Temper only talked to her like that when it had something to do with Isabel.

"Oh, so that makes it okay to bring up shit that we tabooed? Cool, my turn." Temper rushed to the couch. She sat in the center of it like a statue of Buddha with her legs crossed. "I guess you can say you finally broke your ties to your dad then, huh? Who would have ever thought the daughter of a kingpin would be graduating with a PhD in anthropology and history? With all the killing, pimping, robbing—"

"Okay, bitch, you made your point. Never means never, but what I want to know is, when will you forgive yourself for the shit in yours? Whatever your past shit is." Tyger knew a few things about Temper's past from talking with Isabel, though none of it seemed juicy enough to mention. Nevertheless, she didn't hear it from Temper and wouldn't bring it up. Tyger was getting tired of playing the role of the bigger person, but for Temper's self-pitying ass, she'd play nice and play it again. "And I don't know whose daddy you're confusing with mine. My dad was a gentleman and a scholar on his way to excellence in mathematics," she joked, changing the vibe in the room. "It's such a tragedy that he died from complications of his obesity. We never saw that heart attack coming," she giggled.

"Yes, that is a tragic story you've told for years, but I have a question. Who is the nigga you spend Christmas with in Arizona who owns all those hogs? You know, the cat who has a nigga in dark glasses bring you shitloads of money every year on your birthday?"

"That's my rich sugar daddy, slut," Tyger said, rolling her eyes.

"Exactly. Pieces of our lives make the puzzle we're creating prettier when we draw our own pictures on them. Like the piece where we tell everyone about our friendship sparking in a foster home as we both grieved our parents' deaths. It was fate that put us together after losing everything we loved." Temper held her arms up and played an imaginary violin to her own words.

"Whatever, joy killer. There's one question about your past I've meant to ask, and once I get my answer, I'm done with it."

"What, bitch?" Temper yelled, annoyed.

"Why did they name you Temper? What's the story behind it? I'm sure they didn't look at you at birth and know you'd be a temper-having ho at first sight." She laughed.

"Fuck you. There is more than one definition for the word, smart ass. My mama named me Temper so I'd never forget that the heat life throws at me may soften me, but it will only make me tougher. Now are we done with the past?"

Tyger faked sniffles. "Girl, that shit was deep."

"Fuck you."

"No, I'm serious. Your mama gave you a Band-Aid to use for life, but your dumb ass is too stupid to use it. Go ahead and roll that blunt you're itching to smoke. I'm done with the past. Let's smoke and then go shopping. It's freakum dress time. We're celebrating tonight."

"It's always freakum dress time, and we're always celebrating. Don't make the shit sound extra special, Doctor."

"Bitch, I'm about to be a doctor, and I did it two years earlier than in my plans. Bitch!" She screamed and Temper screamed with her. You would have thought they were already at the club as they shook their asses all over the living room.

***

The girls turned into full-fledged women together, living and working with each other for the next eleven years. As they did most weekends, one night they made it to Los Angeles with ten minutes to spare before the club opened at 10:00 p.m. They were ready to party the night away unless somebody tore off their dresses before they made it to the dance floor. Aging had been good to them both. Temper's once-skinny legs were now full of lean meat that curved upward at her thighs and hips to accent her round butt. Her Asian heritage finally took precedence over her looks, thanks to the change of environment, food, and lifestyle, but there were no signs of it when it came to the "W" that formed her butt, nor the golden-brown glow under her fawnskin.

As a teenager, Temper had permed her hair to give herself a nappy look but gave it up when she moved into the court-ordered group home. She had her hair cut down to a shoulder-length bob, and every time it grew, she cut off more of the remaining chemical in it. She let it grow out to her elbows and wore it down, always bone straight. She aged like wine and cheese as she got better with time. She retired the khakis, T-shirts, and blue high-top Chuck Taylors for heels, pumps, and wedges that complemented her professional attire. Her makeup was subtle yet enticing enough to add mystery to her look. She used breath mints to make her kissable because she had paper-thin lips. She invested in body splashes and added a new smell weekly, staying far away from tradi- tional perfumes because of allergies. On a beauty scale with number one representing ugly and ten breathtaking, you'd list Temper a twelve.

However, none of this took away from the ten Tyger was with or without makeup when they were together. Her skin color forced anyone who came in sight of it to reconsider eating black jellybeans. It was too dark and smooth not to have a sweet taste, and the cocoa butter, baby powder, and Blue Magic Hair Food that fragranced her body from head to toe tempted you until you wanted to take a lick. Tyger had never been skinny, but the 203 pounds she carried were still an unexpected addition to her five-foot six-inch frame. This bitch took the word "fat" and upgraded the definition. You would think she'd have a roll or two to hide and tuck in a girdle. However, there were no bumps, dents, dips, or rolls on the dough she was serving. Her bread box was baked firm yet soft like cake, and her limbs were cut in smooth, thick slices. The black strapless dress she was wearing looked airbrushed on, and with her size, no one could say she looked sloppy in it.

If Tyger had any problems at the club the girls fancied once a month, it would be from hating females or overly horny males confusing her with a stripper. Those big watermelon double-D breasts were millimeters away from busting through the one-size-smaller support bra she wore, and there was no way she'd be dancing or even walking quickly with the dump truck she was toting on her backside. If she sneezed too hard, it would unload, and there would be ass to see for plenty of moons.

In the time it took them to find a parking spot, check themselves in the mirrors behind the visors, and pose for a few camera phone pics, the club was packed from wall to wall. It was fan night, and all you could see in the flashing lights were the Lakers' purple and gold and the Dodgers' blue and white dominating the room. The black that Temper and Tyger wore, however, dominated everyone's attention.

"Damn, bitch, you didn't check to see what they had going on in here tonight?" Temper hissed, feeling awkward and overdressed.

"Yeah, I did, and if I had told your ex-gangster, want-to-be ass that it was 'I love LA' night, you would have said you didn't want to come, or you would have walked in here looking like all the rest of these tailgating bitches. Look around, ho, we're standing out in the crowd. Watch me work this muthafucking floor."

Temper leaned back on the bar and rested her elbows. She had her eyes locked on Tyger as she spoke to the bartender over her shoulder. "I'll have a tequila sunrise, please."

A model beating down the catwalk didn't have shit on the prance Tyger was pumping out. It was like watching African cats in the mating season how every man she passed looked at her from front to back as they slowly took a handful of their dicks. It didn't matter what race they were. If they had a dick, she excited it.

"Do that shit, Tyger," Temper whispered, cheering her on.

Each step Tyger took caused the ass cheek on the opposite side to jump firmly, yet both cheeks looked equally soft. Her breasts shook, identical to Jell-O placed on a washing machine on the spin cycle, as she walked over to the DJ. Similar to a mute porno star, she beckoned him with her index finger. As if he were in the last leg of a two-man race, he threw the headphones off and rushed to her. There was no telling what Tyger could have been whispering in his ear as his eyebrow rose and he licked his lip, but Temper knew the flirting and longing they had been doing for each other for months was about to come to a fuck-filled end.

"Here you go, sexy. Your first drink is on him," the bartender shouted over the blaring music as he pointed toward the end of the bar. "By the way he keeps staring at you, he'll pay for your friend's first one too."

The lights were too dim in that portion of the club to see his face. Though the embroidered jersey made him look muscular, she prayed he wasn't fat. She raised her glass in his direction, and a Hennessy glass raised by an iced-out hand responded.

"Where's my drink?" Tyger asked, swooping in on Temper's glass for a sip.

"I hate when you do that, and it was a gift."

"Then you should have told him to buy me one too. Who's the trick?"

"Why does he have to be all that?" Temper snapped and frowned. She looked as though she had tasted shit at hearing Tyger's words.

"Um, because he is. He spent money on a chick he doesn't know. That's called tricking!"

"Can't be, because it's not tricking if you got it!"

"Bitch, please, don't let them song lyrics fuck your head up. There are rich tricks and poor tricks. They both are one and the same. They're tricks. Where is he. What does he look like?"

Temper shook her head. "I don't know. He's sitting at the end of the bar toward the bathroom."

"You can't see shit that way from here," Tyger moaned after feeling defeated from attempting to look.

"I know."

"Then let's go thank him so I can ask for one too."

She snatched Temper by her free wrist and made her way in that direction. At first, Temper showed restraint, but with the room's eyes on them, she threw on a smile and went along with it. Tyger pulled her in front of her when they made it to the end.

"Hey," Temper said to the back of the wide shirt. "I just want to come and say thanks for the drink."

Romantic music began playing, and everything slowed down as he turned in his chair to face her. The mood set itself, and her pulse sped up as she stood face-to-face with her childhood crush. She didn't know if she should run, but once his green eyes met Temper's, she was immobilized and thought she'd turn to stone.

"It's all good, baby girl. You're killing that dress. I had to tip you."

"Tip me?" she giggled.

"Yeah, it's a tip for not conforming to the rules of the night," he said, pointing at his baseball jersey, "and staying true to you. I'm Julio."

He reached out for her hand, and she still couldn't move. Julio Torres was the sexiest Mexican to beat down her grandmother's block, and everybody loved him. Unlike the majority, he wasn't in a gang, but every gang around respected him. He was always hauling wood with his father. They were busy in construction, but he still took the time to stop and speak to whatever familiar face he passed. Back then, Julio's green eyes weren't the only thing that drove the girls in the neighborhood crazy. He had long hair that he kept in a ponytail, yet that didn't stop the good girls, gangster bitches, or hood rats from begging to twist him. None of them wanted the hassle that would come from braiding all that hair. They all were in it to sit him in between their thighs to put their throbbing pussies on his back. It wasn't compensation for the dick. It was looked at as one step closer to getting it, but no one ever was lucky enough to do it. Unlike the other girls in the neighborhood, Temper never voiced to anyone that he was in her line of sight. There was too much competition, which made her lose interest. Seeing him now, with his hair cut low, fifty pounds of added muscle, and his money longer by the look of his dress and jewelry, a different type of crush was forming—the kind of crush that would leave her in need of a change of panties soon.

"I don't know what's wrong with her, but my name is Tyger, and my friend who can no longer talk is—"

"Journee, Journee West," Temper blurted out before Tyger could finish. She raised her hand. It was the dumbest name anyone could produce in a second. Thanks to the decal on the museum's wall she passed a hundred times a day marking the western hemisphere exhibit, JOURNEY WEST stuck in her head. She was sure if she had said her name, he'd rack his brain to the only Asian Temper he knew—her. There weren't too many people named Temper and even fewer who looked Asian and black. There was no way he'd see it as a coincidence.

Tyger looked at her, surprised by the lie, but didn't say a word. "I'm feeling a little jealous about you buying my girl a drink and not offering me one. What's up with that?" Tyger flirted.

"Oh, that's called preference. You're beautiful, bad, and sexy as fuck. Excuse my language but not my preference. If Journee wants me to buy you a drink, I will, but I'd only be doing it for her. What do you say, Journee?"

"I say she needs to find her own man to buy that drink," she jokingly flirted back. "Is anyone sitting here?"

"Yes. You are," he said, moving his leg to give her space to sit.

"Damn, Journee, it's like that?" Tyger asked with her hands up, and Temper gave her a nod.

The DJ was seconds away from walking up. He grabbed Tyger's hand and walked off. Temper looked at the DJ booth, and there was a sign that said he'd be back in thirty minutes. She'd bet he'd spend that thirty minutes in the restroom or behind the tint of his back-seat windows.

"You're beautiful, baby. I'm sure you may take this like I'm trying to spit game, but it seems like I know you or have seen you in a passing moment." Not knowing what to say, Temper let out a short, nervous laugh. "I'm serious. Call me lame, but I never forget a face, especially one that beautiful." He softly turned her face until they made eye contact, then asked, "Will you walk away if I said I think I dreamed of you?"

"Whoa," she sang as she moved her face, attempting to get out of his hand's grip. "Yeah, that's a lot of game you're spitting. I wouldn't walk away. I'd run."

"See, I knew you'd take it wrong," he pouted as he let her face go. "But I'm serious. If you weren't in my dreams, then I'm sure I know you from a past life. Where are you from?"

"Las Vegas." She didn't have to think of a lie. Her first day back in Los Angeles she'd programmed the answer to shoot out of her mouth when asked. Her new appearance was the opposite of how she carried herself as a teenager, but that wouldn't stop her from being prepared for the worst.

"Nah, I've only been to Vegas once and lost everything but my socks on the crap tables. You should have seen me trying to cover my dick and ass on my way to the car. For the first time, I realized I have little hands for a man." His joke caught Temper off guard, and she broke out in laughter. "See, I was hoping I could make you laugh. It makes it easier to keep that pretty smile on your face."

"You're good."

"I'm okay, but I think it's easier to shoot these words out of my mouth after meeting the girl of my dreams. Now I just have to spend the next few years getting you to fall in love with me and take this last name I got. I would give you more, but you've already stolen my heart."

"Julio, you need to put that drink down. It's got you laying it on heavy, buddy."

"Yeah, I think you're right. That last shit I said scared even me. How about we go outside on the patio and get a little fresh air?"

"I'd like that."

Julio reached out for Temper's hand, and she placed her hand in his. It felt nice, it felt right, and it felt meant to be for more than just that night. *Fairy tales do come true,* she thought as he led her through the doorway. When they sat at a table on the crowded patio, it seemed like they were the only people outside. In a sense they were, because their vision wouldn't allow them to see anyone else.

"No, lick it again!" Tyger said as she pushed the DJ's head back down into the clammy skin of her inner thighs. She had meant to shave the night before but had run out of razors. She didn't like rocking a bush in her panties, and when her lover of the night saw it, she said, "That's a throwback joint. Eat it like your daddy, granddaddy, and uncles used to. You ain't a real man if you ain't rested your forehead in the carpeted covering of a good pussy."

"I ain't like these young niggas out here, baby. I don't mind an Afro."

"Good. More licking and less talking. Let your spit make my Afro's soul glow."

"You do know you are crazy as fuck, right?" he chuckled.

"Certified lunatic. Now lick!"

He finished the task of pulling her panties off and then sucked on her hood as his tongue tickled her clit.

"Yes, Mr. DJ." She began grinding her Afro against his face for added pleasure. Plus, it itched. Then she did what she did best. She began mind fucking herself to her climax. She sang every song she could think of, pretending she was face fucking the DJs from the videos of each one. Her legs began to quiver as warning of the explosion that would follow, and she screamed out, "'Cause that's my DJ!" as Lil Wayne's and Mannie Fresh's voices played in her head. Trying to catch her breath wasn't an option as he went again to see if he could cause more.

Three explosions in, he was ready to feel the effect he had on her through his condom. "One more. Do it one more time, and then you can bend me over and fuck me however you want to, Mr. DJ."

"I'm going to do that anyway," he announced, unfastening his belt and pants. "But I'll lick it a little longer since I'm your DJ now." He chuckled as his dick fell out of his drawers like a thick metal detector pole hovering over sands. Once Tyger saw that she reconsidered.

"Nah, DJ. 'You can get this started.'" She sang out the nineties hit, never taking her eyes off him.

He bent her over the third row, lifted her ass in the air while he spread her cheeks, and licked it a little more before digging for treasure. He was three strokes in as her head rotated left, and she got a look at Temper sitting on the guy's lap looking like she found love. The dude she was with was closer to Tyger's taste in men rather than the beanpoles Temper chose. She didn't know what game Temper was playing by lying about her name, but she didn't like it.

"Is that all you got? I want you to fuck me!" Tyger yelled, sounding more pissed than freaky. "Fuck me, DJ!"

"Damn, girl, you got me about to nut talking like that. Hold on for a second." He pulled out and squeezed his meat. To take his mind off the sensation, he rolled the condom band higher up his shaft.

Tyger looked back. "Are you for real? You've been talking all this shit about taming me, and now you back here trying not to nut? Give me that dick."

She grabbed him closer to her and snatched the condom off as she watched Temper and Julio walk hand in hand back inside the club. Like she was thirsty, she took him deep into her throat and bobbed and drooled as fast as she could until she felt the throbbing down her throat. She took him out of her mouth, spit on his meat, and jacked him off until his nut flew past her to the seat.

"We the best!" he screamed as the remaining drops fell.

"No, boo, the rappers on the tracks are. In this situation, that would be me. When you can hang, we can try this again. Watch out. I got to go," Tyger demanded, climbing over the seat to catch Temper before she left. By the time she got herself together and walked back to the club, it was already too late. Temper was gone, and her phone was going straight to voicemail.

"If he hurts her, I'll kill him," Tyger spat and then picked at her tongue to get the stray pubic hairs off.

Chapter Nine

The girls had had a few small arguments here and there in the more than ten years they'd been friends, but none outweighed this.

"I'm going to tell him the truth soon, on my time, and when I'm ready to. You have one job to do, and that's to be my friend and don't call me by my real name until I've told him. Why is that so fucking hard for you?" Temper snapped.

"That's a dumbass question, even coming from you. Bitch, you're taking this shit with him to the next level, and you're lying every step it takes to get there. That shit is dangerous." Tyger damn near spit on Temper as she was getting her words out.

"It's a fucking name I'm hiding and my past ghetto life. You don't even tell people about your past, but you hold me to a different standard."

"I'm not shacking up with nobody I'm hiding my past from. And his ass is a part of that past. That's why I'm holding your ass to a different standard. How do you move in with a nigga you won't even tell your real name? He can't even be listed as your emergency contact if things did go sour. He'll be trying to get help for a ho named Journee West when Temper Chey is the one in need," Tyger screamed as she slammed down the box she was carrying for Temper. "If I had known you were still keeping secrets from him, I wouldn't have broken my nail trying to help you move. Are you dumb?"

"You tell me, Dr. Washington. Am I?"

"Hell yeah. Look in the fucking dictionary, and bam, there yo' stupid ass is with that dumbass smile you get whenever he's around. Wake up, bitch. This shit between y'all has gotten real."

"When will you ever be happy for me?" Temper questioned as she dropped the box she was carrying next to the others. "I can't think of one time you were truly happy for me without it benefiting you, or you had an event of your own to celebrate too. I finally fell in love, and I took the fucking slow route. We've been dating for almost two fucking years."

"Yeah, and you've been lying for two fucking years, too. Where are you from, Journee? What's your real name? Fuck that. Do you have any kids?"

Temper cocked back and slapped Tyger so hard that one of her eyelash strips flew off. She told Tyger about the baby she abandoned when she was drunk, and Tyger, being insensitive, threw it back in her face. It was on.

"Bitch, you hit me for telling the truth?" Tyger yelled, her words muffled as she gripped Temper's hair and gave her three quick, powerful punches to her face. "You've been tripping since you met this nigga. You left me at the fucking club that night," she said as she sent her fist to Temper's mouth. "You broke the 'no men in the house' rule," she said as she gave her one to the eye, but Temper couldn't take another hit. She was overpowered and outweighed. Not knowing what to do next, she bit the fist that kept hitting her and didn't let go as Tyger screamed, "You even broke the birthday pact." She slung Temper from her bedroom to the hallway.

"If I broke the pact, that means he's the one, stupid bitch. You are so fucking smart that your smart ass is dumb. I'm not trying to be besties rooming with you all my life. I want to be best friends with my husband, and I know Julio is him," she made out through sniffles.

"Then I'm glad you met your husband, because as of today, I'm done being your best friend. Get your shit and be out of my house in an hour. Don't say shit to me at work, either. As of today, your ass is dead to me, bitch."

"You say that shit like there was a time when you saw me as alive. It's always been about you and your smart-ass plans. Congratulations, crazy-ass Washington, you made it. You're the first gutter rat slut to become a doctor. I'm sure your mafioso-ass daddy is proud. I'll be out of this bitch in thirty minutes."

"Say that shit while you're packing, ho. You got fifteen minutes now." Tyger stormed by her, being sure to bump Temper as hard as she could into the wall as she made her way out the front door.

Work didn't feel the same without the girls' friendship to brighten the day. For the past three weeks, everyone engaged in their beef because everyone could feel it. It was hard for them to take sides since the girls made sure they didn't say a word to or about each other, and they never discussed what happened. The fact that they used mediators to communicate gave proof that they were feuding. With the girls being everyone's favorites, the joy in the museum was almost extinct.

Besides the hate brewing between the girls, it seemed like a typical Friday. Temper was taking different grammar school students on tours as Tyger got the week's numbers together to email to her boss.

"Does anyone know what these sharp points set in wooden handles are?" Temper asked the group of teenagers who looked like zombies as they dragged their feet, bored by the tour.

"Yeah, an artifact," a voice shouted from the back of the crowd, and the kids roared in laughter.

"Great guess. Does anyone else want a go at it? No? Okay. Well, you are looking at one of the first tattooing machines invented."

"Like tats? That's a tattoo gun?" one of the boys asked, and the kids seemed to wake up, sparking mini conversations among each other.

"Yes. Archaeologists traced tattooing back five thousand years, and historians believe it may go back further. It was discovered that in ancient times, gypsy women would take seven or more needles, tie them together, and prick the skin in a different pattern based on wants or needs. Once they had the design poked into the skin, they used the black of burnt and smoked wood or oil mixed with a woman's breast milk, and then they'd rub it onto the skin."

"Ugh!" the kids exclaimed in unison, and Tyger almost joined them. She had been walking the halls as she heard Temper's voice and decided to take a listen.

It had been weeks since she'd tuned into one of Temper's tours, which was sad because she used to enjoy them. She'd never tell Temper, but she was right about her being selfish and never truly showing happiness for her friend when they were friends. When she sat in her apartment alone, without her roommate, she reflected on their argument and tried to rack her brain to make Temper's words lies, yet she couldn't. She had mastered making everything about her. Tyger was the one with the doctorate in anthropology, but she rarely got to enjoy history and relics anymore in her new position. To hear Temper make history understandable and fun to a group of inner-city youth gave Tyger the same thirst-quenching sensation that a glass of ice water would give a traveler lost in the Sahara Desert.

"Wait, did I hear you all correctly? You're saying that if tattoo ink were still made the old-fashioned way, all of you would pass them up?" The crowd murmured and shot off different answers, but the consensus was yes. "Would you brand your skin or poke holes in it for anything else?" Temper asked, moving them over to the next portion, which gave the history of branding.

Paula, the museum director, was back from her meeting early and caught Tyger eavesdropping in the hall. She walked up behind her and didn't say a word as she joined the peekaboo tour.

"Temper really knows her stuff and how to get those bad-ass kids interested, huh?" Paula said, nudging Tyger.

"Of course, that's why she was hired," Tyger admitted and then turned her focus back to the lesson in progress.

"There are fraternities that make you brand your skin. I'm going to be a Q-Dog. If they are still branding their members, I'm getting branded," a male's voice yelled from the crowd.

"That's one of the most popular forms of social branding there is, sad to say, but that's definitely a great answer." Temper searched the crowd for the future proud Q-Dog, and her heart skipped a beat when she found him. The boy was a replica of the image her mind created of her son at that age.

Though she secretly tried hard over the years not to think about the baby she'd abandoned, the task was too big, and she failed every time. Yearly, on the day she'd given birth, Temper would lie in her bed and imagine what he'd look like with the year of growth. In a few years, she envisioned, he'd look like the young man she couldn't break eye contact with. He was the perfect combination of her and her most hated lover—light skin, dark hair with a slight curl, and smarter than what they both had been.

For a moment she debated asking the boy his name. Sadly, reality kicked in, and she remembered his name would be meaningless seeing that she never knew what Lena named her son. Shaking away the thought and the heavy feeling building in her chest, she asked the group, "Can you think of any other reason people use branding or penetration of the skin?"

"Cows. They brand cows' butts," a girl yelled out, and the room went up in laughter.

"Yes, that's one of the first usages of branding. It was called *brandr,* which derives from the ancient Norse word meaning 'fire' or 'burning sword.' Anyone else?"

"You and a close friend can poke the skin until it bleeds and rub the blood together so that you can be sisters for life," a voice on the opposite side of the room said, but there was no one in sight as the kids voiced their disgust at the example.

In the hall, a man approached Paula and Tyger. "Excuse me, Paula," Julio said, reading her name badge. "Is Journee here?"

"Journee? Who's that? Is she one of this week's volunteers?" Paula, confused, asked Tyger, who thought she had seen a ghost. Julio frowned at her, which meant he knew of the battle between the girls, but she wouldn't let her anger blow Temper's cover.

"I know who he's looking for. I'll handle it," Tyger volunteered.

"No, I'm sure you're doing rounds, and I'm just getting back. I'll take him to my office and look her up. Do you know what area of the museum she's working in?"

"No, not quite, but I do know that she's the docent."

"Are you talking about Temper?"

At the sound of her real name exposed, Tyger ran into the room where Temper was and tried to get her attention. Temper's attention belonged to the rear of the room. There was a lady, heavily drugged, or so it seemed, big and very dirty approaching from the back of the exhibit. She had a smile on her face, but all her teeth were missing except for three. Two teeth lingered at the top of her mouth next to each other and one at the bottom. She looked like a horribly drawn cartoon caricature on crack.

"Remember what you said to me, Temper? We're blood sisters for life, and no nigga would get in between us. You said if we poked our fingers in the bathroom, we'd be real sisters for life, and I did it. Do you remember that? So why did you stop treating me like your sister, Tee?"

Temper didn't say a word. She just stood there motionless.

Tyger ran out of the room and yelled, "Get security. I think Temper is in danger."

Paula ran down the hall, and a confused Julio followed Tyger. He had just shown Paula pictures of him and Journee on his cell phone, and she told him that her name was Temper. If Journee was her middle name, that meant Tyger was saying his soon-to-be fiancée was in trouble. He tucked the engagement ring he'd been holding deep into his pocket, ready for whatever would happen next.

"Why aren't you answering me? Come on, Tee. I know you have a smart-ass line to shoot back at me."

As Kei'Lani took a step closer, tears made their way down Temper's face.

One of the kids yelled, "Run. She has a knife!"

The kids scattered as Kei'Lani rushed forward, but Temper couldn't move. The feel of warm urine running down her leg was the only indication that she was still alive, but she longed to be dead.

"Temper," Tyger yelled, but she didn't blink.

With her arm raised and Kei'Lani's hand tightly gripping the knife, Temper closed her eyes and wished that death would come quickly. However, it never came at all. She didn't visually know what happened next, but she could feel herself moving backward. Five seconds later, Kei'Lani screamed out in horror. Opening her eyes, Temper saw Julio standing over her former best friend with a bloody blade in his hand, security running their way with Paula behind them, and Tyger hugging and holding her. She gripped Tyger and cried. Of course, Tyger cried too.

"I'm sorry, Temper. He made me do it," Kei'Lani whimpered as life took the long way to leave her. "He wants to fuck your life up for what you did to him. He's crazy, and I haven't loved him in years. I swear, I ain't loved him in years."

"Kei-Kei?" Julio asked as he took a closer look at his victim. Then he shot his eyes up to Temper. He dropped the knife and gripped her face. He pushed her hair back, used his hand to make a makeshift ponytail, and then visualized her eyes with black makeup rings around them. He could have thrown up when he recognized her. Instead, he began walking away.

"You're the girl who put my best friend in jail for life over the baby. Oh, my God."

Some people get saved by the bell. For others, it takes walking through the church's doors, but Temper was saved as the security guards tackled Julio to the floor. They carried him out of the room and away from the attacker turned victim without asking any questions.

Tyger could see that Temper was too devastated to tell security or Paula what happened, so she squeezed Temper before she let her go and said, "I can't let them arrest him for this. Promise you won't stand here and watch this junkie die."

Temper didn't promise, nor did she disagree. Her eyes were locked on her childhood friend bleeding on the floor. There wasn't any way for her to tell if the wound was fatal, and she wasn't sure that she wanted her to die.

"You're so beautiful. You were always beautiful," Kei'Lani moaned through the pain while gripping her side.

Maybe it was how she rocked on the floor that allowed the lighting to hit her face just right, causing Temper to see her as her best friend. She snatched off her two-button sweater and applied pressure to the wound.

"Hush, you're going to be all right. Look at me. You're going to make it through this, Kei'Lani."

Kei'Lani smiled. "No, I won't. I have to be dying. The Temper I know would have finished me off for trying to catch her slipping."

She dropped the sweater and stepped back to give the approaching paramedics space. "I'm not that girl anymore."

"Yes, you are. You always will be."

Once the paramedics got her on the stretcher and into the ambulance, they asked Temper if she was riding, and she nodded.

"You can't go with her, Temper. I know you feel bad about what happened, but she tried to stab you, and Julio is being arrested for protecting you. You don't even know this lady," Tyger barked.

"Yes, I do. She was my best friend."

Temper locked eyes with Tyger until they closed the doors to drive off. An apology didn't need to be said. They both knew that Temper's response to her near-death encounter at the hands of a woman she once called a friend made their fight nonexistent.

It took four hours to get things situated enough at the museum for Tyger to leave. Between the schools, parents, and the media, it was a headache that only time could heal. Paula was furious, and no matter what Tyger said to prove Temper's innocence, it wasn't enough.

"Wait, Temper is Journee, the attempted killer is her childhood best friend, and the man who stabbed her attacker is the man she's been with for over a year and a half who doesn't know her real name? She's fired," Paula yelled.

"She didn't lie to him about anything else, and she did it to prevent him from linking her to her past. I told you when you hired her, her teenage years read parallel to a horror story."

"They grew up not too far from the area. Temper chose to lie to him, and you defend that as right?" Paula snarled.

"Of course I don't, and with our personal life on the table, her lying to him for two damn years is the same reason we had our falling out. She's wrong for lying, I agree, but her lies aren't what caused this problem."

"You're right. Her shady past did. How did you meet her again? For being of Asian descent, I'm sure she has disappointed grandparents waiting to disown her."

"This isn't a race thing, Paula. Don't turn it into one."

"Don't try to take it personally, because your best friend made us the front-page news tomorrow and not in a good light. You tell me not to make it about race, but open your eyes and read the headlines. A homeless black woman tries to stab her half-Asian childhood friend in the presence of inner-city youth during a history lesson on tattoos, an exhibit approved by Tyger Washington, the museum's black curator and friend of the would-be victim. An Hispanic man from both ladies' past saves the day by stabbing the perpetrator with her own knife. And do you know what happens next? They go check out the neighborhood, which I bet is gang infested, and do a little digging in Temper's past to find a sealed juvenile record as I did."

"And all of this fucked-up shit happened under the supervision of the director—a white woman and Harvard graduate," Tyger added.

"Exactly!"

"Oh, wait, I forgot to mention an undercover pill-popping animal who can only function on enough psychotic uppers to bring back the dead. Right, let's not forget to air your dirty laundry too."

"I told you my habit is under control. That little incident where you found me in my car out of it was a one-time thing. I accidentally took too many, and my issues will never make it to the newspaper because I don't advertise it like your people do."

"Like my people do? Are you talking about black people? You know what, don't answer that. I'm going to leave before you say the wrong thing, and please, Ms. Undercover Junkie Museum Director who was born white and holds a master's degree from Harvard, please remember that the only full-blooded black woman on staff is the only one who holds two doctorates in two different subjects. One of them is an honorary PhD, like you love to point out, but where is yours? And those two degrees I hold didn't make me one percent whiter, yet they made me a hundred percent more qualified than you to run this museum. All of this shit is part of my plan. You're just too white to see it."

"Again, this isn't about you or me. Next time there is anything out of her, she's fired!"

Paula didn't care what Tyger had to say. It was her reputation on the line. She felt the only way to save herself and satisfy everyone affected by the event was to let Temper go at once. The kids' statements to the police named Temper as the innocent victim, so she'd wait until Temper's next late clock-in or late return from lunch, but Temper was as good as gone.

"You won't have another problem out of her," Tyger assured her. "I'll see you bright and early tomorrow. It's probably best that we get here before the media does."

Tyger didn't know Temper's friend's name, but she did know her injury and was sure she'd be sent to the jail ward. She went into the gift shop and grabbed impressive and expensive trinkets, but then remembered before she swiped her card that the police wouldn't allow the lady to keep the gifts where she was nor where she was going. Instead of trying to win points with Temper by showing her friend love, she'd save the spoiling for Temper directly.

The county sheriff stationed on the floor told her which room she was in. Seeing that the victim was there with the accused and didn't want to press charges, they were waiting to hear back from the museum to find out if they would be pressing charges due to their no-weapons policy.

"I'm visiting on behalf of the, um, museum," she stated as she removed her credentials from her wallet and handed them to the sheriff. "We didn't plan on filing any charges once we found out she was coerced into the act. She was a childhood friend of the victim."

"Who told you her life was in danger and she was forced to do it?" he asked, pulling his walkie-talkie off his side.

"That's what the lady screamed after she was stabbed. She said, 'He made me do it. He's crazy.' Either way, we won't be pursuing any charges against her. Can I please see her now?"

"Yes, you can see her, but don't leave until my sergeant or a detective comes to talk to you. That's the first time I've seen a pass given on a weapon," he added and shook his head in disappointment. "She's the third door on the left."

Tyger wasn't sure if her visit would be welcomed by Temper or if she wanted privacy with the lady because of their fight. They agreed years ago never to pry about anything that happened before them, and Temper's attacker fell into that category. All she knew about Temper's past was that she had given birth to a baby who got the father his third strike, and she only knew that much from Isabel after telling her about the near fight at the courthouse that sparked their friendship. Tyger didn't intend to be nosy. However, she could hear the girl's conversation before she made it to the room. Knowing Temper, Tyger was sure that she would change the subject when she entered if it was about her past. Tyger never cared about Temper's past until today. She lingered out of sight near the door and tuned in.

"How in the hell did you pull Julio's fine, heavy-pockets-having ass? He ain't never fucked with anyone from the hood. Hell, a year or two after you left, rumors started spreading that he was gay. He stopped fucking with everybody, but he gave me a ride back to the hood when I got out of the hospital in East L.A. That *ese* can talk." She laughed, and Temper joined in.

"Yeah, he has a lot to say about everything. Honestly, I ran into him at a club with my best friend, or should I say sister, after all the shit we've been through, including this crap with you."

"Crap, what the fuck is that? You said it right. It's called shit, and who are you talking about? That fat bitch from the museum?"

"She isn't fat."

Tyger was glad she heard Temper correct her because she was ready to walk in and do the correcting herself. "She just took that thick shit and stretched the elastic on it to the max, but that's my girl, and she's been there for me through a lot. Anyways, I knew who he was as soon as he got under the lights, and he didn't have a clue who I was for the last two years. He was going to propose to me soon. I just knew it. You definitely came and changed all of that today."

"No, you're not going to blame two years of lying on me. You're the one who decided to lie about not being black."

"I didn't lie about being black. I lied about coming from the hood because I'm not hood anymore."

"Yes, the fuck you are. Get hungry, lose your job, or let any other bitch beside me run up on you with a knife, and I bet you all the money I'm sure you got that you won't be able to hide the hood in you. I'm just surprised you'd go after him knowing how close he was to Khasema. You say you're not hood anymore, but I see you're still cutthroat. Maybe you're worse than I remember you being. How long are you going to gut punch Khasema for nutting in that thing and then saying fuck you?"

"I don't know anybody by that name, so why would I have remembered?" Temper was going to change the subject, and Kei'Lani knew it, but after all these years, she was done letting Temper run the show and lurking in her shadow.

"You're still lying, I see. Khasema, aka K-Mack, is your son's father who's doing life thanks to you, and he's up for a parole hearing next year after serving sixteen years—the same fuck nigga who had you flip bad on our friendship."

"I don't want to talk about this. Why were you in the hospital when Julio gave you the lift, anyway?"

Kei'Lani adjusted her position in her bed the best she could with one hand and one foot cuffed to it. She wanted to keep talking about Khasema, yet she didn't want to make Temper mad to the point of deciding to press charges to be rid of her for good. Kei'Lani still had a job to do, and if it were only her life on the line, she'd take the risk, but it wasn't.

"I had a seizure. I have a fucked-up seizure condition from a brain injury that you caused. Remember when you cracked me over my head for fucking the same nigga you fucked? As if you didn't fuck every nigga I fucked. You've fucked me up for life, as I'm sure you were trying to do. I ain't been right since. I can't keep a job, am in and out of the hospital, and can't drink or smoke. That will put me in the hospital. And there are days I wake up and don't know who or where I am. You taught me a lesson in friendship that day that I'll never forget, and that's to trust no bitch. What's fucked up is I can't remember how to tie my shoes day to day, but I ain't never forgot you or stopped loving my blood sister who did this to me," she said, holding her finger in the air.

"If you loved your blood sister so much, why did you hide fucking him, knowing how crazy I was back then? You know what? That doesn't even matter anymore. What does matter is how we got here in the first damn place. Why did you try to stab me? Because of the golf club shit? You were telling me the reason at the museum. I was too zoned out to hear it. Wait, how in the hell did you know where to find me?"

For the first time since they had been together, Kei'Lani didn't have shit to say, and Tyger hoped she did. She waited to see if she'd answer Temper's question by telling her someone had sent her to do it, but she didn't, and when the air got too thin to breathe, Tyger stepped in.

"Knock, knock. I hope I'm not intruding, but I had to come to check on you, Temper. Are you okay?"

"Yes, I'm good. Just tying up loose ends with my old friend Kei'Lani."

"Say it for me. Say it just one time," Kei-Lani begged.

"Say what?" Temper snapped.

"Call me Kei-Kei. I want to hear it."

"Never again."

"Oh, you must've told thickums lies about your past too, huh? What did she tell you about the only best friend she had until she was seventeen?"

"Honestly, Kei-Kei, I had never heard of you before to-day. We agreed on anything that happened before us didn't matter. Maybe I should leave and give y'all a moment of privacy," Tyger offered, and to her surprise, both ladies rejected it.

"Have a seat, Washington. This shit only gets uglier from here. It's time for you to know everything about your sister," Temper said as she made herself a spot on the bed next to Kei'Lani.

"You don't have to—"

"Hush, child, she's going to tell the truth. I need to hear this one, and whatever gaps she leaves in the story, I'm filling them bitches in. Yo' best friend ain't shit, big booty, and she about to finally say it. Where's the popcorn? Extra butter, please."

Temper shot her middle finger up at Kei'Lani, took a deep breath, and then started with her parents. She worked her way to her uncle, aunt, and grandmother, and Kei'Lani chimed in.

"She didn't show up to none of their funerals either, but you can continue."

Temper heaved as she accepted that everyone she loved was dead, then took Tyger on a detailed ride full of fights, robberies, sex, drugs, and surprisingly, no money.

"Wait, you got passed around a hood day party like a blunt by choice? Who signs up for that shit?" Tyger uttered in disgust.

"Yo' sister," Kei'Lani answered, winded from laughing. "She wanted to show the big homies that she was down for the hood, but really that bitch went down on the hood."

Kei'Lani was tickled, Tyger looked nauseated, and Temper took it all with her chin up. She held her head high as she continued to tell stories of threesomes with Kei-Kei for weed and beer.

"Hold up. If you're going to tell your story, make sure you tell my truth. I wasn't licking her pussy for pocket change and malt liquor. That might have been why Temper did it, but I was born bi. My daddy was one of the biggest . . ." Kei'Lani stopped talking. She realized she'd gotten so relaxed in Temper's tell-all session that she almost relieved her own hand. She switched her words up. "Freaks on the east side. He had cases of porn that I binge watched like a *Golden Girls* marathon. I did it because I wanted to. She's the hooker," she concluded with a nod at Temper and didn't say another word.

"I'm not trying to be funny or judge you, boo, but I got to know. Are you sure the guy you sent to jail is the baby's father?"

"Yes, I'm sure."

It was the first time Temper felt ashamed of herself. She didn't know how many men she'd slept with in her life, and when asked, she didn't remember when she lost her virginity or to whom. However, she knew without a doubt who she had gotten pregnant by.

"Good," Tyger chimed in, wanting to move past talk of anything that had to do with the baby Temper tossed away. "If you had to guess, how old do you think you were when you lost your virginity?"

"I don't know. Twelve? I think I got dared to lose it at the pool."

"Bitch, stop lying, you had already fucked Spade behind the Laundromat on Halloween before then," Kei'Lani said, breaking her silence to correct her.

"Shit, you're right. Then I don't know, because I was ten then."

"Ten?" Tyger exclaimed, holding back tears and disgust.

"Yeah, I was ten. I got my first taste of dick and couldn't cut it off. There were times when everything felt wrong, and during those times, I would sneak in my granny's liquor and have a shot. The liquor made me hot and dick cooled me off."

"Oh, Temper, baby."

The sadness slipped out of Tyger's mouth, and Temper ignored it. There was more to tell her. Temper went on to tell the truth about the gang tattoo that hid behind the rose on her left breast and confessed that she was never officially put on the Crips hood she represented. Still, after fucking the majority of the men from it, no one made initiation an issue. She told Tyger everything she could remember, but she left out one part.

"Temper won't admit it to you, me, nor God, but that bitch has a real problem. She likes drama, violence, and sex, but I'm sure you already know that, huh? You're sexy as fuck with them big legs and smile. I know she's tickled that kitten," Kei'Lani said, sticking her tongue out and wiggling it from side to side.

"Thank you, I guess, but nah. As a matter of fact," Tyger began, turning to look at Temper, who was fighting back tears, "I told the bitch about a lesbian encounter I had, and she hasn't let me live it down. And I did the shit when I was sixteen."

"You know I be playing with you about that," Temper defended herself.

"Yeah, but why was it so hard for you to say that you had one too?" Tyger questioned.

"Because it made my past real. We said everything was left behind. That was part of it, and so was Kei-Kei."

"Now that right there she ain't lying about. When she found out that I fucked that dog K-Mack, she busted me in the back of my head with a golf club and left me to die in her granny's house. Me and that old woman never got along, but after she found me face down in that carpet, she made it her business to take care of me. Even on the day she died, she had been by the house to check on me and ask if I had heard anything from you. She was sure you'd come back after you got out of jail at eighteen. She said she couldn't die until her Chinaman came home."

That was it. Temper couldn't hold back any longer. The truth needed freedom.

"I got pregnant and was too high all the damn time to care. My baby daddy was a small-time dope boy, and I knew he'd throw me the money for the abortion. I knew it because he had paid for the first two."

"What?" Kei-Kei gasped at the new information.

"They weren't his babies. The first one he paid for was a mistake. There was a Hood Day event where I volunteered to be the homies' piñata, and I let everybody hit. There wasn't a way to find out who the daddy was, and it didn't matter. I was fourteen. Keeping the baby wasn't an option. We both knew who I was pregnant by the second time because it happened at his dope spot. He called himself doing right by his homie when he paid for it, but I wasn't right in the head once it was done. I started having these fucked-up nightmares where I'd be walking across a cemetery, and there would be a zombified baby following and saying fucked-up shit to me. I stopped sleeping, and one night, when I was walking the streets hoping to catch a sale, Khasema stopped me. The funny part about it was that all he said to me was, 'Are you okay?' And I broke down. I told him about the dreams, and he smoked with me until around three in the morning. When he got sleepy, he told me to come home with him. I thought he was trying to fuck, and he surprised me. I started spending the night with him, and he would hold me until it was time to start our day. It was like that every night for three months, and we didn't have sex."

"That bitch is lying," Kei-Kei yelled, cutting her off. She intended to ask Temper who her first two pregnancies were by, except anger entered her thoughts. "I know her baby daddy, and Khasema ain't the 'love on you' type of nigga. Who are you trying to impress? If he was that good to you, why would you get him his third strike?"

"You just answered with your own statement. He wasn't a 'love on you' type of nigga, yet he was for me, and then he found out that I wasn't a 'love on you' type of bitch. I stayed high and drunk twenty-four seven, but I wasn't fucking nobody except for him. It was hard to get him to believe me when he caught me sucking his boy up at his spot. He offered me a quick hundred, and I went for it. Shit wasn't the same for us after that, and then he went to jail."

Temper turned to face Kei'Lani. "I didn't know they'd get him for the baby. The day I had him, he called me talking recklessly, and then he threw you in my face. He told me he was going to have his bitch Kei-Kei beat my ass. That shit hurt. When I got caught in Vegas running away with drugs, I almost died from an untreated STD. That's why Lena's house smelled the way it did when I was in labor. She was right about the infection, but it was worse than she thought. When I told them what happened to the baby, I knew he was going down since I was a minor, and I didn't give a fuck. I put the drugs they found in my bag on him, too. He crossed the line using you to get revenge. I would have killed him if he were free. Why not ensure the bitch got life!"

The room fell silent. Kei-Kei's posture, erect with her arms folded against her breasts, said she wanted to say what was truly on her mind, though she chose not to.

"You don't have the power to sentence anyone to life. If that was his sentence, he was proven guilty in a court of law. You can't hate yourself for the outcome nor wish you could go back in time to fix things," Tyger comforted her, and Temper rejected it.

"I don't hate myself for it, and I'd do it again. I told you all of that to try to explain how I feel inside. It's serious, way more serious than I can explain. I get a high off it, and I thought switching everything up would kill that hunger I have for it, but it hasn't."

"Yes, it has. Look how long we've been friends, and you've been able to hide it. If it were a problem, you wouldn't be able to stop yourself from doing it," Tyger explained as Kei'Lani spoke up.

"She's right, Tee. When I knew you, it was a real problem. It was like you had to be a part of fucked-up shit, and if things were going smooth, you'd mess them up on purpose. The shit that's happening to you now is just karma or bad luck. You aren't looking for it or making it happen this time, but you should have told Julio the truth, not like he couldn't find out anyway. Last I heard, he was a cop."

"A cop?" the other two sang in unison.

"Yeah, he's a cop, or at least I know he was. He had all that cop shit in his car when he gave me a ride. I asked him about it, and he lied, talking about he was going to a costume party and borrowed his boy's shit, but I know a real badge from a fake one."

Tyger looked at Temper, and she shrugged. "He told me he took over his pop's construction business and they had relocated to the valley. He never took me there. I just believed him."

"Um, sounds like you weren't the only person hiding shit in the relationship then," Kei-Kei pointed out, and sadly, that raggedy fact brought Temper a piece of hope. *Maybe we can work things out since we both lied.*

"Let me get this straight. All this time you've been making a bed with a cop around me?" Tyger's voice transformed into a high-pitched tone. "You didn't think to check the nigga out at all?"

"Damn, what are you mad at? Don't tell me you were fucking little sexy too?" Kei-Kei asked like a member of a talk-show audience.

"Of course not. I'd never have sex with anyone my bestie and sister messed with. Hell, they can't even get me to feed them unless she asked me to," Tyger responded in a calmer tone. "I'm just saying it's dangerous to have anybody around you who you don't know anything about. It doesn't matter if he was a cop or a killer. She shouldn't have had him around me until she knew everything about him."

"I didn't know, and you should know I would never purposely bring anyone like that around you. We need to calm down because we don't even know if he's a cop. Kei'Lani's ass doesn't know everything, nor is her mouth a prayer book. Her lying is what got her cracked with the golf club, not jealousy."

"Yeah, I lie but not about this. How do you think Julio is feeling about fucking the bitch who abandoned his godson?"

The timing couldn't have been better. As if cued to walk in, a suited Julio, dressed as if he came from court, with two uniformed cops at his side, flashed a badge at the three women and then said, "We need to bring the three of you down for questioning."

"For what, Julio?" Kei'Lani snapped. "Temper nor the museum is pressing charges against me. It was a misunderstanding."

Julio, with disappointment etched on his face, looked into Temper's eyes. "Is this true? You're not pressing charges on the attack against you today?"

"I'm not." Her words filled Kei'Lani with confidence.

"May I ask why?"

"Because I don't know the truth about anything or any-one around me, that's why, Detective. I'm sorry, what's your last name?"

"It's Detective Torres, Journee West. Or is there an-other name you'd prefer to go by?" When he realized she didn't have a response, he continued, "To answer your question, Kei'Lani, you're all coming in to give any infor-mation you can on Paula Hess. She was found dead in the parking lot of the museum."

Temper and Tyger inhaled in shock. Kei'Lani didn't know who Paula was, but she knew being at the museum with a knife was enough for her to get nervous over it.

"Ay, can one of y'all lend me money for a lawyer? I ain't saying shit without one," Kei'Lani stated. She wasn't a fool to the way things worked, and the other two quickly followed suit.

Chapter Ten

Julio didn't waste time once he got the girls to his precinct. He threw Kei'Lani and Tyger into a holding cell and stormed to his office, making sure Temper was on his heels.

"Why wouldn't you press charges on her, Journee? I mean, Temp . . . Ugh. I can't even say that name." Julio took his palm to his head like it would wake him up from his nightmare. "She tried to kill you," he yelled as he got Temper into the privacy of his office. Unlike the other detectives they passed on their way, Julio didn't have a cubicle. His office sat near the restroom, along the wall in the back. His door was open when they approached, so Temper missed the title painted on the glass. However, the way the others greeted him in his unit confirmed he was ranked up.

"Look at her," Temper yelled, returning his tone. "Life has already been hard enough on her. Why should I add to it? It was a mistake, and she feels bad about it. Maybe you stabbing her caused her to realize it. I don't know, but why would I kick her when she's already down as far as she can go?"

"Because she almost killed you." He shook his head and then said, *"Por favor, dime que no me enamore de un muneco."*

"No, Julio, you didn't fall in love with a dummy, and the fact that you're questioning if you did means you weren't in love with me to begin with."

Julio's jaw dropped at her understanding of his native tongue, and she checked him on that, too.

"Don't act shocked. My dumb ass speaks a lot of languages. It's detecting the pigs around me that I have trouble with."

"You know what? You're right. I wasn't in love with you, because Temper is a dummy and always has been, from your fake gangster bitch days to the dumb decision you're making now. I fell in love with Journee, the intelligent, loving, smart docent from the museum. Temper is hood trash who wouldn't press charges on Kei'Lani," he said, opening his top desk drawer and retrieving the engagement ring. "But Journee, the woman I brought this ring for"—he slammed it on his desk in front of her—"would have, because she'd risk lying to the man she loved about her past to secure their future. You're not that woman."

The hurt in his eyes turned into anger. He waited for a sign of the woman he loved to show. Instead, all he got was a question.

"So now that you know I'm Temper—the hood bitch who had a baby by your childhood friend, the cause of him serving life, and the woman who gave her baby away—you no longer love me?"

"Are you fucking deaf? I've never loved Temper. I would never date anyone who threw her child, my godson, by the wayside. I would never date a woman who dated one of my friends, and if you remember me from back in the day, you know that I've never messed with anyone from that neighborhood, and I wouldn't. They were all hoes, hood rats, and chicken heads from the bottom of the barrel."

She took a deep breath and let it out slowly. She needed a blunt but hadn't smoked one in two years because she'd given it up for him. He smelled the scent on her once and expressed his dislike. That was all it took for her to kick the habit.

"Is that how you see me?"

"Temper, that's the only way I can see you. You aren't Journee."

"Then, Detective, can you please start your interrogation on the death of my boss? I'm ready to get it over with. I have places I need to be," she requested in a tone absent of emotion.

"What? Are you not hearing me? Am I not speaking English? Are you going to press charges on your attacker or not?"

"Not."

Julio rushed over to Temper and almost snatched her out of her chair. He gained his composure as she jumped to her feet. With his finger pointed in her face, less than an inch from touching it, he whispered, "I almost killed her for you because I love you, and this is the repayment? You won't even open an investigation to find out why she did it or who sent her. Damn, I guess I was wrong about you all this time. You are that same little hood-rat bitch who used to blow all my homies in the hood for a sack of weed and a forty. You did a hell of a job pretending for the last two years."

"Are you saying that you knew who I was?"

"Yes and no. I knew your real name wasn't Journee. I tried to pull you up when we first met. I was bored and thinking about you. That's the same moment I had to be honest and admit that I had feelings for you. Fuck, it couldn't be real. Me, fall in love with Miss Perfect? There's no way in hell love would come that easily for me. I ran the name you gave me to make sure I wasn't dating a criminal, and nothing popped up in criminal, traffic, or warrants. I assumed it was a middle name you preferred to go by and left the shit at that. I didn't hunt to try to figure out who you were, which was idiotic of me. Blame my stupidity on my heart. I thought I was in love. No, I didn't have a clue that you were Temper until today. I even convinced myself that you lied because you loved me and that I shouldn't hold your actions as a kid against you. Boy, was I wrong. You're just as dumb as you were back then."

"Wow, listen to you. Big, badass Julio with the badge thinks he's better than me because he made slim to no mistakes in his youth. He had a strong, providing father and a mother who prepared three meals a day for him while instilling morals, traditions, and family values. I didn't have any of that fairy-tale shit. You were my first knight in shining armor, and I lied about who I was the moment I saw it was you who bought my drink. I was a kid back then, Julio. Lost, confused, and fucked up, but I get it. I'm below you, and if I don't press charges, you're done with me. Okay then, I'm not. So I guess I am that little bitch who sucked all your homeboys' dicks to stay high so I wouldn't have to deal with my fucked-up life. You know what, King Julio, aka Mr. Perfect, after kissing, licking, and fucking me for the last two years, you can say you blew your homies too."

Julio cocked his hand back and froze in the stance.

"What would that make you if you slapped me, knowing I'm a ho? A pimp?" Temper egged him on and went so far as to turn her face to give him more coverage to slap.

After seconds of waiting, he began to walk back to his chair behind the desk. "Temper Chey, I'm clearing you as a suspect. Now get the hell out of my office."

"What about my two best friends?"

"They will tell you their situations when they can. One more thing." He stood up and sat on the corner of his desk. "Earlier today, when I found out who you were, I remembered going to the first Hood Day celebration after Khasema got sentenced, and your name was the topic of conversation. I just want to know this—does Kei-Kei know you used to fuck and suck her daddy, too?"

"Fuck you!"

"Me and the rest of the east side already did. Get the fuck out of my office. I need to disinfect the ho from that seat."

"No problem," she said as she removed her keys from her purse. "I'll see you when you get home, Detective. I've been living there for over fifteen days. If you want me to go, bring home an eviction notice with you. I have ho juice to spread throughout it." She rushed out of the office to get in the view of witnesses, not knowing what he'd do next. Julio stood in the doorway, fuming as he watched her leave.

"Send in Tyger Rae Washington next," he said to no one in particular. He waited ten minutes, and then he was informed that Tyger was still waiting for her counsel to arrive, so he called Kei'Lani instead.

"Whatever Temper said to you, Julio, is a goddamn lie. Up until today, I hadn't seen her lying ass in years, and I didn't even know her boss." Kei'Lani gripped her side, praying for a little sympathy since he was the person who'd stabbed her. "I left there in an ambulance. I don't know what happened after that."

"Why were you there?" he asked calmly.

"I heard about the tattoo exhibit and went to see it. You know, I'm tatted up and was like damn, let me go check out the history of this shit. I didn't know she worked in there."

"If that is true, why did you have a knife? There's a sign on the door that's visible and says that it is a felony to possess a weapon in the museum."

"Come on, man, you know how rough those streets are and where we grew up. I don't leave the house without one. I can't."

"So your story is that you wanted a piece of history and ran into your childhood best friend. Honestly, I remember y'all being closer than that. Why did you try to stab Temper?" His voice cracked as anger overtook him, and he knew he should have recused himself. He was too emotionally attached, and that made him unqualified to perform the legal duties required. There was a conflict of interest, but he couldn't walk away. He was in love with Temper and determined to get to the bottom of it, whether they were in a relationship or not.

"Revenge," she bellowed. "She's the reason I'm like this, the reason I stay in and out of the hospital. She found out I was messing with Khasema after she had the baby, and she beat me over my head with a golf club. I had to be put in a medically induced coma for months because they couldn't get the seizures to stop, and when I saw her, I snapped. I wish it had been a gun in my purse."

For a woman who was stabbed less than twelve hours earlier, Kei'Lani's reflexes were intact as she dodged the items that flew off Julio's desk as he flipped it over and darted her way. He scooped her up by her shirt.

"Cut the fucking lies, Kei'Lani. I heard you say someone sent you to do it. You said 'he' sent you. Who is he?" he yelled as she curled up into a ball to protect herself from the ass beating she was sure would follow.

"I was lying. I didn't want to go to jail. I was scared, just saying shit that I thought sounded good. Please, Julio, don't hit me. Don't hit me for lying."

"I'm not going to hit you for lying because I can't prove it, but what I think happened was you gave a deathbed confession. You thought you were dying and told the truth. I can't prove it yet. However, I'm going to arrest you and let the State of California pick up charges against you for your attempted attack with a deadly weapon on a museum worker."

"You mean for the attack on your future wife, the bitch who ruined my life in so many ways I can't even count, right? The baby mama of your best friend who you stopped writing once you made the force, but you continued to help raise his son? But I thought I was brought in for questioning on her boss. I didn't know that you could handle your own personal affairs with that badge. Aren't you supposed to recuse yourself? I was told that if Julio's sprung ass got involved, he would recuse himself, but it looks like you're all in." Her laugh couldn't be touched by any wicked witch from any side of town or movie. She scooted away from him until her back was parallel to the wall.

"You're not smart enough to know what recusal is. That's confirmation that you were coached into doing this. I also know you moved in with Khasema's mother a few years after she moved to Victorville, and I know you are still in contact with Khasema. Your last visit was two months ago. Be smart, Kei'Lani, and work yourself out a deal on this attempted murder charge I'm about to throw on you. Did Khasema send you to the museum to kill Temper today?" He paced his words as he came to her.

"Temper has done a lot of people wrong and has a lot of enemies, Julio. She thinks she can fuck and fuck over anybody she wants, but she can't, and it's her time to get fucked. You need to be smart and get away from her, or you're going to find yourself like me. That badge won't protect you."

"And how are you, Kei'Lani? Are you being black-mailed?"

She laughed. "Blackmailed by a black male. Is that what you think? No, Julio, I'm dead and have been dead from the moment I made her my friend. I'm sorry, but remember, I tried to warn you."

Julio wasn't sure what she was about to do next, but he flew across the room to stop her. Before he was halfway there, Kei'Lani slammed the back of her head into the wall with all the energy she could muster and instantly hit the floor in a full-blown grand mal seizure.

"I need help in here," he screamed, and immediately his office filled with his colleagues.

Temper had fallen asleep on the couch waiting for Julio to return home to continue their conversation. She packed and cried. Once again, her past forced her to throw away the love and happiness in her life. She hadn't felt this kind of pain since Isabel died. Even then it didn't hurt as much. It wasn't the same feeling as losing a parent or sibling. She'd lost her soul mate because of her foolishness as a child.

"Why can't you see that I was young and dumb then if you're so fucking smart?" she yelled at the framed picture on their dresser of her and Julio. After staring at it for a few minutes, she waved the white flag and curled up with the memory of them on their first trip to the cabins in Big Bear. They never got a chance to play in the human-made snow. There wasn't time. They were making love from the moment they arrived, and neither had a problem with the change in itinerary.

"Hello."

It was 1:30 in the morning, and Julio hadn't come home. Temper was sure he wouldn't show once she informed him that she'd be there waiting. When her phone rang, she only answered the private number because she thought it might have been him.

"Girl, where are you? I just knew you'd be at the house waiting for me." Tyger's voice was shaky, and that alone was enough to scare Temper.

"Putting on my shoes, and I'm on my way."

"Okay, hurry up and bring a wrapper with you. I had to get a bag."

"I already have a pack in the car." She ended the call and grabbed the duffle bag she packed.

When she got into her car, Julio pulled up behind her and blocked her in. He got out and came over to her. "We need to talk."

"Yes, we do, but not tonight. My hood-rat ass has a dick to suck for weed. Can you move your car?"

"It's about Kei'Lani, Temper."

"I don't give a damn who it's about. Move your car, or I'm calling the cops. Oh, wait, you are the cops," she sneered.

"Your best friend said Khasema sent her to kill you," he lied. "And then she rammed her head into the wall to cause a seizure. Last I heard, she wasn't going to make it, and I don't care. That's not why I'm telling you. What I do care about is that you're in danger, baby. Let me protect you," he said, trying to reason with her. "Let me save Journee from Temper's mistakes. She doesn't deserve to suffer because of your past."

"'Baby'? Listen to how crazy you sound. There ain't no Journee. There's only Temper, and there will always only be Temper. Calling me by another name is still betrayal to your best friend. I made mistakes—me, Temper. I'm the girl who fucked up your homeboy's life, and either you can forgive me and let it go or do what you already did and let me go. Can you please move your car, or do I need to call 911?"

Julio stared into her eyes, and they were as empty as she was forcing his heart to be. He got back into his car and moved out of her way.

On her way to Tyger's apartment, she cried as fear came over her. How in the hell would she protect herself when all it took was friendly words from Kei'Lani for her to be foolish enough to let her back in? True, Khasema was in jail, but Kei'Lani mentioned he would be going in front of the review board next year. If she decided to press charges on Kei'Lani, would that keep Khasema in jail, and would him being in prison stop the attempts on her life? How much pull did he have in the streets? She wondered about it, and then she remembered the security blanket she'd given herself years ago. She hit the gas and did a hundred miles per hour until she pulled up at her old apartment. She had to knock because Tyger had had the locks changed.

"Are you okay?" the girls asked each other in unison as they hugged.

"I'm fine. What happened at the police station after I left?" Temper blurted out before Tyger could say another word.

"Please roll that shit up. I've been sipping this vodka, but it ain't doing shit. Paula's under-the-table, racist ass is dead and gone," Tyger said, shaking her head.

With all the other shit on Temper's mind, she'd completely forgotten about it. "How was she killed? What did they say happened?"

"They didn't tell you?"

"No, Julio didn't tell me shit. He wanted me to press charges on Kei'Lani. When I refused to, he told me to go fuck off and cleared me as a suspect."

"Oh, yeah, Julio," Tyger said, rolling her eyes. "The second fucking cop you had around me when I told you never to have any around me," she started up, and Temper shut it down.

"This isn't the time for that. I already told you I didn't know, didn't mean to, and that I was sorry. What happened with Paula? You must have been cleared as a suspect too, or you wouldn't be here."

"There can't be any suspect in a damn overdose. The bitch died from a drug overdose. We shouldn't have been asked to come in anyways. I answered your question. Your turn. Can you please tell me why we had to sit at the station for all those hours and get questioned about everything but the fucking overdose?"

"She overdosed?" Temper repeated, confused.

"Why do you sound surprised when we both knew she was addicted to pills?"

Temper didn't know if she should answer honestly. Paula had trusted Temper with the information she didn't want anyone to know. She wanted to have children and told Temper that her husband's sperm wasn't up for the job.

"Nor is your addiction to prescription medicine," Temper noted.

"I know," Paula whispered as the janitor pushed the trash bin past her office door. "That's why I gave them up."

"Sure you did."

"I swear I haven't popped any pills or taken anything, not even cough syrup, for the past six months to get my system clean enough to conceive a child."

"Who's helping you beat the addiction? I sat in one too many Narcotics Anonymous classes at the shelter I used to work for to know support is key in kicking any habit. Is your husband helping you with this?"

Paula closed and locked her door. "He's never home to pay attention to me. I started drinking wine to deal with his absence, and then this long infomercial came on about depression and a drug that did away with it. I visited my aunt, and she had a bottle. I've been stuck on pills since. One night, when I wasn't expecting him home, I took two pills with a glass of wine. I wasn't thinking straight. I just wanted to relax. Brad walked in and found me on the kitchen floor, mumbling. He saw the bottle and blamed it on the wine. He doesn't know about my addiction, and if he did, I don't think he'd care."

"Sad story," Temper said, facing her. "If you're not sure if he cares, then why are you trying to have a baby? Y'all need counseling, which makes beating the addiction that much harder. Are you attending meetings?"

Eventually, in secrecy, Temper attended a handful of NA meetings with her. She was the first person Paula called when the pregnancy test returned positive. Marriage counseling was working, and she and her husband started having a date night once a week. It wasn't impossible for her to relapse. It just wasn't probable.

"I'm not surprised, just confused why we were brought in for questioning on a drug overdose too," Temper answered, deciding it was best to lie.

"Then you should ask your boo. He had Kei-Kei and me in the same waiting room while he talked to you, and to be real with you, I don't trust him or her. She seemed like she was still holding whatever happened in the past against you, and it was driving her crazy to get it out. Your boo called her in for questioning, and the next thing I know, the paramedics were rushing in to get her because she had a huge seizure that she brought on herself. Are you going to fire that blunt up or just keep standing there holding it?"

Temper lit the blunt, hit it once, and then passed it to her. "Is that all that happened?"

"Do you think I'd be this amped up if that were all? Hell no, that was just the beginning. Your boo came back like he was ready to kill my lawyer and me. He started asking me about our past and how did we meet. He wanted to know why you left Las Vegas and what happened to Isabel."

"Why would Isabel come up?" Temper asked, reaching for the blunt.

"I don't know, but I do know something is up, and your past seems to be the cause of it. Are you sure you told me everything about your past? All I heard was fight, fuck, and get fucked up."

"I'm sure, but now it's your turn, don't you think?"

"Um, no. I didn't ask you to tell me any of that shit. You wanted to. You needed a therapy session, and I gave an ear. I don't have a past. My parents died and then we met, that's it."

"Save that shit. You just said that you think my past might be after me. Well, what if it is? What if there's bullshit going on I don't know about? Is there something in your past that could help me, or somebody you can get to look into all of this?"

"Oh, no you didn't, bitch. You're trying to use me. There's that fucking perk I knew your ass was after way back when. Here we are, years later, and now you want me to pull a card out that I threw away at sixteen for a new life. Ho, you're not my friend. You ain't nobody's friend. It's just like Kei-Kei said. It's always all about you. Get the fuck out!"

"I've been thrown out of better places by better people. I'm not leaving." Temper was so firm and straight to the point that Tyger wasn't sure how to respond. She'd told Kei-Kei that she had never met this version of Temper she was introduced to today, and she wasn't sure how to feel about her.

"That's the only version of Tee I know—cutthroat, heartless, and selfish. She doesn't give a fuck about you. Y'all have been friends for a long time, and that's why you probably don't believe me. Just wait until she gets a man. You'll get to see where you stand with her," Kei-Kei had warned.

Tyger didn't agree with her verbally, yet she did agree. She had witnessed the switch up when she met Julio. She didn't know precisely how far Temper's change in attitude could go, but the little she noticed was enough to know that dick had the power to make her best friend do flips.

"Are you listening to me?" Temper snapped, hoping she wasn't being ignored. "I said you can beat my ass, but I'm not going anywhere. I don't have a clue what's going on. I was only asking you if you had your sister's back at all costs, and you just made it clear that you don't. I'm okay with that. Everything that I said to you earlier today, I meant. I'm fucked up on the inside, and I've done a lot of terrible shit in my past, and the more I try to let it go, the bigger my problems get." She hit the blunt Tyger was holding and then snatched the bottle out of her hand.

"Then I should kick your ass for questioning my loyalty since you're going to let Kei-Kei off the damn hook for trying to kill you. I was locked in the room for an hour with that bitch, and I hate to tell you, but she ain't your friend. I don't know about how you hoes were in the past, but she was trying to team up with me to pin whatever came our way on you. Both of y'all bitches ain't shit."

"If she weren't about to die anyway, I would press charges to prove the relationship we have is more than I ever had with her."

Tyger shot her hands up to her mouth. "She's not going to make it?"

"Not from what Julio said."

"Ahh, Temper. I'm so sorry for your loss."

"Not my loss. She ain't you." She shrugged. "Do you know why I never told you about my lesbian experiences with her?"

"Yeah. You a secret-holding-ass bitch, and that's what your kind does."

"Wrong. I didn't tell you because that day you spoke up for me on our way to court, I wanted to fuck you so bad to show my appreciation. Nobody had ever done that for me, and in less than three hours, you did it again with those Blood bitches. You would have thought I was crazy if I had said what I wanted to say. That's why I settled for that best friend shit, because asking you to be my woman would have killed the opportunity you gave me to get to know you. Getting to know your super-smart ass is why I could let go of a lot of shit I did. So telling you that I love pussy would have led on to me asking to taste you."

"Bitch, I should swell up your muthafucking eye for try-ing that weak-ass shit on me. First off, I'm straight. That 'fuck her to get what you want out of her' bullshit you're trying to run ain't gon' ever work. Put your dick back in your mouth, pimp. It's going to take more than hot words and a wet tongue to get me to fold. Next, I have your back to the fullest. You shouldn't have to question my loyalty, but protecting your ass comes at my discretion, not your recommended methods. Lastly, I lied."

"About what?" Temper's heart felt like it would explode in her chest while she waited for Tyger to answer the question. It never crossed Temper's mind that Tyger lied about who her father was, or that it wasn't Tyger's quick wit that saved her at the courthouse. There was a rich man Tyger visited in Arizona, but that could have been anybody. Thinking back, that was the only time Temper had witnessed Tyger act in that manner or talk that way. She had to know. "What did you lie to me about?"

"About that damn experience. I ain't never licked no pussy. When I was writing you back, my roommate was standing over me reading my shit, and I wanted her to think I was bisexual so she'd mess with me. Instead, she saw me as a player like her and didn't try to do shit with me."

Temper tried to hold it in, knowing Tyger was pouring her soul out, but it was too funny not to laugh, and the liquor and weed thought it was too.

"Then why did you let me hold on to it for all that time? You could have come clean years ago," she said, flopping down on the couch next to her.

"I thought about it but couldn't decide which was more embarrassing: lying about eating pussy to get my pussy eaten or lying about eating pussy and not eating any at all. I don't know, girl." She joined in on the laugh. "I just needed you to know the truth, so you can stop trying to play me with that 'I wanted to fuck you' shit. You sound like one of those weak-ass niggas I went to school with. They used to throw eggs at my head for being a nerd, and now when they see me all grown up, they want to throw their tongues at me and give me more head than my pussy can handle." She laughed, but Temper did not.

"I love you, Tyger, you already know that, but you're going to have to whoop my ass. I wasn't joking. I wish I were, I really do, but why would I want a husband when I felt like I met my wife before I was eighteen? I only did that shit with Julio because I got tired of hoping things would pop off between us. I decided years ago that I would never initiate it, and you never did. I was like fuck it, let me go find love."

Tyger hurried over to the arm of the couch, leaving a vast space between them. "Yo, I think you might need help, Temper."

"I think we both do. Why did you map out your entire life with me and not a husband? I had time to think about all of that on my way over here. You made a plan for us that involved no serious relationships and us being attached for life. Why is that?"

"Because you're my sister and my best friend. What do I need a man for besides dick and head when I got you for everything else? I don't want no damn kids, and I'm not about to share a bed with nobody." She snatched her drink. "Give me my damn bottle back. I got you one. It's in the refrigerator. This shit is starting to creep me out. We need to change the subject back to the important shit and try to figure all that out. This lesbian heart-to-heart stuff is too much."

"Yeah, you're right. Grab my bottle for me. I'm going to roll another blunt."

They smoked and talked, drank, and talked a little more, and since Tyger already announced the museum would be closed for days because of the many events of the day, they planned out their moves for tomorrow.

"You need to call Julio and play the role with him and see what all he knows. When his chief found out he knew us, they took him off the case. He stabbed Kei'Lani and shouldn't have been on it in the first damn place. I don't know what happened in that office between him and her, but I know that whatever did got his ass suspended," Tyger announced, way past drunk.

"What do I say to his punk ass? I hate him."

Temper laid her head in Tyger's lap like she had always done when frustration took over, and Tyger began to scratch her scalp with her nails.

"I don't know, but we will come up with the exact words in the morning. You will have to play that shit cool. You can't be over there talking crazy and . . ." Temper took Tyger's words away as she sucked on Tyger's braless nipple through her spaghetti-strap shirt. "Um, what the fuck are you doing?"

"Getting these cravings out of my system," Temper said as she lifted the top to reveal two beautiful seedless watermelon–sized breasts. She hurriedly stuffed the nipple in her mouth before Tyger told her to stop.

"But I'm not gay," Tyger moaned as she slowly resumed running her nails through Temper's hair.

"Neither am I. You cured me."

Her mouth was replaced with her fingers as she pinched Tyger's nipples slowly and moved up to her mouth. She kissed Tyger like she'd never been kissed before.

"I'm not gay. I'm just high. Okay? I'm only letting you do this because I'm fucked up, and my pussy thinks you're a man."

"Whatever your sexy ass says, that's what it is. We're both fucked up for all I care. Come up out of those shorts. I've waited for years to taste you."

Tyger almost ripped the shorts off as she moved faster than light traveled to take them off. When they hit the ground by Temper's foot, she grabbed a handful of Tyger's pussy and cupped it tightly until she could feel the juices mist in her palm.

"Damn, that pussy is fat. Man, I've wanted you," Temper moaned, and the grip she had on her pussy made Tyger shake.

Temper wasn't lying. She'd wanted to fuck Tyger for a long time, though the desire to do it didn't start until recently. She'd had a wild night in bed with Julio and thought it would have been better if she could have shared the taste and feel of another beautiful woman with him. It was the first time that the lesbian beast within had shown its face in years, and she blamed the unwanted visit from her old chum on the new wine Julio wanted them to try. It made her feel 16 again. It made her feel alive, sexy, and fuckable by either sex.

She'd wanted to fuck all night, but she only experienced the pleasure of sex all night with a woman, and then Julio changed that. He fucked her so good that she wished she had a pretty pussy in her face to lick while she enjoyed the dick he repeatedly rammed in her, and that was when she saw Tyger's face. It was beautiful, but the titties she knew she owned from watching her get dressed in front of her turned her on. As Julio pounded her from the back as if she were a random bitch he'd wanted to fuck, she shoved her face into the pillows until she was sure he couldn't see it and pretended she was licking Tyger's pussy. From her clit to her asshole and back, she was on Temper's menu but was imaginarily being served. What was taking place between the women was a dream come true for Temper, even if it was only for this one night. She'd enjoy the moment like it was hers to have forever.

"That feels so good," Tyger screamed out as Temper switched positions. She went from lying across the couch as she sucked on Tyger's clit to helping Tyger ride her face. Then she got on her knees as Tyger fucked her face to an imaginary rhythm only she could hear. Both girls were in triple X mode, and then Tyger said what Temper was hoping to hear.

"I've been waiting for us to fuck around like this for years too. I can't lie. If I had known you could fuck me this good, this pussy would have been yours."

"Then let me have it now. It's not too late."

"I am," Tyger moaned.

"Naw, I'm talking about whenever and however I want it. I want you to be mine."

"I am yours. I've been yours, but what am I going to do about dick? I can't go forever without it."

"Me either, so we'll just have threesomes from time to time with a throwaway nigga."

"Okay, but no more outsiders. It's just you and me from here on out. Fuck Isabel, Julio, and anybody else you've tried to put before me. Like that bitch Paula. I knew you were creeping to that ho's house. Did you fuck her?"

There was the truth Temper was looking for dished out in drunken lust.

"No, and I promise you that after this shit is over with Julio, I won't let anyone else into our lives. It'll be just you and me forever."

"I like that."

"Me too, baby."

"My turn," Tyger announced as she reached to the sides of Temper's yoga pants to pull them off.

"Do you know what you are doing?"

"No, but I love you, and if it's going to be just us, then I need to learn."

"You don't have to," Temper assured her, but Tyger did have to. She needed Temper to do everything she asked of her and to get all the information she could on Julio's investigation. Everything Tyger had told Temper and anyone who asked about her relationship with her father was a lie. They were and always had been best friends. They had a rough patch, but the incident made them closer. Tyger would kill before she let Temper's past send a tail after her father, but she needed to be sure that was the case. She didn't want to fully alert her father until she gathered everything she could on her own. Involving her father could get Temper buried at the bottom of the ocean. Tyger had to be sure that she deserved that fate.

"I want to, Temper. Let me please you, baby."

There it was. Tyger gave Temper the treatment that many men had given her before, but none ever sent her to the heights Tyger did. As she came back-to-back on Tyger's tongue, she thought her plan to use sex to get Tyger's help might backfire. Tyger was a pussy-eating natural.

Chapter Eleven

Tyger watched her. Julio watched her. Now that Kei'Lani's death made the news as the buzz of Paula's overdose became public information, the whole state of California's eyes were on Temper. So were the undercover cops Isabel worked with in Las Vegas. It was like a western movie, or better yet, the untold story of a mobster's daughter. Too bad Temper wasn't affiliated with either. There was death, murder, suicide, imprisonment, assault, gangs, drugs, sex, disease, undercover cops, and to top it off, a thrown-away baby. There was too much orbiting around Temper's name for Isabel's partners not to take a closer look into things.

Matthew, the undercover officer who drove the van the day of Temper's Las Vegas arrest, never felt comfortable with the facts surrounding Isabel's death. He was told that Isabel acted alone on a tip she received on the john she had been hunting. Whatever happened when Isabel arrived at the location given to her by this tip forced her to call for backup. By the time Matthew and his partner made it, Isabel was applying pressure over the hole that allowed blood to ooze from her neck. Ballistics couldn't trace the gun to anyone, there were no fingerprints or DNA found on the scene, and Isabel's call to dispatch was too calm to say she was in pursuit of a suspect. She didn't even draw her weapon, but what bugged Matthew the most about the murder was that everything surrounding her murder was speculation. There was no proof that she received a tip on the case she had been working. The trace done on the last call she received was made from a burner cell phone and had only been used to make that call solely. The cell phone service provider tried to trace where the phone was sold, but that was a dead end. The trace tied the phone to a pharmacy chain with stores domestic and international.

Even the last people to see her alive, those at the runaway shelter, were no help because all their stories were identical. They said her phone rang, she stepped away to answer it, and returned in different clothing saying that work had called. Matthew spent day and night doing his own investigation, and nothing added up. Why would she respond to a call alone? Who was the informant who gave her a tip? Most importantly, why would she decide to leave Temper, especially on her birthday, when she never placed anything else before her, not even a case?

He wanted answers and would start his search for them by questioning Temper about any possible fallings-out they may have had, but she was too devastated by Isabel's death at the time. He'd wait until after the funeral to ask, but Temper didn't show up for it. From what Matthew gathered when he spoke with Isabel's parents, Temper was too heartbroken to attend, and everyone felt that with all the hurt and pain the little girl had gone through in her life, it was best she didn't attend.

The cold case he labeled his partner's death as never sat right in his heart, and then he received a call from the head of homicide in Los Angeles to prove his heart was right.

"I know this comes as a surprise, Detective," Julio whispered.

"You can call me Matthew. The tone of your voice tells me this little investigation you're running isn't officially on the books, Detective . . ."

"Torres, and you're right, so you can call me Julio. There's not enough solid evidence to officially open a case or for me to give you to reopen Isabel's, but I have a gut feeling there will be."

"I'm in, anything I can do to help."

Matthew volunteered the information surrounding Isabel's murder and told him everything he knew about the relationship she had with Temper.

"One more thing I have to ask of you. Can you please scrape up all the information you can on Isabel's life insurance policy, pension, and the total of her estate? It all goes to Temper in a little over a month, and I want to know everyone who knew Isabel named her as the beneficiary and the stipulations she placed on Temper's inheritance. I don't believe it's coincidence that an attempt was made on her life on the eve of her becoming a millionaire," Julio concluded.

Matthew couldn't speak. He'd never thought to question who would receive her pension and if she had a will in place, because she wasn't married, nor had she birthed any children. He assumed her parents would receive it all after watching them get handed the American flag at her funeral. Knowing that it would go to Temper was enough to take to his sergeant to reopen the case.

"Hello, are you still there?" Julio asked for the third time.

"Yes, I'm here. Can you fax me the insurance company's name and anything that might help me? I'll look into everything else and get back to you as soon as I can."

"Sure, and you might want to talk with her parents and siblings, if she has any, to see what they knew about it. I hate to reopen their wounds, but it might be the only way to catch her killer finally."

"Gotcha. I'll be in contact soon. Wait. Isabel was my partner for years, and I loved her. Why is her case so important to you?"

"Because her case may help me solve the investigation around Temper."

"Personal," Matthew mumbled.

"Excuse me, I didn't catch that."

"I said, 'Personal.' You called her by her first name instead of her last. In this case, your stake is personal, and that's why it's off the books. I'm glad to see that someone else loves Temper as much as Isabel once did. I'll be in touch."

Being in touch took a back seat once Matthew received the okay to reopen Isabel's murder case. Now that he had a contact in Los Angeles, he decided to work the case backward, starting with the newly involved first. Detective Julio Torres was first on his list, and he didn't like the information he found. Julio grew up on the same street as Temper, and after cross-checking names and affiliations, he found visitation records linking him to the man Temper named as the drug dealer when they arrested her all those years ago.

After digging a little deeper, he found out that the drug dealer struck out due to a rape case that produced a child birthed by Temper. It didn't take more than a Google search of his name to pull up the articles involving the museum's stabbing to protect the docent, Temper Chey, and three added names for him to investigate: Kei'Lani, now deceased, whose last known address belonged to the mother of the drug dealer serving life for raping Temper; Paula, the museum director who conveniently overdosed in the museum's parking lot the day of the stabbing; and Tyger, the museum's curator he'd questioned the night of Isabel's murder. She was Temper's best friend, whom Isabel had planned the surprise party with for Temper. Isabel told him she was unsure about her because the girls' friendship was built behind juvenile hall's walls, and Tyger's bloodline linked her to well-known West Coast criminals. She was also the girl Temper skipped town with after Isabel's murder.

Not knowing who he could trust, he publicized the reopening of the murder investigation and had every newspaper and station announce new leads. The word spread quickly, and soon he found himself dodging phone calls from Julio by having his secretary tell him that he would call him back at his earliest convenience. Trusting Julio didn't seem right, especially after finding the eviction notice he'd filed against Temper.

He did take Julio's advice to contact Isabel's parents. They were a tremendous help when it came to being character witnesses for Temper, but ultimately it was the piece the local news station ran on Isabel that gave him the solid lead on the case he had waited to solve for years. He had a confession and a man in custody. It was time for him to have a face-to-face with Temper.

Armed guards packed the foyer. The invited media outlets took their places while those relevant enough to make the guest list mingled. Whether any of them cared for the lady of the hour or the event itself didn't matter. The opportunity to network was too grand to miss it.

The day had finally come when the museum's board, along with the mayor and city council, honored Tyger for her courageous part in saving Temper's life. She had saved the museum after Paula's tragic overdosing, and it was also the day she accepted her role as the new director. Although the promotion had taken her years to reach, it happened two months after Paula's death, which also happened to be the best two months of her life thanks to her and Temper's secret relationship.

"How do I look?" Tyger asked as she adjusted the hem on her slacks over the back of her heels for the umpteenth time.

"Overdressed for what I have in mind," Temper responded as she rubbed the curves of her hips.

"Stop," Tyger snapped. "We already talked about that, and you're violating the rules. No public display of anything that anyone could take as affection. I keep telling your horny ass I'm not gay unless we're home with your face in my pussy." She looked over her shoulder at her office door to make sure it was closed and then cupped Temper's face. "I love you, you little freaky, sex-crazed bitch."

"I love you too, you little freaky, straight-acting bitch."

The words rolled off Temper's tongue as Tyger's tongue replaced them in her mouth. They kissed while Temper rubbed on Tyger's ass as if it would bring her good fortune. There was no way Julio would ruin it, so he silently closed the door and knocked.

"It's open. Come in," Tyger announced as Temper made her way to the connecting restroom to wipe off the traces of their kiss that the lipstick left behind.

"I just wanted to come by before the event and congratulate you on all of your accomplishments and tell you that it's an honor to present you the award for bravery. This museum and the city of Los Angeles are lucky to have you." He extended his hand for hers, and when she gave it to him, he kissed it slowly and softly. "You look amazing, as usual."

"Thank you," Tyger said, unable to conceal the smile that grew on her face. "I'm honored that you are the one presenting it, and I hope everything that happened in the past—"

"Is water under the bridge," he confirmed, cutting her off. "My goal was to make sure that Temper was safe, and she is. I owe an apology to you for not trusting the bond that you and she have."

"Don't be silly. We all make our share of mistakes."

"Yes, we do," Temper said, stepping into the room. "Hello, Detective Torres. Long time no see. You look like life is still treating you well."

"You as well," he said, extending his hand for hers and then repeating the kiss he'd planted on Tyger's. "I just wanted to come by to congratulate your best friend before the event, but I'm glad you're here, too. Now I can congratulate you on being promoted to curator. That's a long journey. I mean, a long way from the old neighborhood. I'm sure it doesn't matter to you, but I'm extremely proud of you."

It was hard for Temper not to want that man standing in front of her, but everything happened for a reason. Tyger had sent her to play nice with Julio, but he hadn't been in the mood. Instead of meeting at the house as she'd planned, he switched the location. They'd met at a diner close to his home.

"Am I no longer welcome at our house?" That was the first question she asked as she took her seat.

"I assumed you no longer saw it as your home since you stopped coming to it. I wanted to make sure we met to talk where you felt comfortable."

"You assume everything and never seem to know anything. What's this little meeting all about?"

"Your protection."

After begging to interrogate her for her safety and being denied, he handed her the eviction notice.

"What's this?"

"The official termination of us and everything we had."

She tore open the envelope, read the contents in their entirety, and slammed the order down on the table. "You are so weak it's pathetic. Can't get me to jump through your little loops like the dog you were hoping to train, so you took your little punk ass to the courthouse and lied on me?"

"There goes that mouth everyone loved to fuck. Where's the lie, Temper? You knew Kei'Lani was a criminal, and you refused to press charges on her. What illegal shit are you tied to that had you scared to snitch to save your ass?"

"Fuck you, Julio. You're the real criminal in all of this. Since you brought up Kei'Lani for the thousandth time, why don't you tell me what happened between y'all behind your office door? You cocked back and almost hit me. What did you do to her? Did you ram her head into that wall? I'm just saying her whole life has been fucked up. Why would she wait for that moment alone with you to commit suicide?" she asked, flipping the interrogation.

"I don't know. Maybe she realized that I was the first man to love your stupid ass, and the shit she's been pulling on you for years wasn't going to work anymore."

"Or maybe you killed her to stop her from telling Khasema that you fell in love with the bitch who got him his third strike. Wouldn't want to look bad to your boy, right?"

"Not possible. We don't love hoes. We get our nut and then pay them for services rendered." He dug in his pocket and threw $200 at her. "That throat was good. Keep the change as a tip, bitch."

Those in the diner had turned their attention to Temper as Julio left her sitting there staring at the eviction notice. The grounds for eviction were suspected criminal activities. That alone was enough to make her never speak to or think of him again. When she'd made it home and shared her trip to the diner, Tyger was pissed that she hadn't played along, but Temper didn't care. She no longer trusted anyone, including Tyger, but she knew if she showered her with love, Tyger would ensure that she stayed safe.

"No, I can't say that you being proud matters to me one bit, but I do thank you for the kind words. If you don't mind, I need to get my best friend ready for the day. I'm trying hard to say this as nicely as I possibly can—get the fuck out."

"It doesn't have to be like this, Temper," Julio said, begging with his eyes as knocks rang on the door.

"Come in. It's open," Tyger stated, starting to feel annoyed by the interruptions.

Matthew walked in with two other men, all three wearing suits and holding badges. "I'm sorry to inter-rupt, especially on a day like today. Temper, I need to transport you back to Las Vegas for questioning related to the murder of Isabel. We wore suits to throw off the media. Nobody knows who we are nor why we are here. I thought the both of you would prefer it that way." He nodded toward Tyger to acknowledge her day.

"Am I under arrest, Matthew? If not, then I refuse to go. It's my best friend's special day, and I don't understand why Isabel's death is coming back up after all this time. You all said you didn't have any evidence back then, but you act like you have a shitload of it now. What's up with that, Matt? Did important evidence get overlooked?" Temper stood firm in her questioning.

"There was nothing to overlook. We didn't have any ev-idence back then, but we do now, and you, better than anyone, should know there's no way I wouldn't dedicate my life to solving this case. I don't want to arrest you. It would be like arresting Isabel's only child, but we do have a motive in the sum of $1.7 million, and the fact that you ran away after her death is suspicious. I want you to come in by your own free will and not by force. Answer a few questions, and let me clear you as a suspect, Temper. I'm sure Isabel is cursing me out from up there for bring-ing you in as it is, but she understands the job, and that's all I'm trying to do. Are you walking out of here with me, or are these LAPD officers arresting you and then you spend a couple of nights in L.A. county jail until we can get you transported to Las Vegas?"

Temper shot her eyes up at Tyger and saw fear in its purest form. Then she moved them to Julio, who took her glance as her wanting his opinion.

"Go with him. If he doesn't arrest you, you can walk away after this, but don't talk to him without your lawyer."

"You must be Julio," Matthew said, extending his hand. "So we finally get to meet."

"You're a hard man to reach," Julio said, shaking his hand, and immediately Temper walked up on Julio.

"Do you have something to do with this, with Isabel's case being reopened?"

"No, Temper. I reached out to Matthew to see if he could help me protect you, and honestly, this is the first time I've heard anything back on it. I didn't even know he had enough new evidence to reopen the case already. I promise you that's the truth."

"You keep saying that you want to protect me. Who or what do you think you are protecting me from? Isn't it obvious that Isabel's killer can't be out to get me if Vegas detectives see me as a fucking suspect? What the fuck are you protecting me from?"

"From yourself," he screamed, letting his emotions take over. For months, he'd been going nights without ends trying to reveal the bigger picture by putting together this fucked-up puzzle that Temper called life, and every piece he picked up seemed to have been altered or manipulated for someone else's good. But whose? That question was the reason the bags under his eyes were full, and the reason he could no longer hold back his feelings. "I'm trying to protect you from these dumbass decisions you keep making until I can find out who is benefiting from all of them."

"That's the dumbest shit I've ever heard. How is calling Vegas to open the murder case of the only fucking mother I've had and making me look like a suspect protecting me?"

"I didn't have that fucking case reopened, Temper."

"Stop fucking lying to me. That's all you ever do. That's all you've ever done."

"He's not lying," Matthew declared as he made a wedge between the two undeniably heartbroken lovers. "Once I found out about y'all's relationship and the grounds for the eviction Julio placed on you, I knew he was trying to protect you, but I wasn't sure of his motive after learning his connection to the man you admitted to selling drugs for as a teen."

"Please tell me how lying about me being involved in criminal activity to have me thrown out of a house that I didn't want to live in is protecting me, Matt? Please help make all of this shit make sense." Temper looked at Tyger, expecting her normal smart-mouth adlib to let the room know she had Temper's back. However, she was silent and still in her stance.

"If he used that as a reason for eviction, it puts eyes on you, and I'm sure wherever he filed the paperwork knew who he was and exactly what he was trying to do. It seems stupid, but that was the only way he could legally use man-hours to protect you without breaking the law to do it. I'm not here to vouch for his feelings or if he has lied to you. I just want you to know that it's a known method among those wearing badges to keep those domestic to us safe."

"That's a fucked-up method," Temper hissed and rolled her eyes.

"Well, in the end, I felt like it was best to try to protect you myself, the way Isabel would want me to, but I was left to question, how well did you protect Isabel?"

"I loved Isabel," she yelled.

"Then there should be no reason why I'd have to keep you after questioning, right?" He opened the door. "Ladies first. Take the hallway to the kitchen, and we will slide out the back door. Congratulations on your achievements, Ms. Washington. It's an honor to be in your presence again. I only hate that every time I come, it's to bring bad news," he said as he followed Temper out the door. "I hate to have to take her away from you."

"Thank you. I understand," Tyger stammered as she locked eyes with Julio. When they could no longer see Temper, Matthew, and the LAPD escorts, Tyger ran and closed her office door.

"What the fuck was all of that? Is that legal? Can he just force her to answer questions about stuff she doesn't know anything about? You know she's playing hard, Julio. You can look in her eyes and see she's scared."

"Calm down. I know you're scared for her, but there's a lot of fucked-up shit around her, and we need to know how long and far it goes."

"So you are in on this?" Tyger accused as she stepped away from him. "You stood right in her face and lied again. Why do you keep doing her like this when you know she loves you?"

"I'm not in on nothing Matthew has going on, and I'm not working with them. I'm working for Temper, whether you or her see it or not. I love her. Why don't either of you see that? Maybe if we can get all this past shit flushed away, the flies circling her will leave. Then I can have my wife and you . . ."

His words stopped abruptly as he recalled the passionate kiss he'd watched them share, and he wondered what type of relationship the women had. If he did resolve all the problems around Temper, would Tyger and their relationship be next? There wasn't a need to lie. Tyger was one of the sexiest plus-sized women he had ever laid eyes on, and although he didn't wear it like he wore his badge, BBW was his preference. If he had laid eyes on Tyger first, it would have been her drink he bought that night at the club. But he hadn't, and it wasn't her heart that had stolen his outside on the patio. He wouldn't mind a threesome here and there if Temper wanted it. A few fucks from time to time was fine, but he wouldn't accept them being in a relationship with each other. This situation gave him a new investigation to open, and he'd use Tyger to get the information to solve it.

"You can have your best friend in the best state of mind like she should've always been in," he finished.

"Then I want in. Tell me what's going on with her so that I can help. If she's in danger, then I'm in danger too, because whoever attempts to take her out got hell on their hands. They will have to kill me to get to her because nobody, not even you, will ever hurt her as long as I'm breathing."

"I can't let you get involved."

"Why? Don't tell me you made me a suspect against my best friend." She threw the bone, and he pretended not to see it.

"Of course not. Look, let's get out of here, handle this event, and then sit down and talk. Maybe you can help me, okay?"

"Yeah, okay," she returned as she began to ponder what it would take to get him to expose his full hand.

"I'm sorry I asked you to go through all of this, but I don't know who I can trust, and it feels like everyone around me has me under a microscope," Temper said as she slid out of her heels as they walked through the kitchen doors.

Temper hardly ever ate anything they served at the museum because the lines were always too long and the food was overpriced, so she wasn't familiar enough with the kitchen staff to know a paper bag brown god was working the grill. They weren't museum employees. They were cafeteria workers employed by the City of Los Angeles and had their own HR department to report to. Otherwise, Temper would have run to the closest computer to look up his name. He had to be at least six feet two inches, 220 pounds or better, judging by the width and firmness of his frame, and younger than her, but it was hard to tell by how much with his face covered in hair. There wasn't another way to put it. He was handsome and worth eating every bite of an overpriced meal or two to get to know. There was something familiar about him, but she assumed that she might have seen him in the museum and thought he was a guest. She didn't realize she was gawking with all the looking she was doing until he gave her a smile and a nod. His teeth weren't that white or straight, but that was what they made dentists for, she thought as she nodded back and asked her question. "You said there was a huge break in the case?"

"There is, but I think it's best we talk once we get back to Vegas." Matthew locked eyes with hers until she understood that he didn't trust the people around him either. "Thanks for backing me up on this, fellas. I have her from here," he assured the two police officers who were appointed to accompany him to escort her.

Once he got her in the car alone, he told her of the detour. "We're going up the coast for a day or two to sort everything out. Everyone thinks you're headed back to Vegas with me. Let's see if anyone reveals their hand."

"What about clothes, food, and hygiene items? I planned on shopping at the outlets once we got there for all of that."

"Then I guess we will need to stop on our way to Santa Barbara. Don't worry about food. I've already shopped for groceries."

"I hope it isn't that stakeout food you and Isabel used to eat. Hamburgers with a side of pizza don't sound good to me at all."

"Then I guess those hot dogs and egg rolls I planned for us to eat tonight are off the list, too." He chuckled as they drove off, leaving the chaos in L.A. behind.

The event was one that Tyger would never forget. For her acts while the museum was in peril, she was honored with the key to the city and named historian of the year. She had never been big on crying. Her father didn't allow it, and her mother was too busy plotting ways to get out of her father's grip to pay her any attention.

"I'm sorry, but when I'm nervous, I don't feel comfortable anywhere on earth except within the comfort of the four walls of my room. It's from being incarcerated. I'm sure you've heard of it before—PICS. I believe my doctors said that, from time to time, I suffer from three out of the four clusters," Tyger shared as she sat on her bed after inviting Julio to have a seat on the loveseat where she did the majority of her studying.

"Post-incarceration syndrome. I'm very aware of the mental disorder. Not to pry, but you weren't in jail for that long, and wasn't it a juvenile facility? I did a little digging in all of your backgrounds. I didn't think you could get the disorder that fast."

"Time is understood by no one. It is rare to get it that fast, as you put it, but if you're not mentally stable enough to handle a day in jail, hell, even in the holding tank, you can fall victim to it. Come to think about it, I don't think I've ever told Temper I have it, but I'm sure she's picked up on a few of the symptoms. My room and books are all I need." She giggled.

"Then if this makes you feel any better, this is the nicest room I've ever been in. It's like you have every room in one bedroom. Where did you find the mini refrigerator and stove? They look like they belong in a dollhouse."

"Online. I don't remember the site. Not to be rude, but I've met my limit on small talk. If I don't have a brain stimulant soon, you'll be watching me read. I hope you don't mind."

Tyger took off her pants and shirt and walked to her closet in her strapless bra and high-cut panties. There would be nothing sexy about an average-sized woman in plain-Jane granny panties, but with hips, thighs, those fat legs, and a fat ass, it was like watching amateur porn. Assuming she was searching for clothes to put on, he said, "Whatever helps your PICS, I don't mind."

"Good," she said as she turned around with a lighter and blunt in her hand. "I know you're a cop, and even though I have a weed card, y'all trip at times."

"Oh, no, I probably should step out while you smoke that. I thought you had psych meds or something like that to take. Catching contact could cost me my career."

"Are you serious? You were dating Miss Mary Jane Farms, and you don't smoke?"

"No, I don't, and when Temper and I were together, she didn't either. We'd relax with a drink. Do you have any wine or liquor? I could use a shot of tequila right about now."

"The kitchen cabinet over the fridge is the bar, and since we don't cook, the fridge is the wine cellar. Knock yourself out. I'll go smoke in my bathroom and call you when it airs out."

Tyger wasn't lying when she called the cabinet the bar. There was a variety of liquor ranging from top-shelf to

$5 hookups, and Julio didn't know what to choose. After rummaging through everything the ladies owned, he grabbed the whiskey and poured himself a shot. He swallowed it and poured another to knock out the thoughts of pulling his dick out and spanking Tyger's ass with it.

"What are you doing over here, man?" he asked himself while pouring shots three and four.

By the time Tyger said she was ready, he'd had a coffee mug full of it and was drunk off his ass. It wasn't long before he pulled out his dick and stared at her.

Tyger was shocked. She couldn't believe he'd pulled it out and didn't say shit like she knew what to do with it, but she needed him to tell her if her dad was involved in Temper's past. She had been curious about his dick game since the first night Temper came home bragging about it, but not curious enough to risk their bond over trying to take it for a test ride. She needed the information, and if giving him some pussy would give it to her, she'd take this risk for her father. Still, he'd have to initiate it. The thought of her betraying Temper wouldn't allow her to make the first move.

She lit her blunt, and when he didn't whine like a badge-wearing bitch about the weed smoke, she took her panties off, spread her legs, and did him exactly the way he had done her. When she noticed he was slowly rubbing and squeezing his meat, she said, "This pussy will feel a lot better than your hand, Mr. Officer." Another Lil Wayne hit played in her head.

"Oh, shit," Julio growled as drool fell over his bottom lip. He staggered over to Tyger, and after seconds of a drunk struggle, he slid his dick inside of her. Julio was drunk and aimed to live out his sexual fantasies in Tyger's pussy. He wanted to ram his dick in her and treat her like his slut of a sex slave. The other part of him craved to enjoy the moment with deep, slow strokes and a mouthful of titties.

He imagined his dick would meet Mrs. Right after seeing the different shades she came in on pornos. However, he never imagined he'd get to beat her down by way of the woman he loved and planned on marrying. This beautiful, big bitch had it all—perfect titties, a wide, round ass he could grip for stability from the back, and a wet little pussy she knew how to tighten and control. He couldn't nut if he wanted to. Both of his heads had waited years to fuck a bitch like this, and the unbelievable sensation to get back to his police work wasn't going to mess it up. It was the hood nigga living inside of him who loved to fuck hoes. Not even his badge could force him to kick the addiction.

"I can't lie. I think I love this dick," Tyger moaned as she detached his mouth from her nipple to enjoy his kiss while she came for the umpteenth time.

"I was just thinking the same thing, baby. It feels like you were made for me, like this pussy is supposed to be mine."

He kissed her until the shaking in her walls ceased, giving her the freedom to speak again.

"Then treat me like I'm yours. Fuck me like this pussy is yours."

He slid his steel out of one mouth, mounted her face like he was about to hit a set of jailhouse push-ups, and then rested his nuts on her chin as he fucked the other.

"If you want this dick back in that pussy, suck my shit clean. Spit shine the head, freaky little bitch."

Tyger, motivated by his words, curved the width of her tongue around the width of his dick and let the spit flow while her throat accepted penetration.

"Oh, shit, yeah, bitch. You're mine now."

He snatched himself out of her mouth and spanked her lip with his hard head as pre-nut glistened his hole. Before he could no-hand his way back inside of her, she used her weight to overpower him and climbed on top.

"No, you mean you're mine now," she dictated, sliding down on his dick like it was in a fire station, and when the space between her ass cheeks was filled with his balls, the shaking in her legs and thighs commenced.

"Ay, don't talk shit if you're going to come that fast on my dick. Moan, bitch. That's what I want to hear. I want to hear my name come out of that pretty-ass mouth."

"You want to hear me say, 'Julio'?"

"Nah, I want to hear you sing it."

He pulled her hair down to the center of her back, forcing her to face the stucco on her ceiling as he sucked from one breast to the other. She gyrated on his lap, and then he forced everything that dangled in his drawers inside of her.

"Julio," she screamed.

"Sing my name just like that."

The pair spent the next minutes playing a moaning tug of war and using each other's names as safe words.

"What about Temper?"

The question came out of the air like a fly whispered it in his ear. Love should have made Julio hit the emergency brakes and eject her from his lap, yet strangely enough, it boosted his mood, and Tyger could feel him grow half an inch inside of her.

"We can fuck her too. The pussy ain't as good as this, but she still holds a few heartstrings."

"What? I'm not—"

He cupped her mouth with his hand, preventing the lie to exit her mouth. "Two rules: never lie to me, and don't keep secrets," he demanded, using his thigh muscles to switch positions. He was on top, pounding her as his nuts spanked her for the attempt. "I saw y'all kissing in your office earlier. I didn't like the shit, but if that's how you get down—"

It was her turn to stop his words. "I wasn't about to lie. I'm not gay. I like my pussy licked, and in return for her licking this pussy like a good little kitten, I'd kill her cat."

Julio's eyebrow raised. "You mean, lick the pussy like this?"

In a quick move, he snatched her up like she was as light as college-ruled paper, and dived into her pussy, resting the back of her thighs on his shoulders.

"Yesssssssss!"

He licked, sucked, and pulled on her clit until her juices moistened his chin twice. "You still need her for that?"

"Hell nah, but we can keep her around. I want you to fuck me while you eat her pussy and she sucks on my titties."

That was the straw that broke the floodgates. Julio jumped up and shot his dick at her face as his nut came shooting out. He could have died when he felt her lips wrap around him to replace the hand he was using to squeeze his head. With thirst, she finished drinking his load. After watching her lick and play with his shaft, he was tired of the games.

"Look at me," he demanded, but her eyes never met his. With his free hand, he grabbed a lock of her hair and forced her to. "Bitch, you heard me. Look at me when you suck this dick, you hear me?" he asked, securing his grip and tugging at her hair. She looked into his eyes with helplessness etched in her own and nodded. It was a turn-on. The power of watching one of the baddest bitches he'd ever nutted in taking pride in her submissive role polished his ego. "Now suck the head faster." She bobbed, and, feeling like Tony Montana in a Florida floral button-up in front of a mountain of cocaine, he lit and hit the blunt. He was sure the weed would assist her with getting him back hard.

If he'd had that ring on him, he would have proposed. Both of their plans to crack each other for information were thrown out, at least for the moment. They found something better to focus on than Temper. They found their secret fantasies in each other.

Chapter Twelve

The beach house was lovely at night, though it didn't compare to its beauty in the daylight.

"Do you remember Kevin?" Matthew asked as he poured them a glass of orange juice to go with the breakfast he'd cooked. Eggs, bacon, hash browns, and toast made for a good breakfast any day, but they tasted a lot better as Temper ate alfresco by the pool with a view of the ocean.

"Yeah, the scrub I dated when I lived out there. We broke up because Isabel caught him trying to buy pussy. Oh, my God, he didn't kill her, did he?" Shock stole her breath and held it until he answered.

"No, he didn't kill her, but we do have him in custody, and he will be charged as an accomplice to her murder."

"Oh, okay, so . . ." she said, winding her hand for more information. "It can't be that cut-and-dried, or we wouldn't be here. What's Kevin's part in it?"

This was the part Matthew wasn't looking forward to, the part where he had to tell Temper she was in danger and, in that same breath, tell her that was all the information he had.

"We used media outlets to announce the case was reopened and that we had a huge lead on the people involved. For seventy-two hours after that, we ran everyone who bought a plane, train, or bus ticket out of there with any ties to Isabel or her past cases, and we came up empty-handed. About forty-eight hours after that, I got a call from the television station. They said they received a call asking if there was a reward for information on her death and if they could get off for their part in it if they shared what they knew but hadn't killed her."

"How stupid is he?"

"Real stupid, because the station asked him to hold on while they looked into it, and his stupid ass did. By the time we tracked down the address and made it over there, he was still sitting on his couch with the phone to his ear. Even after he confessed his part, he asked if he'd still get the reward."

"And what was his part?"

Temper had never been the sharpest knife in the drawer, but she did speak and comprehend bullshit on an advanced level. She knew Matthew was dragging his feet, and she was ready to hear the truth.

"From his statement," Matthew said, retrieving a folder from the stack of them on the chair to his right. He handed her Kevin's written statement so she could read along as he summarized it. "He received a text message. Under the impression that it was sent from you, he went to the location, but you weren't there. When he made it back to his car, there was a car parked next to his. Supposedly it had broken down, and the driver needed help. He lent his phone, a text was made, and a text came in. He was given his phone back, and he went home."

She applauded. "Great act, but I'm here for the full show. You're holding back. There's something you ultimately don't want to tell, but we both know that you will and that you have to. How about we skip the pussyfooting and you give me the gut punches? Trust me when I say I can handle anything at this point in my life. Now go back. Why did he think the text came from me?"

"Read his statement—"

"No. I want you to tell me."

He took a deep breath. "The text said, 'It's me, Temper. This is my new number. Can you please meet me?' Kevin said he ignored it like Isabel instructed him to—"

"What do you mean, instructed him to?"

"She ran him off. When she found out he was buying prostitutes, she put her gun in his mouth and told him if he didn't leave you alone for good, she'd come up with a legal reason for pulling the trigger."

Temper couldn't believe what she was hearing, and if it hadn't come out of Kevin's mouth, she wouldn't have. "Kevin told you that lie? He broke up with me because I didn't tell him she was a cop, and he was paranoid because he smoked weed."

Matthew shook his head. "That's not a lie. I was there when she did it. Isabel saw you as her daughter, and she made it her job to protect you. Kevin didn't want to call it quits with you. He was threatened. He even begged her not to tell you that she had caught him in bed with a prostitute."

Unsure of what to think or feel, she asked, "Was that all the fake text from me said?"

"No, it said that you knew he was done with you, but it was your birthday, and not even Isabel's controlling ass could stop you from having him as your birthday gift."

"And he showed up?"

"Yep. The mention of sex was all it took, and that alone made Isabel right for banishing him."

"I didn't say she wasn't."

"You didn't have to. The look on your face said it all—relief that that scumbag didn't reject you."

"Whatever. So he gets to the place, and I'm not there. He helps someone get help and makes it home. Fill in the gaps. If that's all that happened, why is he in jail?"

"Because we can't prove his statement is true. As for the gaps in the story, he said that twenty minutes later he received a text that said, 'I'm here, Kevin. Where are you? What tip do you have on my case?'"

"Isabel texted him?"

"We don't have a record of that text, but if his statement is true, he would be the last person besides her killer to communicate with her."

"Why would she randomly text him about her case or assume that they were meeting?"

"This is just speculation, but I'm guessing the text that the stranded person made from his phone was to Isabel and the text back was her response."

"All this technology and y'all can't track those texts down?"

"I said the same thing when I was given the report back. Kevin uses one of those refillable-minute phones from the grocery store, and because of Isabel's undercover status, only the number the text came from was available. When we found her body, her phone had been factory reset, and there was only one number in it."

"The number that you tried to trace back to the manufacturer."

"Right."

"So Kevin's story can't be proven?"

"Yes and no. We are holding him under that charge as protection, just in case her murderer has this planned out and executed. He kind of fucked himself when he said that the moment he found out she was dead, he knew the girl had set him up from his phone. He never said anything before. It took him all these years to come forward with that."

"Did he describe the girl?"

"Yes, chubby with huge breasts. He said everything about her said she was from Cali, but he couldn't remember her face."

"Did you show him a picture of Tyger?" Her stomach flipped as the words came out of her mouth. All it took was those descriptive words, and she was ready to throw her best friend in jail for life. She hurt her feelings as the truth told the story.

Thinking back, Tyger was in town for her birthday way before she knew it, and she did know her plans with Kevin for her birthday were canceled because of Isabel. *Tyger could have sent him the fake text begging him to meet me, but Tyger was at the shelter with me when Isabel left early. Even if she was the girl pretending to have car troubles, Kevin gave a twenty-minute time frame from the incident to Isabel's text. It sounds like Tyger, but if she did it, she couldn't have been working alone.*

"I see your gears turning. All the dead ends you reached on naming Tyger as a suspect I reached as well. Who else did you tell about the circumstances surrounding your breakup with Kevin?"

"No one. Tyger was my only friend back then. Could he have told someone, and is he sure of the twenty-minute time frame?"

"He is sure, and I checked. His number was the other unidentified number that came up on the transcript of Isabel's phone, and all of his times and time frames add up. He said twenty minutes. The records show twenty-six minutes. Still not enough time for Tyger to have been the girl. Around the time the first text came in, you and Tyger were out test-driving your car."

"Wait, how do you know that?"

He pinched the bridge of his nose and then swallowed his cup of orange juice whole after letting it go. "Because I was Isabel's man."

Temper blurted out, "Yeah, right. She hated you." She laughed uncontrollably.

He waited for her to finish before correcting her. "If you believe that, then we did a damn good job of undercover work together. Come on, Temper, think back to all those nights we said we were working on a case and locked ourselves in her room or the nights she called to tell you she wouldn't be home because she was on a stakeout. Hell, even the night we caught Kevin walking into a hotel room hand in hand with a prostitute, we were there for a quickie on taxpayers' dollars, but on paper, we were there to get a feel for johns' hangouts."

She was speechless. It all made sense now that he'd revealed his hand. She remembered that she wanted to surprise Isabel by cleaning her room and private bathroom and saw a used douche bottle in her trash can next to an empty box that once housed condoms. She thought Isabel might have met a man she wasn't ready to introduce her to, but when she called to check on her an hour later, Matthew answered her phone and gave a weak line about her talking to the sergeant. She chalked the items up as necessities for the undercover job she was working.

"I loved her, and I'm not resting until her killer or killers are dead or in jail. I don't have a preference which way justice is served. My badge means nothing without her." Temper squeezed his hand, and he smiled at her. "When I get you back to L.A., I'm going to wait a few days and then bring Tyger in for questioning. I think we are barking up the wrong tree, and with her background and ties, it's a dangerous tree to shake."

"How dangerous?"

"Are you kidding me? Do you know who her father is?"

"Honestly, I don't. I don't know anything about her or her past."

"I know you don't, and that was always a concern of Isabel's. Here, take this stack of folders. It contains her records, with info on both her parents and her uncles. You and Tyger are more closely tied than I believe either of you knows.

"I have calls to make and leads I need to follow up on. Yes, I'm in it to solve Isabel's murder, but your safety comes first. You're in danger, and I don't know the ins and outs quite yet, but I do know whoever is calling the shots doesn't want you dead. They want to hurt you and then force you to rot in jail. Killing you seems to be their last option. We will regroup and go over everything at dinner tonight." He pushed the chair with the folders closer to her. "Don't skip any details. Read everything line for line. I'm beginning to think that, in the end, you're the only person who will be able to save you."

"Good morning, baby. After all the work you've put in over the last two days, I thought it was only right to feed you goodness other than me." Tyger giggled.

"I ate last night." He smirked. "I think I prefer my food covered in your juices. Bring your sexy ass here."

Julio reached for her thigh, but she stepped back.

"Eat, horny little man, while I get my clothes out for work tomorrow. Then you can do whatever it is you want to me," she said, leaning in for a kiss.

"I like how you said that." He chuckled.

They both had been sober for over twelve hours, and the energy between the two had intensified. However, her intelligence and his skills as a detective reminded them both that there were rocks neither could leave unturned.

"Come here, baby, before you get your clothes out. Come lie on my chest."

"No, Julio, you need to eat. Your food is going to get cold."

"I'll get up and put it in the microwave. I promise I'm going to eat it. Come here. I'm serious. I want to talk to you."

Sighing, she placed the plate on the nightstand and got into bed. He held her, rubbing his hands through her hair until the energy was right.

"I'm a cop."

"Yes, this I know," she giggled.

"Tyger Rae Le'shay Washington, I'm a cop."

"I hear you, and what do you want that to mean to me?"

"Nothing, but it means I know your past. Your father's, mother's, and hell, I grew up with your uncle."

She sat up. "You grew up with my uncle? My daddy's little brother? I barely even know that dude. What does he have to do with me? Hell, what does that have to do with any of them?" Finally, he was talking Tyger's language. It looked like having sex to loosen Julio's guard worked.

"Do you remember the two rules?" he asked.

"Do you remember them? No lies, no secrets. I guess you've dug through my life, or an FBI agent gave you intel that I've reunited with my father. So the fuck what? The restraining order expired on my twenty-first birthday. I've seen him once a year since then, and he sends me a shitload of money. That's not a relationship." She'd rehearsed her words three times before she said them. She wanted to gain his trust by making him feel like she was trusting him with her secrets.

"Tyger, you are the only person who ever got close enough to kill him, and from what I read, it was only his money that kept him alive. Eight shots, from the chest to his jaw. No one lives after those types of bullet wounds, nor is anyone forgiven for pulling the trigger on that type of man."

"Are you trying to figure out what makes me so lucky? How did I come close to killing the first true black monster of the mob and get to live afterward? Simple. I'm his daughter, and that's the only reason I'm alive. As sick as it may sound, he respected me more for having the guts to pull the trigger. That solidified that I had more of his blood flowing through me than my mother's."

"Who told you to take him out? I don't believe eight-year-olds even have those types of thoughts yet."

"An eight-year-old who never sees her father because he's preoccupied with killing, drug smuggling, and fucking up politics does. I was certified as gifted young. Smarts mixed with his DNA made me feel like a ticking bomb. I loved spending time with my nerdy-ass uncle because I forced myself to. Nothing in this world, and I do mean nothing, felt better to me back then than knowing I can control life based on what I do with my hands or speak with my mouth. I'm Capone's daughter. You can't fathom the power that came with my birthright. If you want to know my past, then erase everything you read in the books the government wrote about me. The first time I watched my father shoot a goodhearted, hard-working family man in his face over a parking spot that belonged to no one but the city and tell the cops to clean it up, I knew I wanted to do the same. The only difference was that I wanted to do it to all the bad guys in the world. My daddy was first on that list. No one had to pay me, although I'm sure checks would have come flooding in if I had."

"So you did have a gun that day at your mom's?"

"Wrong again. After I shot my father, they placed me in witness protection. Everyone there was already on my daddy's payroll and happy to tell me that I was only alive because he forbade retaliation. That's how I got PICS. My uncle brought in the best therapists from all over the world on my father's dime, and after years of sessions, I was handed a clean bill of mental health. Now that there was a restraining order in place, it gave my mom the freedom she needed to get away from him. By that time, she'd already grown to hate me."

"Why?"

"Because I was a part of him. I shot my dad to rid the world of an evil villain. I hit my public defender to get away from my mom. Those are the only crimes I've ever committed in my life."

"What about this shit with Temper?"

"What about it?" she snapped, standing. "I want to solve it. I want to fix her life and make sure she's straight, then cut her off. She told me that she's a bad guy. After all these years of her thinking that life chose her to fuck over, I found out a lot of it is her karma. That's why I got you to come here, because I didn't know if you are friend or foe—"

"What?" he interrupted, climbing from underneath the covers.

"You heard me. Are you a good guy or another evil villain? I asked my dad's people to look into you, and because I was given the same book the government gave you on me, I decided to bring you here to make my own decision. You got secrets you're hiding too. Must be why your two rules are based on your own inadequacies. I don't know. I'm here for Temper, and once I know she will be okay without me, I'm transferring to a museum out of the country. I made my plan the day I met her, and I've reached the last step. You're the only part of all of this that I'm questioning."

He fell back on the bed, laughing and shaking his head. From the moment he saw Journee, it was the mystery around her that attracted him. Less than five minutes later, she'd approached him with the woman of his dreams at her side, and he knew he had made a mistake, but he rode it out. Learning that Journee was Temper, the girl who had cost his closest friend everything, was the irony that showed the depth of his mistake, and so was Tyger.

"What are you questioning when I already told you that you were mine?" he said in between his laughs. "I don't have any secrets. You can ask me about anything your pop's people gave you, and you'll only get the truth from me. Temper is caught up with people she didn't do her homework on, and I found out she had a tie to those people living under her roof. I'm here for the same reason you invited me, beautiful. Is sexy, smart, warm-spirited Tyger my friend or foe?"

"Friend. Until she finds out about us, I guess," she giggled as she got back in bed, straddling his lap. He gripped her breast and pulled her in for a kiss. His meat rose, and he slid it back inside her. She rode him slowly and then froze.

"My uncle—why did you mention him?"

"We can talk about it later," he moaned as he tried to pick up the pace.

"No, we can talk while I ride this dick." She came to a complete stop.

"Okay, but why does it matter?"

"Because everything matters. Now tell me." She got off his lap and took him into her mouth. It took him a second to get his words together, but before he could say a word, Tyger's head popped back up.

"Did you hear that? It sounded like Temper's bedroom door just closed."

"I didn't hear shit. We're talking about her. It has you paranoid. All you should be focusing on is us," he said, pointing back at his meat.

"Is that right?" she flirted.

"That's all I'm focusing on, especially since I know you aren't working with your uncle."

The door slammed against the wall loudly like a demolition crew bringing down an old building. Matthew tightened his neck to pretend he was unbothered by Temper barging in. He knew the exact cause of her intrusion.

"Big Keith is Tyger's uncle?" she came through the door, shouting. "Tyger and Kei'Lani are first fucking cousins."

"Does this mean you're ready to talk?"

"Hell yeah, I'm ready to talk." Temper plopped down on the couch next to him, looking defeated. "Does Tyger know?"

"No, she doesn't. She's had a restraining order against her father since she was eight. Before that, she didn't have a relationship with her uncle because he and her father—"

"Are from rival gangs," she finished. "Infamous Capone is her father, and she's the legendary person who shot him eight times in the face."

"Not all the bullets landed in his face, but yes, Tyger is the shooter."

"Her dad did a lot of bad shit globally. She shoots him in the face, and thanks to his team of million-dollar-an-hour surgeons, he lived. I thought they said a big drug lord sent shooters who caught him sleeping."

"At the time, he created that lie to save Tyger and his ego. I'm sure you read her reasoning for doing it."

"Yeah, typical Tyger. She wanted to rid the world of evil." She shook her head. "That clears her from all of this shit with me. If she isn't close to her uncle and her dad even hates him, then she wouldn't team up with Kei'Lani or anyone else to get me."

"I'm in agreement with you on that one, but to not bring her in would alert whoever is trying to frame her that the jig is up."

"Am I missing something? Because it sounds like the case is solved to me. Her uncle, Big Keith—or like we called him in the hood, Beast—is calling all the shots. He hates his big brother and is setting his daughter up to take the fall."

Matthew raised an eyebrow and moved over to the armrest to get a good look at her before asking his next question. "You think it's an open-and-shut case? Okay, what's his motive?"

"Khasema."

"Khasema? Your child's father?"

"I don't have any children," she snapped.

"Okay, I'll play pretend with you. The guy you told us you were selling drugs for—what's their tie?"

"The gang. Big Keith is Khasema's OG. They'd do anything for each other. I fucked up Khasema's life, so Keith is out to fuck up mine."

"You're saying that Keith would send his only child to kill you in honor of Khasema? That just sounds a little farfetched."

"I'm sure it does. You're a pig. No offense, but you're overqualified to understand this street shit."

He chuckled. "Oh, am I? You might be right, but I came up with my own little theory as to why Keith would be orchestrating this. Stop me if I'm wrong." He pulled out his legal pad and flipped through the pages. When he found what he was looking for, he slid the notes to Temper and showed her the bubble cluster with how everyone involved was linked.

"Temper is best friends with Keith's only daughter. Temper gets pregnant by Keith's little homie and gets him his last strike. Temper is the reason his daughter has horrible seizures. He puts out a hit on Temper in juvenile hall, and Temper gets saved by Tyger, his only niece, who doesn't know him from the brother who hates him. Keith gets word Temper is back in California living it up, and he sends Julio, Khasema's best friend, to the club to set her up. Instead, Julio falls in love—"

Temper cut him off. "Keith sent Julio after me?"

"I'm not sure, but Julio has been meeting with Keith once a month since Khasema was sentenced. Not sure why, but he has."

"What? He told me he didn't mess with any of the lowlifes we grew up with."

"I'm sure he did. He started his career on the drug task force and ranked up from there. You don't want ties with those types of people where Julio is trying to go."

"This just keeps getting weirder. Do we have any alcohol?" Temper asked, but she was already checking the cabinets before he could answer.

"There are bottles of red and white in the fridge."

"Thank heavens. Keep going. He sent Julio and he failed."

"Right. Then Kei'Lani wanted a go."

"You think she volunteered? I don't know if that part is right. She said something along the lines of him sending her to kill me, and she hadn't loved him for years. She could have been talking about her father, but I was under the impression she was talking about Khasema."

"I don't know why she would say that either, unless it were to save her own ass. Khasema is her husband."

"What?" she bellowed, but he kept going.

"They married three years after the incident. When Khasema's mother moved to the Inland Empire, Kei'Lani moved in with her. From what I was able to uncover, it seems his mother nursed her back to health, and then Kei'Lani helped raise your . . . I mean, his son. Cancer took his mother's life a few years later, and Kei'Lani filed for custody of her husband's son and was denied because she was in and out of the hospital for long periods at a time. That's when his honorary grandfather stepped in. That makes you the chick who dogged his grandson."

"If you only knew."

"I will when you tell me. What am I missing?" Matthew flipped through the pad and stopped at a blank page. "I have to know everything."

"You do, and I'm shocked at how much you seem to know. If Kei'Lani had killed me, I'm sure Khasema's son would have been listed as next of kin, and since Keith is his guardian—"

"You mean he *was* his guardian. Truth is eighteen years old. The money would go straight to him."

"His name is Truth?" Her voice cracked as she said it. The weight that rode her shoulders and rested in her chest at the thought of her son was back. He wasn't just a baby she'd birthed and abandoned anymore. He was a man with a name, a portion of which she'd given him as she'd made her great escape.

Symmetry Truth was now Truth Charles. Her son was alive. Joy and pain filled every gap of space between her joints, and her body went stiff. The joy of knowing there was still a chance she could make right of her wrongs and the pain of the truth that it was too late to mother him stole her mobility. Diagnosing her with arthritis due to her symptoms made sense but it was maternal love that disabled her. It was a gene found in women that Temper assumed she lacked, although she'd fought to suppress it for eighteen years. She loved her son and regretted her decision to leave him. Still, she felt she'd done what was best for him. Knowing his name gave her an opening to tell Truth the truth once she knew they both were safe.

"Yes. If you would like to see a picture of him, I can—"

"No, I think it's probably best I don't." Changing the subject, she said, "Keith has more than enough motive, and I want Julio and whoever else is involved thrown in jail until they turn into dust. I knew Big Keith was obsessed with me, but damn, I'd have never thought he'd go this far."

She tried to stand up, and Matthew pinned her back down. "Explain 'obsessed.'"

"I . . . I was pregnant by him twice, or so I believed, but I'm sure of at least one. I'm not proud of anything I did before meeting Isabel, and I don't need you judging me because of my childish mistakes."

"I'm not Julio. I understand change, and don't you forget that I witnessed it. You're not that little girl I met at the Greyhound station." He placed a comforting hand on her back. "You are a woman, not that foolish child. Finish when you're ready."

The glass of red wine sat there sweltering as she grabbed the bottle and turned it up like forty ounces of malt liquor. She needed to put herself back in her old mindset to tell the story correctly. After balling her hair up in a bun at the top of her head, she continued.

"It was their Hood Day, and I was given as a gift to all the OGs. Most of them only wanted head, but Keith wanted it all. He fucked me with a condom in front of his boys. But when I made it home that night, he was parked in front of my house."

Temper's eyes focused on the bottle next to her, and seconds later, that bottle was blurry and replaced with a scene that happened long ago.

"Come here, Temper."

"What's up, Big Keith? You need a sack?"

"Nah, baby girl, I'm good. I just wanted to come by and check on you after those Hood Day activities, make sure you're straight."

"Aw, that shit. Yeah, I'm good."

"You sure? Get in. Let me talk to you for a second."

Without hesitation, Temper opened the door and sat on the passenger side. He handed her the blunt he had burning in the ashtray.

"I know me and my niggas can get a little buck wild when it comes to celebrating Hood Day and all. I know you're hella young and—"

"It ain't rape if I'm willing, big homie. Fuck my age," she said, interrupting him. *"Shit, I'm feeling good about today. We're straight, and I already know what you got going on at home. I'd never speak a word of this shit to Kei-Kei. I put that on the turf."*

"Okay," he chuckled. "Want to ride with me then?"

Taking a long pull off the blunt, she buckled her seat belt and said, "Hell yeah."

They rode from the east side of L.A. to Long Beach, smoking and talking about the hood the entire ride.

"What you know about Long Beach, baby girl?"

"Not shit. Every now and then, Kei-Kei and I will ride the train to the end of the line and smoke a blunt at the beach and then head back. Besides that, I ain't never really fucked with it."

"Word, but do me a favor. When you're with me, let's not talk about Kei'Lani. That's my baby, and I know y'all are the same age, but she isn't as mature as you. You feel me?" he asked, cupping her face and then tongue kissing her. The car behind him blew its horn to let him know the light had changed. "Hold on, faggot, I'm macking on my new little girlfriend right now."

"No, you're not. I don't do boyfriends, but you definitely can be my boo," she said, rubbing his dick through his extra-creased khakis.

"Yeah, I want to be your boo as long as you can keep this shit between us." She looked at him like he had lost

his mind and then reached over to unbutton his pants. "Hell yeah, baby. I want you to suck it and my balls like you did earlier, but let me get you in this room."

He made love to her and then promised her the world. He swore to take care of her as long as she remained his boo. She got a taste of his nut, but he preferred to shoot it in her other mouth. When she found she was pregnant, he ensured the abortion had been taken care of only because he wasn't sure if it was his baby.

The room became clear again, and Matthew was calling her name.

"Temper, you said, 'pregnant by him twice.' What happened the second time?"

"By the second time, he used Khasema as a diversion to spend time with me. We were fucking almost every day, and there were times he was willing to share me with Khasema, and then he didn't have time to creep with me anymore and gave me to Khasema. About a month after that, we found out I was pregnant, and Keith begged me to keep it. He said that me and the baby wouldn't want for shit, but I couldn't do that to Kei-Kei. She wanted to be an auntie, but I couldn't let her become an aunt to her little brother or sister, and that shit right there wasn't right. Plus, Khasema was trying to clean me up." She giggled. "He wanted to make a woman out of me, but I wasn't ready. Months after I had the second abortion, I fucked that up by sucking another one of our homeboy's dicks for a hundred dollars."

"Is that what you meant by 'obsessed'?"

"No, that's barely scraping the surface. Keith started popping up on me everywhere, even when I was with his daughter. He came and got in the bed with me one night at my grandmother's while I was asleep. He woke me up by kissing me all over my face, confessing feelings, and asking me why I killed our baby. I had to threaten to tell his wife to get him to leave, and you'd think that was the last time he'd try anything, but it wasn't. For, like, three months, he rolled by me, sniffing a pair of his boxers he put on after we fucked that smelled like my pussy.'

"Okay, I get it. Obsessed.'" Matthew sighed and fell back into the couch. "Yeah, obsessed. But wait, Khasema didn't know you were a minor. Isabel told me. Why wouldn't Keith tell Khasema if they were that close?"

"Are you serious? Even known pedophiles don't go around bragging about fucking minors. You're a cop. You should know that."

"Right, they don't. Not until they get caught in the act, and depending on their mental state, not even then." He took a deep breath and let it out slowly. "What you just told me changes everything. Go shower and get your stuff. It's time I take you back."

"Why? I thought we had at least another day here."

"Kei'Lani murdered Isabel. She used the same gun they found in her house after her death. I got word from ballistics right before you came in. The gun was a match, and I had my partner show Kevin a picture. He confirmed her as the girl who needed help. Other things have to be done with the case that I can't do from here. Other than that, case closed."

"What about Keith? Are you going to arrest him for his hand in her murder?" she asked, choked up.

"After what you just told me, probably not, but there's a job I need you to do for me to help speed all of this up. Nothing about this is cut-and-dried with Capone involved, but we will get to the bottom of all of this soon. And, Temper, stop lying to yourself. Those older men in your neighborhood molested you. It doesn't matter if you were willing. They were all at an age to know better."

Chapter Thirteen

The light illuminated Julio's side of the bed, but it was a vibration that ultimately woke him up. It was Temper, three missed calls in the last two minutes, and if he didn't answer soon, it would be four. He grabbed his boxers from the nightstand and swung his legs out of the bed to put them on. Tyger was knocked out. He could barely see her in the moonlight that crept through her blinds, but he knew by the way he beat her down, she would be sleeping well. Not wanting to disturb her while she recharged from the riding she'd taken before they went their separate ways to sleep, he opted to call Temper back from the living room.

"Are you okay?" he whispered into the phone. It was closing in on three days since she was taken to Vegas, and he'd been worried about her since she left, though his time with Tyger did well to keep him occupied.

"Are you?" she snapped.

"Um, yeah, I'm good. I was asleep, but—"

"Asleep where?"

"In bed," was his safe response as he shot to the living room window to see if he could spot her outside. When he was sure she wasn't out there, he asked, "What kind of question is that?"

"Whose bed, liar?"

In nothing more than the boxers he'd slid in and out of for the past three days, his V-neck T-shirt, and ankle-length socks, he stepped outside the apartment door, and a car's headlights flashed off and on at him.

"I can explain, Temper."

She hung up and jumped out of the passenger side with Matthew at her heels, but by the time she made it up the stairs, Matthew ran back to his car, leaving her to confront Julio alone.

"Explain what, nigga? That it's two in the fucking morning and you just walked out of my apartment in fucking boxers? Or that yo' ass has been in my apartment since I left town, apparently fucking my best friend I had a physical fight with over you?"

"It's not like that."

"Then what is it? A second ago, you said you were ready to explain."

"I . . . I came over to . . . to—"

"A stuttering muthafucka is a lying muthafucka. Isn't that what the streets say?"

"I don't know what the streets say, and I'm only stuttering because I thought I had more time before I would have to explain this to you."

"You thought wrong. Get to explaining."

He lowered his head to the floor, closed his eyes, and took a deep breath. "Tyger and I are a couple. We got together to try to figure out what we needed to do to protect you, and I know it's going to sound crazy, but we fell in love in the process."

His head being down was a blessing and a curse because he never saw the vase she threw at him coming.

"You were talking about marrying me, and now your ass is standing in my face with blood all over you, screaming you're in love with my best fucking friend?" she screamed.

"You're the only one screaming . . ." he started and then stopped. As the word "blood" cycled through his head, he saw the blood she was talking about at the tip of his sock. He grabbed his shirt, and there was blood there too, and on his hands. "Tyger," he yelled, rushing toward her room.

"Julio, don't take another step. Put your hands up and turn around slowly," Matthew demanded with his work piece pointed at Julio as sirens blared in the background. Temper noticed the blood as she was walking up, but the anger nestled inside of her. It was brewing from the moment Matthew told her what he needed her to do for him.

"I had a feeling we'd witness weird activity going on in your absence, so I had my friends keep an eye on Julio and Tyger after we left. I got a call that he followed her home after the event and that they've been together since. From what I was told, neither vehicle had been moved."

"So what are you saying?" Temper asked, folding her arms defensively.

"I'm saying that they've been in that apartment together for almost three days, and neither has left."

"That doesn't mean they're in there fucking."

"I didn't say they were. That's your speculation, but they are in there doing something. I want you to call her phone and see if she answers. If she does, see if she tells you Julio is there on her own. If she doesn't, call Julio and see what you can get out of him."

"Fuck that. I live there. Just take me home. If I pop up on their asses, they won't have time to compose a lie together."

"If they are together this long, the lie was already composed. Besides, we need either one of them to lie. It can help the case."

"No, I like my plan better. Take me home, because if I find out they are fucking, I'm going upside both of their heads."

"Did that work for you with Kei'Lani?'

The shot was fired, and Temper felt it in her gut. It hadn't worked with Kei'Lani. Her going upside her head with that golf club fucked up the rest of the girl's life, and though she would never let the words out of her mouth, it wasn't worth it. It felt good at the moment, but it hadn't resolved anything if Kei'Lani still ended up as Khasema's wife and stepmother to her son. She failed at her attempt at revenge. Seeking it again against the smartest person she had ever met and a highly decorated detective seemed ludicrous the longer she thought about it.

"What do you need me to do?"

"I didn't mean to—"

"Yes, you did. Don't lie." She held her hand in his face, stopping him in his tracks and stealing his next words. "Just promise me one thing—don't lose your badge over any of this. Isabel wanted to retire from the force. You have to let her do that because she still lives in you. I can feel her."

"I can always feel her." He grinned.

The blood covering Julio should have been the first issue Temper addressed, but seeing him in his boxers and his attempt to hide his location sent her into a jealous rage. Staring at him frozen in his stance by a gun sent a new feeling over her—the feeling of fear. She remembered how aggressive he was with her in his office and the unclear circumstances surrounding Kei'Lani's death minutes later. She wasn't sure whose side he was on, yet she knew for sure it wasn't hers.

She ran to Tyger's room with Matthew attempting to stop her as the backup he called walked in. "Noooooooo!"

Her agony sent chills down the spines of everyone who could hear her scream and recognize it as pain. Tyger's eyes were wide open and slightly pushed passed the limits of the sockets that housed them. The sclera of her eyes was red, covered in dark burgundy veins. Tyger had been strangled to death. A medical examiner wasn't needed to announce that as the cause of death, especially with the belt looped around her neck. What was stranger was that both of her wrists had been slit. Her arm hung over the bed, inches from the floor, as blood steadily flowed onto the carpet.

He was going to make the shit look like a suicide, Temper thought as one of the police officers was a step away from grabbing her to remove her from the crime scene. She pushed past him, and with all the power she could muster, she punched a handcuffed Julio in his mouth.

"You killed her. You killed Tyger, you dirty pig bitch. I hope her daddy has you gutted before you ever see a judge."

She was tackled to the floor before she could get in another word or punch.

"I didn't kill her. Temper, you have to believe me. I'd never hurt her," Julio pleaded. Still foggy, and maybe even high, he was positive that whatever had happened to Tyger didn't happen at his hands. As the homicide team walked in one by one, they made eye contact with him and lowered their heads. As he was dragged out of the apartment, he pleaded with them.

"Armstrong, Jackson, come on, fellas. You both know I couldn't have done this. Rodriquez. . . ." None of them gave him another look as they entered the bloody room.

Forty-five minutes passed. Outside, the biggest dick sword fight Temper had ever witnessed was taking place as she sat in tears inside of Matthew's car.

"If that's Capone's dead daughter in that bedroom, this is now a federal case, end of discussion," a tall, well-built white man no more than 35 announced to the still-building crowd of uniforms.

Temper had spent the first five minutes outside fuming, ready to kill everyone involved, but since then she'd been grief-stricken over Tyger's death. She had noticed the full-blown agency battle underway. Thanks to Tyger's father being anything but an upstanding citizen, the FBI pulled jurisdiction. However, so did the local authorities, so of course, the homicide detectives and Matthew from Las Vegas didn't have a leg in the fight. That didn't stop them from joining in on the argument.

"We have a cold case we reopened, and it ties into all of this. We'd like the Los Angeles Police to hold him until we get approval to transport him to Vegas," one of the homicide detectives Matthew worked with begged as Interpol flashed their badges, listening in on the commotion. Within minutes, internal affairs pulled up with every media channel you could name on their rear.

"This is going to turn into a media circus starring us as clowns if we don't agree soon," Matthew said, pointing at the uniformed policemen making a perimeter around the scene. It seemed like everyone who lived in the apartment came out when they saw the news vans. "FBI has jurisdiction, so let them take him, but if it's not too much to ask, can we listen in on the interrogation?"

"I think we can make that happen," an agent from the FBI agreed.

"What about the body?" one of the LAPD homicide detectives asked.

"Go ahead and let her leave with the coroner. We'll send for it later, but if anyone comes with questions about it—"

"We know how the Bureau works. What about the girl?"

Everyone turned and stared through the windshield at Temper. She hadn't stopped crying long enough to talk with anyone yet.

"You guys can have your go with her first, but when you are done, we expect you to transport her to us. Who's the Vegas detective who arrived on the scene first with her?"

"I am," Matthew said, stepping up. "I've been working this case with Detective Armstrong for months. I understand that we both need to be interrogated."

"Good, then you'll understand why you and the lady will leave your vehicles here at the crime scene and ride in the back of a squad car until you're cleared by LAPD, after which you will be transported with the girl over to us. Which squad car is Mr. Torres in?"

No one answered him, but heads nodded toward a squad car up front. It was suspicious that no one, not one officer or detective, not even internal affairs, thought to question the FBI agent's authenticity. Nor did they bother even to ask a name. When the real FBI pulled up to the scene, they reported their stolen vehicle was found less than two blocks away with the imposter agent shot by at least four different weapons. There was no sign of Julio.

The night was long and ran over into ten daylight hours of the next day before Temper was released. Between the different agencies coming in to question her, the only thing that was agreed upon was that Tyger's and Isabel's murders and Kei'Lani's and Paula's suicides had to be merged into one big case centered around Temper. There was no choice. Almost everything was tied to Temper, and what wasn't was tied into Tyger, forcing it to connect back to Temper. The FBI wanted her placed in protective custody because, with Julio missing and now the wedge between feuding brothers, Temper wasn't safe.

"If Keith convinced Julio to kill Tyger as an act against you, Tyger's father won't only send hit men after his brother, they will be on their way to you, too."

They brought in a female FBI agent, thinking it would be best to have a person Temper could relate to explain the dangers. She had a calming voice and seemed very caring, but they never factored in Temper's past when they asked her to step in.

"Agent McCoy, you did a beautiful job of playing the woman card, and I'm sure you're right, but what is it that I'm trying to preserve my life for again? My cop of a fiancé just fucked and killed my best friend because his best friend is serving life because of me. I have no family. After Tyger's death links to me like all the other shit at the museum, I won't have a job, and I'm already homeless because there's no way I'm moving back into that apartment now. What am I supposed to keep going for? Why would anyone in my shoes want to live?"

The room went quiet as everyone racked their brains to produce a satisfactory answer. From face to face, you could see blanks being drawn, and then Matthew spoke up.

"About an hour and a half ago, almost two million dollars cleared in your banking account. Isabel made sure that you had a reason to live. Isabel wanted Las Vegas to be a pit stop on your road to a new start. She was killed by people who want you to feel trapped in old circumstances. People who don't understand that children make mistakes. If you let them win, Isabel would have died in vain. I'm retiring my badge at an old age because I can feel her inside of me. Are you that dead already that you can no longer feel her love?"

"That sounds good, but there's no beating Capone. All of you have failed to arrest him, and when you did, he escaped. The only person who ever came close to killing him was his daughter, and where is she? In the morgue. The fake agents who left with Julio are dead, and you don't know by which brother's orders because you've never been close to either, but I have. I've loved Capone's daughter since we were teenagers looking for a way out of this—and she's more like her father than your missing information files will ever know—and Keith loved me. I've felt what it's like to have their blood growing in my body, and it doesn't feel good. Keith may be a well-known Crip with a lot of pull, but he's no Capone."

"What are you saying?" Agent McCoy asked.

"I'm saying you need more detectives at that crime scene, or you need to be interrogating the detectives who were there. By the way, Matthew, whatever happened to Detective Armstrong? How long has he been helping you put this case together? Wasn't he first on the scene?"

"Yeah, what are you saying? He arrived with two others, and he's been at the scene longer than anyone else. He's down the hall now."

"Then you all should get him, because when I punched Julio, he shot him a look of remorse."

"And?" the balding officer from internal affairs asked, speaking up for the first time.

"And I think he found evidence that might show Julio didn't do it but needed to report it to his true boss first." She turned her attention to Matthew. "You told me that you were starting to think that I was the only person who could solve this case. Do you remember telling me that?"

"Yes, I do."

"Do you still feel the same way?"

He looked around the room and didn't see one sign of hope, nor was he sure who he could trust. "The same way."

"Then listen to me. I know Keith, and he doesn't have the power they are trying to give him. I think Capone was tipped on what happened to his daughter and said Julio did it. I think that same person found evidence that proved Julio didn't and called to retract his statement, and out of frustration, Capone sent a peon he could throw away to drive off with Julio, and then his real goons snatched him up to get the truth. I think Julio is alive telling everything he knew and has known from the beginning of all of this." She fell silent. "Or he *was* alive long enough to tell it."

"That's a pretty farfetched story, don't you think? An LAPD detective on Capone's payroll when rumor has it that he's hiding in Mexico or South America?" Agent McCoy spoke up, sounding irritated with each word.

"All that money, high-tech gadgetry, man-hours, and know-how, and y'all don't know shit. Capone lives in Tacoma, Washington, with the biggest hogs you can find on the face of this earth." In unison, much of the room stood up in shock. "You can ask the obvious, but I've been best friends with his daughter since juvenile hall. I make his Christmas card list every year, and if you think I'm going to repeat all that or give you any more information on Capone, you are wrong. I can't tell you more than I know, and I'm sure one of you in here is on his payroll, too. Make sure you let him know I'm on a mission to kill every nigga involved in this. That's my word."

Matthew was speechless, and Temper wished she could say the same, because three hours of questioning followed her outburst. The only reason she was released and not forced to accept protective custody was that she vowed to return to Las Vegas under Matthew's protection.

When they were in the parking lot and at least 200 feet away from any cars, she tested her luck again. "I need you to swing me by the museum so I can grab a few things out of my office and get my car to follow you back to Vegas."

"Isabel said you used to try talking fast thinking it would help you be slicker."

"I'm not trying to be slick. All of my clothes are in that apartment, but I have a few sets at work. All of my backup documents are locked in my locker. When I couldn't trust Tyger anymore, I started filling up guest lockers just in case I had to get away."

"I'm talking about the 'follow you' part. You're leaving that car there until all of this is over. I'm your taxi."

"That's fine with me," she pouted, defeated.

Thirty minutes before closing, the museum staff was piled in the food court, riding out the clock until the end of their shifts. Temper didn't expect anyone to be in the building when she asked Matthew to wait in the car. Otherwise, she would have felt more comfortable having him as an escort. It hit her that Tyger was dead and couldn't make phone calls from the afterlife to advise employees that she wouldn't be there to open the museum to the public. It was her murder that prevented Temper from playing backup and making the phone calls for her.

"Hey, everyone, I'm sorry no one called to tell you the museum would be closed today. Tyger was . . . wasn't feeling good today, and I couldn't get around to making the phone calls myself."

"Is she okay?" a voice near the back asked.

"I won't lie to you. She's had better days, and I will leave it at that for now, but I can assure you that there will be no work tomorrow, and all of you will be paid. Go ahead and leave," she said, mustering up a smile as she headed toward Tyger's office first.

Thinking her workplace was empty wasn't the only reason she wanted to come inside. She wanted to feel and see Tyger one last time. Her office was covered with memories of the two. The cold gust of air blowing in her face like smoke as she got closer to her door was a surprise. Tyger's office window was missing. It had been removed without breaking it because there wasn't a shard of glass in sight. Her walls were empty, and every drawer housed in her desk was stacked neatly on top of it. She checked her office closet and bathroom, and both had received the same treatment. She knew she'd have to notify the police of the break-in because that meant the alarm was disabled, but she knew the job was an act of professionalism, and they wouldn't find a fingerprint or a strand that could have fallen in the movement. Capone had beat all twelve agencies that named him most wanted. He wouldn't lose now because of emotions from the loss of his only child. She wondered if her office had received the same cleansing.

From the look of it, everything was in place except for every picture she owned of her and Tyger. They were gone, and her office had a sterilized look. Capone's cleaning crew had been there.

"Psst." The beckoning sound caused the hair on the back of her neck that didn't make it into her lazy ponytail to stand at attention. She wasn't facing the connecting restroom in her office, but in her peripheral vision, she could see a big and tall silhouette summoning her with its limbs. The stranger's face became more familiar, which made his presence even more uncomfortable.

"Don't you work in the cafeteria? What are you doing in my office?" she asked nervously as his smile brought a strange blanket of comfort around her. There was too much going on for her to pretend that it was customary to find an attractive man she could only recall seeing once when she was leaving with Matthew almost a week ago hiding in her restroom.

He didn't answer her. He placed his index finger over his mouth and motioned for her to come to him. She looked around her office and down the hallway but couldn't find a source for him to be hiding from, and then she took two steps near the restroom. She didn't go in.

"Who are you hiding from, and why are you hiding in here?"

"I saw her trying to put these in your desk, and I can't let you go down for Paula." The man was holding a medicine bag full of prescription bottles with Tyger's name on them. "They are covered in Paula's fingerprints. Tyger used to sell them to her or whatever, but he put a gun to Paula's head and forced her to take them all. Now she's about to set it up like it was you. This shit is coming to an end fast, and after you're out of the picture, I know I'm next."

"What are you talking about?" Temper asked, followed by a nervous giggle. "Who is this she and he you're talking about? Hell, who are you?"

"I'll tell you everything once we get out of here. We have help. I did my research, and when we get to him, we both will be safe." He begged with his eyes more than his words.

"I'm not going anywhere with you. You haven't told me anything, and I don't even know who you are."

"She made Keith kill Tyger with the belt Capone sent him so Capone would know that it was Keith who did it."

"What belt? Capone sent Keith a belt? What are you talking about?"

"Damn, you don't listen to shit like everybody says about you. Capone tried to reach out to his little brother Keith a while back. He sent him an engraved belt that said, 'A hard head makes for a soft ass. Are you done being hardheaded, old man?' Keith didn't respond, not because he didn't want to, but because he couldn't. Your foster mother, or whoever she was to you in Las Vegas, had already been killed, and her plan was in motion. It was too late to rekindle shit, or at least that's what my granddaddy told me. He called my godfather from my phone last night, but he didn't answer. When he was done leaving his message, he told me her plan. At first, it was just to put you through hell like you did her and then kill you, but when she found out about your money, her plan changed, and then everyone who had ever saved you from one of her attacks became her pawn. But Granddaddy told me where to find help and then put the pistol in his mouth."

Nervously she asked, "Can you please repeat it all, but this time can you name the people you're talking about?" She paused and stared deeply into his face and saw herself. Nervously she mumbled, "Are you Truth? Are you my—" Her racing heart cut her off as tears formed in her eyes.

"Yes, my name is Truth, but from what I heard, you didn't want a son."

He lowered his head as the text message alert went off on her phone. It was a message from Matthew telling her to hurry up.

"I still can't believe she named you Truth. You're so handsome," she said through sniffles.

"Naw, Granny said you named me Truth, and she honored the request, but this ain't the time for that. I'm eighteen years old, and that family shit ain't never worked for me. All I ever had was Grandpa Keith and my godfather Julio. One is dead because of her, and the other is missing. I was a kid when most of this shit happened, but Granddaddy told me that she said Tyger had to go because she always saved you. First Tyger, then my granddaddy, then you, and once I inherited your bread, then me."

"Who is she, Truth?"

The energy in his face disappeared as a gun cocked and pressed against her temple.

"Truth, why haven't you been answering my calls, boy? You had me worried sick about you," a familiar voice said.

"Kei'Lani?" Temper asked, seeing the shadow growing larger on the ground as the person neared. "But I thought you were dead."

"How did you think that? Kei-Kei might have died, but Kei'Lani will live forever." She snatched Temper up by her ponytail, forcing her to face her as she pointed at her heart. "My daughter will live forever in my heart."

Bridget, no more than 57 years old, stood in front of Temper as the older, more beautiful clone of her deceased daughter, Kei'Lani, minus the harshness the street life and illness had caused her daughter. She looked tired, but the thought of getting revenge gave her a false sense of energy that had allowed her to keep going all these years. Her hair had yet to be touched by gray, though you would have assumed the stress that life had planted her in would have her mirroring a snowflake. Her body looked like she had been training with MMA stars through the fitted, strapless African-print dress she was wearing. With her hand still locked on Temper's hair, she turned to her grandson.

"I went through all of that trouble to plant those pills myself. I even risked being seen on these fucking cameras, and you scoop them up to save a mother who ain't never mothered you. Is that how you do me, grandson?"

"You're not my grandmother. You killed my grandmother. My granddaddy told me."

"Cancer killed your grandmother. That's what it reads on her death certificate."

"Yeah, but you're the bitch who switched all her cancer medicine out with over-the-counter medicine."

Bridget stepped up and slapped him with her free hand as the guy she had with her reached his gun past Temper's head to point it at Truth.

"Don't you ever bite the hand that feeds you. I understand your granddaddy killing himself hurt you, but I'm still your grandmother and the woman who raised you. I thought they said the other bitch you called granny was a nurse. It wouldn't be my fault if she ignored pharmacology."

She looked back at Temper in time to see her trying to text Matthew back. "Still a sneaky-ass snake, I see," she said, taking the phone. As she typed, she read off what she wrote. "'LOL, I'm coming, just making sure I have everything. I'll be out in less than ten minutes.'" She hit send, and immediately Matthew sent a text back. She giggled as she read it. "'Make it five. I'm coming in after that.'"

She didn't bother replying. She powered off the phone and handed it to Truth. "Will you do Granny a favor, baby, and take the battery out of her phone and leave it on her desk on our way out? Oh, and for laughs, leave a little note close by that says, 'I have my mama.' That should make for good press. I guess we should go ahead and move this reunion to somewhere more nostalgic."

Truth did as he was told at gunpoint, but Temper didn't get a chance to see it as something tight was placed over her head and face.

"Now show us how to get out through the kitchen. If you try anything on our way to the car, you're both dead."

Out of respect for her privacy and the tie he knew she had to the museum because of Tyger, Matthew extended his five minutes to fifteen. It gave him time to check in with his team for updates. He wasn't expecting much. They were there to solve Isabel's murder, and with her killer known and dead, they didn't give a shit about Temper, seeing that she was the cause of it.

"There's still no sign of Julio, and being honest with you, we are about thirty minutes outside of Vegas about to eat. That California shit has nothing to do with us,

Matthew, and everything to do with Capone. It's going to get worse before it gets better. I know you loved Isabel. That secret relationship shit y'all thought y'all had was only a secret to those not paying attention, but Temper wasn't her daughter."

"Watch your words," Matthew snapped.

"I'd rather not. You need to hear them. From the moment we caught that girl at the Greyhound, I could feel this deadly feeling about her. My grandmother, my dad's mom, would say that if you see an owl, someone around you will do you harm. Call me superstitious if you want to, but I saw one as you drove to the drop-off. An owl in fucking Vegas just staring at me as we rode by with Temper in the back. I saw another owl outside the crime scene, and I won't allow there to be a third. She's bad news, and you may not want to hear it, but it's her shit that killed Isabel. If you want to be next, then that's on you, partner."

Matthew knew the Mexican superstition. He learned it from Isabel, and truth be told, he saw the same owl his partner mentioned because it sat on the roof of his car as Temper sat in it alone as they decided their next move.

"Can you just tell me if you ran the staff information at the museum like I asked you? And you're done with this case."

"Yeah, and drama like usual. Temper's son, Truth Charles, is a cook there and has been for the past year. Always on time, never a problem, and he's never missed a day, but I wouldn't be foolish enough to call it a coincidence."

"Thank you, brother. I will see you soon," Matthew said, walking into the museum.

"I pray that's true."

His partner hung up as Matthew walked into the security office for help locating Temper's office.

"I can do you one better. I'll take you there. I hate walking by that exhibit by myself anyways." He chuckled. "Those stuffed owls give me the creeps."

"There's an owl exhibit by Temper's office? I don't recall seeing it."

"Yeah, you can't miss it. In my opinion, it's creepier than that snake exhibit across from it. Are you sure you've been to her office before? You can't miss it. And to think she's the one who requested the exhibit be placed there."

"No, I came in through the kitchen the first time. Hey, can you do me a favor? Tell Temper I solved and closed the case I came into town to work. My job in Los Angeles is done."

Matthew smiled at the guard as he assured him he would pass Temper the message. He walked out of the museum, mentally preparing for his four-hour drive home to Nevada. Temper's fate was in her own hands.

Chapter Fourteen

Hollywood directors with years of experience would need to take notes after seeing how perfectly Bridget had set the stage with no time to plan it out. She wasn't expecting Temper to be at the museum when she asked her grandson to sneak her in, but she hadn't expected him to betray her for Temper, either. Bridget didn't know where her husband went after killing Tyger until her grandson called her crying hysterically. If it weren't for eavesdropping on his conversation with Temper, she wouldn't have known what her late husband had told him. However, with the little time she did have, taking them to the cemetery was the perfect place to turn this drama into a tragedy.

Bridget loved Truth as if he were her flesh and blood because Kei'Lani had. To watch her daughter play mother to a child born to the woman who transformed her from healthy to handicapped broke her heart. To think the night would end with her killing him turned her stomach, but she wasn't left with a choice. Her husband had told him too much.

When Bridget first learned of the child, she wondered if it was indeed Khasema's baby or if he was taking the rap for her husband. She knew about his affair with the little Asian girl she hated whom her daughter became friends with, not because the streets were talking, but because Keith was.

"*Do you hear yourself? You walked into our home and announced that you plan to leave our daughter and me to be with her best friend. She's sixteen. What, are you high? Because you can't be this sick,*" Bridget yelled at Keith as he showered.

"*You asked me where I've been sleeping the last few nights and who I'm fucking, so I told you. If you were half the woman she was at sixteen, we wouldn't be having the conversation. It would be your pussy I just got out of.*"

Bridget couldn't snatch the shower curtain down from its rail fast enough. Usually when they got into it, Kei'Lani was home, and she would have to watch her tone and actions or put it off until she left, but knowing their daughter, she was probably out there praising Temper too. Keith was naked, covered in soap, and to say he claimed he had just gotten out of another woman's pussy, his dick was fully erect. With nothing else to grab, she stuck her nails in that.

"*You think you can just stand in my face and tell me you just fucked another bitch?*"

Keith screamed in horror as she dug her nails deeper into his manhood, before slapping her as hard as he could in the face. She hit the floor.

"*You asked. I answered. I'm not trying to disrespect you. I'm in love, and she's carrying my baby. I know I can't have two families, so I made my decision. I'm rolling with her and taking Kei-Kei with me.*" He stepped out of the water and grabbed his towel. The water mixed with the soap had his fresh cuts feeling like they had been filled with salt. He wrapped nothing but his meat as the water from his body dripped on her. "*We are from two different worlds, Bridget. I love you, I do, but you ain't never respected or accepted my hood. I'm Big Keith out in these streets, and Temper doesn't ever* let me forget it. She knows how to treat a thug and how to respect the turf."

"You have smoked your whole damn mind away. I'm sure of it. She's a fucking minor, stupid, your only daughter's best friend, and you got her pregnant? You think you can hide behind the power of that blue flag forever, don't you?"

"The flag don't make the man!"

"What's that, more of your sick philosophy? I don't believe that any of the men—and I'm not talking about those little boys who ride your khakis, but the real men from your hood—would allow this, and I'm going to take it straight to them and see. There's a bunch of them who are fathers with daughters, and I know they ain't havin' this sick shit in their hood."

"Shut up, bitch. How are you speaking about gang life when you hate it? You don't know shit."

"I don't have to because I know being a man comes before anything, and I've been around your homeboys enough to know your hood is full of them. There are two I always thought were pretending to be boys, and now I know you are the third. I hope the niggas beat yo' pedophile ass."

He reached back and locked on her neck. "You're not going to tell my homies shit. I tried to tell you the truth, but I knew you wouldn't understand." He threw his hands up, walking into their bedroom.

"How in the fuck did you expect me to understand that you're not only cheating on me and have a baby on the way, but you're a child molester, too?"

Keith grabbed his clothes out of the drawer and was out of the house before she could get off the bathroom floor. She wasn't even sure if he was dressed before he left.

He had come clean, but all of it was in vain, because when he pulled up on Temper the next day, she had just come back from the abortion clinic, sick and in pain. He could have killed Khasema for taking her, but he understood why. Bridget had come by his house that morning with the abortion money and the threat that she'd have him arrested for the rape of a minor if it wasn't done before sunset. She also told him that if he didn't convince Keith to keep his family together until Kei'Lani turned 18, she'd lie and say he'd hit her to get his probation violated. She knew it wouldn't just get him disciplined. He'd be put out of the gang. Keith never knew how Bridget learned the rules, but he knew to take her seriously if she took the time to research them. That type of shit was in his bylaws. He couldn't talk himself out of those consequences.

Things seemed to look up from there. Keith was back at home and refused to hang out with his homies. He put his wife first, and they built a stronger bond. It wasn't a surprise to either of them that she was pregnant with their second child after almost eighteen years. When Keith got the news he was about to be a father again, he became her shadow, even protecting her while working until his job sent him on the road again. The distance was hard on them both, more so on Bridget than Keith, and when she got the call that Kei'Lani was in the hospital having back-to-back seizures, the stress had her placed three floors above her daughter in labor and delivery. She miscarried as Temper's name rang in her ears again.

Whenever she thought she'd get a break from hearing the girl's name, it came again, but this time it was through the young man who went out of his way to keep her family together and protect her husband. Temper had gotten him his third strike for the same charges she told her husband a little over a year earlier that the girl would get him. It was time to avenge everything, and this time, her husband agreed. Khasema was his son more than his little homie, and seeing that the bitch who broke his own heart did his boy in, it was time to sit her down. Keith called around, and a jail hit was placed on Temper, but that was shut down, too.

When Keith learned his niece had linked up with her, he was done trying. He feared no man except for his brother, and that made Bridget sick. She reached out for more hood rules and laws and found out that Temper was living the good life in Las Vegas in the midst of it all. She had a job and was doing well, while Kei'Lani was just awakening from her medically induced coma to stop the seizures. Her daughter was gone, and all she saw now was a slow-thinking neurology patient who only lived to raise a little boy she hadn't birthed. That was it, and after all these years of waiting to kill Temper, that little boy her daughter kept fighting to live for was going to make her filthy rich. It took setting her own daughter up to do it, but it was done, and now she could run off with the new love of her life. She'd get a fresh start at life before she turned 60.

"Truth, take her blindfold off."

Truth reached down and untied the sweater that was wrapped around Temper's face. When the light hit her eyes, she felt a foot kick her in the back. She tumbled over onto the grave.

"Grandson, let me introduce you to your family. The grave your mama is on belongs to your great-grand-mother Jo. She was your mama's granny and the woman who raised her. To the left of that is your grandmother Dorothy, the neighborhood prostitute, and your crack-head granddaddy. I think the grave says, 'Davi.' To the right is your great-granddaddy. No one knows much about him, and next to him is Wiggles, but she was famous. The world knew her as Shirley Blu. She was married to your crackhead uncle Troy, but last I heard, he was killed by a couple of *eses,* and they buried his body in the desert. You see, baby, you come from a long line of nothing-ass people, and that's why Kei'Lani made it her duty to take you in." She reached down and turned Temper over. "Today, you will join your mama and the rest of these lowlifes in the dirt. Get on the grave with your mama."

Truth hesitated. He was a big guy, and although there was a gun pointing at him, he didn't feel right submitting. He wondered, if he rushed the man holding the gun, would Temper have what it would take to run away to safety, or would he die in vain?

"There's people out here. Are you sure you want to kill us right here?" Truth asked.

Bridget looked around, and about half a mile away was a car with two men standing next to it. It looked like they were there to pay their respects and weren't paying them any attention.

"I think he's right, baby," the man said, speaking up for the first time. "This shit here just don't feel right."

He had been Bridget's lover for the last five months, but with Keith in the way, they didn't get to spend a lot of time together, but she trusted him. Ironically, they met the day she dropped Kei'Lani off at the museum to stab Temper. His Benz was blocking the exit, and he was nowhere to be found. When he came running back to his car, he apologized and begged to treat her to an early dinner for wasting her time. Seeing that he only wanted to take her across the street, she agreed. They did more talking than eating.

"Did you enjoy your time at the museum?" he asked, making small talk.

"I was only there to, um, drop off my grandson. He's a chef there."

"Okay, tell me he learned his way around the kitchen from you, and we can walk out now."

She laughed. "Of course he did, but I'm like him. I don't cook for free, so we are probably better off eating here. And you, did you enjoy yourself?"

"Family sent me in there too. The baby was on a tour with the school, and I had to make sure she had everything she needed with her. You know how these kids are. They trust everything in their hearts and don't put nothing in their heads."

Bridget spent every free moment she could with him. She knew he loved her in the same fashion she loved him. He told her about his ups and downs in life. How he was rich, then bottom-of-the-barrel poor, and now well-off for a man who endured the pains he went through, and she told him all about Keith. He understood the marriage problems and had confessed that his wife's death taught him how to live. From the day they'd met, he had been open and honest with her like no one she had ever known.

When her grandson called to tell her that her husband committed suicide, she didn't know what to do. She was sure his brother would be the person to take his life. She didn't know what to do with the body, and she didn't want the police to be alerted just in case it caused the security to tighten up around Temper. Helplessly, she called on him, and he met her at the body.

"I need you to get yourself together. Go home and wait for me. I'm going to have my people take care of this."

"But what if—"

"It's too late for all the what-ifs. Let me handle this, and then we will talk about everything, including your part in this. I know guilt when I see it." He kissed her and sent her off. When he made it to her house, she confessed to all the evil she had done to live out her plan

against Temper and how his suicide may have messed it all up.

"So you think he confessed to your grandson before he did it?" he asked, smoking a cigarette.

"I know he did. My grandson's eyes have never been able to hide how he's feeling."

"Then you're going to have to kill him too. I know you wanted him to end up with the money, but if you want peace in your last days, you're going to have to kill them all. Anyways, you don't need any living reminders of the pain you've been through."

He promised to help her clean up the last of it so they could get away.

"What, baby?" Bridget asked, looking around the cemetery again. "What doesn't feel right?"

"I don't know, but the shit ain't adding up. If being born gives us ten feet . . ."

Temper could have snapped her neck the way she turned her head to see the man who was talking. The sun was setting, but his familiar face wasn't familiar enough in the growing shade.

"And if we changed everything in our lives, including our environment, then we should have more than the twenty feet we need to get over that wall."

"What wall? What are you talking about?" Bridget questioned, growing more confused with every word as Truth planned his attack.

He told himself that the next time the man started speaking, he'd attack him and take the gun. He looked over at Temper, hoping she could read his eyes, and after she did, she shook her head no. But who was she to tell him what to do?

"The thirty-foot wall, Bridget. The only way out of the hood is over a thirty-foot wall."

"But none of us live in the hood anymore, baby. I'm confused," Bridget exclaimed.

"Temper, I think I got it. I finally think I know how to give you those twenty-plus feet."

Truth jumped up to tackle him. Instead, Temper tackled him as her uncle let off every round in the gun into Bridget's head.

"Troy. I told you my damn name was Troy, not 'Roy,' not 'baby' for five damn months. Bet you heard it now."

Temper let go of Truth and stared at Troy. "Is that really you, Unc?"

"You bet your Chinaman ass it is, Temper Taz."

They embraced as he landed kisses all over his niece's face as she cried into his arms.

"It's all over now, baby. It's done," he whispered.

"But where did you come from, and how did you know?"

"Shirley died on me, and the drugs didn't help with the pain. I was smoking rocks, but I wasn't getting high, so I checked into a shelter, and a man came looking for men willing to work. I worked, started saving money, and got me an apartment. Think I was in it three months before firefighters were carrying me out. Bad wiring. I guess that's why the rent was so cheap.

"Steroids and skin grafts changed my look, not to mention the weight gain and muscles from slanging metal fences all day. I found out that complex had been cited, and since I was the only person hurt, I walked away with a large sum. I tried to check on you and couldn't find anything, so I took a stroll through the old neighborhood and ran into Keith looking stressed out. It took a while to convince him who I was, but he brought me up to speed on this bitch Bridget when I did.

"For five months, I stopped myself from killing her until he said the time was right. Keith made that call, then Bridget called for help with him, and then I got one more call. It was Truth. He said he was told to call me for protection for him and his mama. I told him I could only save one of you, and the other would probably end up dead, and he told me to save his mama. I didn't think loyalty like that was still around." Troy faced Truth. "You're a big-ass boy. I prayed you wouldn't realize that and try to take this gun."

"The thought crossed my mind," he said, looking at Temper.

"I'm sure it did. You have our blood flowing through you."

"The boss wants to see her now." A man dressed in business casual in solid black with the skin tone to match appeared from out of nowhere and nodded toward the one man standing by the car half a mile away.

"That's the call I made. Keith gave me his brother's information and told me to bring him up to speed. I don't know much about you now, Temper, but you'd do good to watch your tongue and take your son with you."

"Will you be right here when we're done?" she asked.

"Probably not," he said, looking at Bridget's dead body. "But now that you got your feet, make me a new promise."

"What's that?"

"If you get your crazy ass on the Greyhound again, go farther than Vegas," he chuckled. "And this time, make sure you take your son with you."

"I plan to," she said, smiling at her uncle. She ran to him and hugged him tightly. "I love you, Unc."

"I love you too, Temper Taz."

She reached for her son's hand, and to her surprise, he grabbed it and held it tight as they walked across the graves.

"I see the two of you decided to reunite." The back window on the car rolled down slightly, but not enough to see a face. "I got your message, and I love you for the loyalty you showed my daughter for many years."

"Her death is a loss to us both, Capone," Temper added.

The man who summoned Temper handed her the gold hunter watch, her and her parents' picture, and the MOTHER charm Lena had given her.

"Where did you get this?" Temper asked, holding in tears.

"Tyger's jewelry box. She had a note in it that said to give it back to you when your heart was healed."

Temper thought back to the day she threw it all away and how Tyger had passed her with an approving smile. It took all these years to find out what that smile meant.

"Our business is done, but there is one pending matter I need the two of you to decide on. Detective Julio Torres. He is standing in the grave behind you, alive. I believe he is a good guy who picked the wrong people to be around, but he has a lot of snake-like ways. What would you like done with him?"

Temper didn't want to respond because Truth had already named him and Keith as the only family he had. She would agree with whatever her son decided.

"It's just us from now on, right?" Truth asked her. "You're not answering his question because he's one of the people who hurt you, like my pops?"

Temper shook her head. "No, not like your pops, but you and I both know that's where his loyalty is. Look at how good of a godfather he was to you."

"Sir, you can kill him," Truth announced.

"No, son, it doesn't quite work like that. If you want to rid your mom of the last piece of her past, you will have to pull the trigger." Capone handed him his gun, and he walked over to the grave and looked down.

"He's already dead," Truth announced.

"Yes, he is. I just wanted to make sure I was leaving your mother in good hands. Tyger would expect that.

Although you shouldn't have run your mouth about Tacoma, I'm keeping you on my Christmas card list." He rolled up his window, and the car pulled off. Temper and Truth were left standing there without a ride.

"Is your life always this tossed?" Truth asked, grabbing her hand as they began their walk across the graveyard.

"Yes, it always has been, but I have a really good feeling that this is the end of it being that way."

Everything around her felt cold as she thought about the lives that had to be lost for her to gain her thirty feet. However, the fresh start she gained, who clutched her hand, gave her the warmth that she'd never again live without.

The End